Amani: Remember

By Lydhia Marie

Copyright © 2015

Lydhia Marie

Copyright in work number: 1119733
ISBN: 1508812284
ISBN-13: 978-1508812289

Many thanks to

Jean-Sébastien Raymond
Gabriel Gosselin
Marie-Claude Bolduc
Marie-Michèle Rosa-Fortin
Caroline Morin
Kelsey Allan Down
Guy Roy and Marie-Andrée Bolduc
Ryan Gosselin
Lynda Rosa
Nathan Orie
Solange Gosselin
Michel Giroux
Jacques Morin
Antuan Vance
Isabel Matias
Carmen Brady
Michelle Bolduc
Barclay Bram
Ammie James

& all my family members and friends!

To Bookie, the best of friends who stayed by my side—or slept on my lap—during the whole writing process.

Table of Contents

Chapter I

I DARED TO LOOK BACK and could still discern a dark shadow following me, so I pushed aside the sharp pain building in my lungs and head and kept running. I could not afford to risk my life again. This had been going on for two days and I had to make it stop.

To make *him* stop.

My eyes were blurry from the pouring rain and I felt disoriented, even though I'd been walking these alleys for a couple of months now. *Left. Another left—no, right!* I tried to remember. Panic was slowly eating the small amount of hope I had left. There was no way I could outrun him.

"Stop, please," he screamed at me, as if I could ever trust him again.

I knew that my movements were betrayed by the wet thuds of my feet on the concrete. I therefore feinted a right on the next corner and turned left instead, hiding behind a red brick wall. It was Wilf Hall, which meant that I was only a couple of steps from my dorm, Lauritzen Hall.

I waited a few seconds, debating whether I should crouch on the ground until my assailant was gone or keep running and hope to reach my dorm before him. Fighting the urge to surrender, I decided to walk slowly in the shadows of the buildings. I attempted a reluctant step forward, then two steps, but immediately started walking faster and faster, as I feared being intercepted.

And then only my unsteady breath and clumsy feet could be heard against the heavy drops of rain. *Where did he go?* With no more shouting or running, I couldn't tell if the man was nearby. Or was he gone for good?

Keeping a good pace, I grabbed my phone and started texting Samera. If anything happened to me, someone had to know. I had barely written two words when the man reappeared in front of me.

***

I came to in a spurt of emotions: fear, helplessness, despair.

What happened?

Where is he?

Where am I?

Am I still on campus? I need to leave or he'll find me!

My mind swirled and the panic gripping at my stomach increased as I tried to move and open my eyes but couldn't. *Why am I unable to do anything? Am I asleep? Or maybe I'm dead. Maybe the dream wasn't a dream and the man actually killed me and I'm stuck in some kind of purgatory, forever caught in a feedback-loop of memory!*

I could now hear my heart beating in my head and realized that my heartbeat was also mimicked on a machine next to my left ear.

Beep, beep.

Beep, beep.

Beep, beep.

A heart monitor? Am I at the hospital?

Instead of appeasing me, this knowledge made everything worse. I had no recollection of how I could have ended up in a hospital.

Perhaps I'm still dreaming. Why was I feeling dizzy all of a sudden? Was I drunk? *Don't panic, Amya. Calm down*, I told myself, which in turn encouraged the irritating noise next to me to grow faster and faster. My head was spinning and I felt nauseated trying to remember what I had been doing the night before.

If my parents see me like this, I'll be dead for real. Focus, Amya. Why would you be in a drunken coma?

No memories of overdrinking came to me, which wasn't a good sign at all. However, a drunken coma was very unlikely, as the only time I ever drank was with Samera when we watched a movie on Saturday nights. And it was only a glass of wine, so there was no way I'd get drunk enough to end up in a coma.

With that hypothesis put aside and with the fact that no one seemed to be threatening me anymore, I soon realized that I was in no imminent danger. The tension keeping me on the edge diminished until my breath steadied and my entire core seemed to relax.

I tried to form rational thoughts.

Something or someone brought me into this hospital and I need to find out why.

My incapability of remembering anything important was soon forgotten when my nose filled with a scent of flowers—lilies, my favorites—followed by a familiar essence of soap and aftershave. I also acknowledged a pressure on my left hand. Was someone here with me?

Again, my heartbeat grew faster and I tried to remove my hand.

In vain. My muscles felt so heavy, as if thousands of rocks kept my body from any movement. Even the tip of my fingers were numb.

"Amya?" someone said. It was a man, but I couldn't recognize his voice as he merely whispered my name.

Who was this man and what did he want with me?

My thoughts were disrupted when the pressure on my left hand grew a little stronger. It didn't hurt, though. It was soft and delicate, like a feather going up and down my palm while the rest of my hand was being squeezed. My first reflex was to squeeze back, but my limbs were still frozen.

This person holding my hand, whoever it is, must be here for me, wherever I am. I found the idea very comforting.

You might as well enjoy the feeling, a voice inside my head told me.

And I did. I embraced the relentless movement of the fingers brushing my skin and found myself breathing at the same pace and rhythm as the gentle touch: slowly, like the water of the ocean going up—and down the shore. Up—and down again. And then my heartbeat decreased a little at every movement and my head cleared of any anxiety or confusion.

My eyes were still closed but I could discern a purple spot coming right at me. It grew bigger and larger and I felt myself moving toward something.

Or somewhere.

***

My eyes are open and I am not in the hospital anymore. I am walking in a green and yellow meadow. My sight is a little fuzzy but it gets better every second; however, the sun is so bright that I have great difficulty seeing where to set my feet. I suddenly and unwillingly turn around and look at my surroundings mainly composed of high grass, tall yellow flowers, a few sheep and horses, and forests gathered around treeless mountains. I don't need a glimpse of what lies behind me because I know that there is a beach and an ocean waiting there. But I'm not going back just now. The day has just begun.

I look down and admire the rays of light on the water left from yesterday's storm. After a quick look around, I can actually appreciate the glittering droplets, each leaf containing its own rainbow. The smell of the misty nature surrounding me is so pure, as if no human being has ever been here before. There is nothing to distract me from the green, the mild wind, the sun—

Except for one thing. I suddenly feel really excited at the thought of glancing behind the enormous oak standing a couple of feet from me. My eyes admire the beauty of this old tree. One of its branches is too heavy and has to support its weight on the ground, but the whole still looks healthy and vigorous.

However, that's not why I am staring at it. I know that someone is hiding behind its trunk: someone I love. My legs come to a halt and I bend to pick up a yellow flower.

It's not a lily, but it'll do, *I muse.*

I am not in control of my body, though the movements I make and the thoughts I contemplate seem natural.

A branch creaks from behind the tree, followed by a

woman's voice. *"Are you coming?" it says, and I realize that it is my own voice.*

"Yes, Amya. I'm right here," I say. *The sound coming out of my mouth is deep and hoarse. I look down.* Why are my hands so large? And why am I wearing a man's clothes? *The questions are lost when a more powerful emotion invades my mind.*

Excitement. I am thrilled that I get to be with her today. Everything is perfect, from spending some time alone with her to being here, in Blue. Nothing can go wrong. No worries about the world outside, nor him.

I walk the rest of the distance between me and the old oak and I am rewarded by the sight of her silky black hair over her right shoulder.

"I'm right here," *I repeat quietly, in a deep voice that is not mine.*

Confused, I feel my heartbeat accelerating and my eyes getting blurry again. What am I doing here? Why am I in a man's body? And more importantly, why is this place so familiar?

***

I was thrown back into my own body as fast as a bullet pierces flesh. It was only a matter of seconds before the heart monitor went crazy, my heart pumping fast. Too fast, I guess, because in the lapse of about two respirations, my hand was released, a man screamed for help, and several new voices arrived, every one more frantic than the other.

"Did you touch anything?" a woman inquired.

"Tell me what happened," another said.

The man next to me babbled a few words, not knowing how to explain my reaction. "I didn't… I—I was holding her hand and…" is what he managed to say.

His voice! His voice was the same I had impersonated while walking in the meadow. *What is going on?* I wanted to scream.

Anger boiled through my veins as the questions piled and no answer was given to me. My mind shut out everything happening around me and I focused on the past. On what I could remember…

I recalled the first time I had watched the movie *Ghost* with Samera. We had created a recipe for a perfect movie night: AllCheeses, a piece of cheese between two all-dressed chips. My parents had gone on a trip to California and they had nicely lent me the house for the whole weekend. Faithful to our tendency to experiment adult behaviors, Samera and I had decided to open a bottle of red wine. I can still remember that it was a Camporignano from Italy because after drinking the entire thing, we wrote to the Italian ambassador in the US to tell him that his beverage had gotten us all fuzzy, sick, and emotional. Samera and I cried throughout the entire movie and finally decided to stay single for most of our lives. I had never had a serious boyfriend anyway, and disliked the saying that "when you are with someone you love, you become one with them." I hated the idea of being half of an individual who could only be completed by someone else, the other half. I liked my independence. So my best friend and I made a vow to stay single at least until we had real jobs or were over twenty-five. However, as everyone knows, no one is ever safe from love. Love always fights its way to you until it knocks you over. A couple of months later, I met Wyatt Anderson. My first love.

During my first semester at Princeton University, Wyatt was assigned as my tutor, as he was one of the best students in English literature and I was probably one of the worst. Anyway, Wyatt was a twenty-three-year-old guy with royal blue eyes that put a night sky to shame. He probably had shoulder-length blond hair, but its curls shortened it to his ears. His strong jaw made his mouth look thinner though his lips were full and appealing. I learned during my time spent studying at his side that he was from Australia, though he did not really have an accent.

I'd never understood what Wyatt had found in me as he was flawless and I—well, I was a book geek failing a literature course.

After a truly awkward first meeting in Dr. Rubby's class,

we started studying together and hanging out, and two weeks later, he was calling me his girlfriend. He was even accepted into my close group of friends, only composed of Samera Cohen and Xander Macfrey, a boy I'd met at a boring party in high school.

My relationship with Wyatt had always been perfect. I remembered that cold day of November when he'd invited me to the movie theater and we'd both fell asleep watching the worst movie of all time. We'd woken up an hour after the credits and had laughed at ourselves for days… Or so I thought. Waking up next to him was the last thing I could remember.

I was trying to push the memories further, to the day before I was admitted at the hospital, when a sharp pain like a knife in my brain made me want to rip my head open. And then, appearing out of nowhere, I saw three sets of images in a sudden flash. The first one was a window followed by red eyes. The second showed Wyatt in front of a beautiful lake, the one nearby my parent's chalet. Finally, the third depicted a blurry face disguised as a ninja turtle and a giraffe. The more I dug for information, the less I could bear the excruciating pain starting in my brain and making its way to my neck and shoulders. I felt like every cell in my body wanted to explode.

"Amya," someone whispered, bringing me back to the present, to my hospital bed.

The agony instantly diminished until it was only a tingle in my temples, and then nothing.

"Amya, I'm right here." It was the same voice who'd screamed for the nurses' help earlier. "I don't know if you can hear me, but I'm right here."

I wished he would speak louder so that I could recognize his voice.

He seemed to shift into his seat and open a bag. An odor of metal mixed with vanilla filled the room and even though I couldn't remember when or where I had smelled it, my nose recognized the aroma. And I somehow felt threatened by it.

My jaw tensed and my eyeballs began to shift from left to right, like an automatic response.

Wait, so my muscles don't mind coming to life, but only when I'm not asking for it? My entire body actually felt less rigid and my gut told me that it would only get better with time.

The odd mixture of metal and vanilla grew stronger until it was all I could think of. The familiarity of it made me try to reach for some lost memory. I dreaded that the pain would come back, but I had to try one more time.

What does this smell remind me of?

Home, perhaps? My father was a writer and my mother worked for a bank. They both hated cooking so we often—if not always—called my grandmother to see if she had something left for us. She always did. She loved cooking for the whole family and my parents were thrilled not to have to prepare dinner every day. But there was no way Grandma would cook something with vanilla in it; she was allergic, as was my mother.

The clinking of metal was interrupted when two female voices grew closer to the hospital room. I instantly recognized one of them. My mother. Everything happened so fast afterward. The man next to me took his backpack and seemed to disappear on the left side of my bed, even though, after hearing my mother step into the room, I realized that the door was on my right.

Chapter II

"HER VITALS WERE OK. It must have been a bad dream," the nurse told my mom as they entered my room.

"Thank you, Nina," my mother said before the nurse left. "Hello, my darling. I brought your favorite flowers," she said and then paused. "Oh. Someone else had the same idea."

After—according to the noise—arranging the new lilies with the older ones, Mom sat on the chair to my left and slightly touched my forehead. She seemed to breathe slowly, as if to hide unwelcome emotions.

"I really wish you would come back, you know," she began in a tiny voice. "Your doctor, Mr. Bennett, told me that you were getting better. He keeps saying you can hear people around you, but I'm starting to think he's just trying to comfort us." She paused, took several deep breaths and kept going. "It's been almost five months, Amya. It is time now. Time to come home... Don't you want to come home?" She finished her sentence in a sob.

I had never seen my mother cry—not that I could see her now, either, but her words broke my heart. She and my father were always so happy and sweet with each other. It was like the honeymoon stage never ended. Always teasing one another and kissing tenderly, much like the high school sweethearts they were. If I had believed in soul mates, I would have said that my parents were meant for each other. My father spent most of his time in his study, writing novels, and my mother was the VP of a bank, which meant that she was often working, attending meetings, parties and such. Because they could not see each other often, they prioritized quality over quantity. And every moment was spent with a smile.

So hearing my mother in tears at my bedside was a new experience—one I'd rather have never triggered. Of course I wanted to come home, especially if I'd been in this state for five months. But how was I supposed to wake up?

My mother cleared her throat, which she always did when trying to push aside her emotions, her feelings. When she spoke again, her voice was steady and her words chosen with precision, as always.

"You were absent for your own birthday two weeks ago and even missed Nevada's memorial. It's the first year you miss her memorial… Xander and his father were there. Samera and the Cohens attended as well…"

She kept talking; however, my mind was already

elsewhere. Nevada…

The flash with the images came back, but this time, it lingered on the window and the red eyes. The two, I now knew for sure, were connected. Nevada…

I tried to focus on Xander's sister's name. Nevada…

I pictured the window and the red eyes, again, and held onto these images, searching for a connection. Nevada…

The window frame was beige, but you could see that the paint was old and needed some work done. If I took a closer look, a couple of teenagers were kissing on a chair nearby and several other students walked hastily. Nevada…

And then I remembered. The day of my sixteenth birthday. The beginning of the Transition.

***

"Nevada!" I shouted as soon as I saw the medium-length red-haired girl in the hallway. She had inherited her mother's hair, while Xander's was brown like their father's.

She looked up from her notebook and smiled. It wasn't her usual ear-to-ear smile, though. And she didn't jump up and down and talked faster than sound itself, as she made her way to me. Her eyes were sad and her shoulders a little hunched, so I hugged her, not knowing what else to do.

"Hi, Amya," she said, with the same half-smile. "Happy birthday."

"Thanks! But tell me about your summer in Florida. Is Xander back as well? God, I missed you guys!"

"It was fun," she replied, her pale green eyes glancing around, as if looking for somebody. "Xander is here. I think he was looking for you and Samera. You should check your phone. Excuse me."

She touched my right hand before heading to the bathroom and as soon as her skin made contact with mine, I felt bitter and pessimistic. Oblivious that it was part of a Transition, I had started to experience people's feelings a couple of days earlier; therefore, I knew these weren't my emotions. They were hers. I suddenly felt the urge to understand them and decided to follow Nevada to the bathroom, where I found her in tears.

"Hey, what's going on?"

She shook her head, not wanting to talk about it, but I wouldn't take no for an answer. I'd never seen her like that. She was the bubbliest person I knew, always laughing and teasing everyone. When she tried to leave, I gently seized her arm.

And that's when it happened.

A chill ran through my body as a purple spot shadowed my sight. And then, I was in her head. I could see me looking at her. But that's not what grabbed my attention. Her thoughts did.

Is she ever going to leave me alone? I—she—thought. *I didn't ask for her to care for me. I don't deserve it. She is just*

like mom. One day she cares, and the other she disappears.
Never to come back.

I should do the same. No one will ever realize that I am
gone until they find my body. And even then, what will they say?
I should make it easy for them. I should make my body easy to
find.

And she snatched her arm from my grasp, sending me
right back into my own body. It was the first time I had
experienced a Sojourn and I had absolutely no idea what it was
and how to react. We stared at each other for a few seconds,
until the bell rang, and then she stormed out of the bathroom.

I should have followed her that day. I should have tried
to talk to her, but I didn't know that what I had experienced was
real.

During the last period, someone shouted for help and
every student in class gathered around the window. As soon as I
saw what was happening outside, my head went blank. Next
thing I knew, I was kneeling on the school lawn, looking at a
distorted Nevada, and Xander was bent over her lifeless body,
somehow still trying to protect his little sister. His eyes
wandered through the crowd and as soon as they found mine, I
choked back my guilt and fled the scene.

Later that day, while I was crying into my mother's
arms, she told me about our family's ability to send our souls to
Sojourn into people's bodies. One member per generation goes
through the Transition starting on their sixteenth birthday. She

wasn't certain if I or my sister would be the "lucky one," so she never told any of us. Plus, she absolutely hated to bear that special power. Mother never listened when Grandma begged her to inform us. In her mind, if none of her daughters knew about the ability, it would never manifest itself.

I'd been mad at her for months after that. Were it not for her omission, Nevada might still be alive. But if Xander was able to forgive my Mom after he was told the whole story— including my new capacity—I too had to make an effort.

Even though the image of my friend's red eyes would forever haunt my conscience.

***

Recalling that memory made me want to shake some sense out of my mother. How could she have hidden such important information for sixteen years? However, I also remembered how responsible she had felt—and must still feel—for Nevada's death. My mother had never truly recovered; always offering her help to the remaining of the Macfrey family, Xander and his dad. After the incident, their well-being soon became of high priority to her. And Xander and I grew into even closer friends as he and Mr. Macfrey often had dinner at our house.

I also learned that year that the essence of vanilla blocks

the ability to Sojourn, which is why both my mother and grandmother told me they were allergic.

I tried to push the memories further, to remember how I had learned to control the Sojourns, but the headache threatened to come back, so I stopped at once.

At least, the Sojourn I'd experienced with the man earlier made sense. It also made sense that he had put on something sprayed with vanilla afterward, in order to obstruct me from his thoughts.

"I need to go back to work, darling," mother said, as if sensing my agitation. "But I will be here tomorrow at lunch, as always. Delilah also said she'd pay you a visit this week or the next. She came back from England just three weeks ago. She worked in a hotel in London during the entire summer. She'll probably tell you all about it herself. I almost didn't let her go because of everything that's going on right now... I know you and Wyatt wanted to go there after you both graduated, so when you wake up, she'll be able to indicate you which places to visit.

"Speaking of which, I spoke with your dean yesterday, and he assured me that you would be able to start your second year at Princeton as soon as you wake up. He said you were a good and studious student..."

My mother went on with her sentence, but my thoughts stuck on the phrase, "*you would be able to start your second year.*" How could I begin my second year of college, when I hadn't completed my first semester?

Information I had heard today but not fully comprehended came to me all at once. *My mother said that I have been in a coma for almost five months. Plus, we celebrate Nevada's memorial every year on my birthday. I was born on September 1st. If my birthday was two weeks ago, like my mom told me, and the last thing I remember was going to the theater with Wyatt in November, it means that I have no recollection of the last eleven months of my life!*

Chapter III

Ian Cohen

*THERE ARE ONLY A FEW THINGS I like about working with
my family. For one, I get to see them every fucking day of my
life, which allows me to find out the weak links for when the time
comes I take over the family business.*

That's pretty much it. No other reason, really.

"Ian," Amanda said, standing beside my desk, her arms
crossed. "Mrs. Cohen wants to see you in her office. Didn't you
get her calls?"

Of course I did. I simply chose not to answer. I knew
very well what Michelle wanted. *"Ian, would you please go to
Yellow and help the kids build their tents?"* or *"Ian, can you
write to the governor and tell them I am sending special forces
to help with whatever problem they're dealing with?"* The world
is falling apart and we're stuck here, in America, unable to do
anything. Such a pity.

Amanda grabbed a lock of her blond hair between her

fingers and started toying with it. *Here's a fact. She likes to pretend she doesn't care whether I give her a reply or not, but I know better. She's been sending me anonymous love letters for months now. And she thinks that if she ignores me, I'll start caring.*

"Out of my way," I snapped, rising from my chair.

"Oh, right," she squeaked, almost stepping over her own foot.

I walked past her without even a glance and headed to Michelle's office. It was small and decorated with pictures of her husband and daughter. But I didn't care. *This office'll be mine someday.*

"Mrs. Cohen, you wanted to see me?" I said with as much gentleness in my voice as I could fake.

"Yes. Ian, there's been a bombing in Washington. Take my husband and four other Protectors and pursue your own investigation. I am afraid that Becky and Marlow are behind it."

Becky and Marlow are teenagers who escaped from the Red Dimension a month ago by following a Protector. They've done damage to our society ever since. The rules are different here, in the Dimension of Amani, and Becky and Marlow don't seem to understand that.

If we lived in Europe, Michelle's suspicions wouldn't even get near Becky and Marlow. Actually, that's not entirely true. She would blame anyone other than her own family, the Cohens, even though she suspects that something is off with the ones living in Europe.

I am personally not Jewish. My father was, but my mother only converted after having me and my twin Jemina, so we were technically born non-Jewish. I chose not to convert to Judaism simply because my sister had, and I hated her. I hated her more than I loved my family. And soon after, I hated my family as much as I hated her. Before rejecting me and leaving America, my father kept saying that I did not feel the strong sense of the community because I had refused my family's religion. He tried to convince me that converting to Judaism would help me, but I didn't listen. Today, I wouldn't mind if my great-great-uncle killed innocent people or even started a war or if my distant cousin converted to Christianity. It is their own shame, not mine.

But for Michelle—and for the rest of the Cohen family in New York—it feels different. Everyone is on the edge, all praying for the rumors to be unfounded. For their family members to continue to follow the instructions of the Torah.

"What should we do if we find them?" I asked.

Personally, I would simply have Becky and Marlow killed. Problem solved. But Michelle will act on her emotions, as always.

"Bring them back here and we'll have a trial."

There you go. A trial. What a waste of time and energy.

I walked out of her office with a smile on my face and crossed the large space where everyone was working *so* hard at their computer. Inattentive to my surroundings, I ran down the stairs to the third floor and notified Michelle's husband, Karl, of our mission.

"When are we leaving, Ian?" he inquired.

Even though I am only twenty-five years old, the Protectors respect me. I am, after all, the right arm of our leader as well as her nephew.

I smiled. "In ten. Bring three of your people and I'll ask someone from upstairs to accompany us."

Someone from upstairs meaning another Protector who could Travel between Dimensions. Another Cohen.

The name "Cohen" is given to everyone with that ability, whether the ability comes from the mother or the father. For me, the name came from my father's side and was given to both my sister and me.

Karl didn't waste any time to gather three bodyguards trained to protect my family. I didn't know their names and I didn't care. As long as they were good at their jobs, that was all that mattered. I texted Jim to meet us outside the Headquarters in five minutes. Jim was the only Protector who answered to me, not Michelle. He was loyal to me.

The drive to Washington was quite productive. We discussed ways we could apprehend Becky and Marlow without attracting too much attention from the detectives investigating the bombing. *Not everyone knows about the Dimensions, so even though Michelle probably received permission from the president himself to investigate, our true intentions are classified to most people.*

We were going as FBI detectives and would have to deal with the real ones already on-site. Karl suggested that we wait until nightfall and then start searching the scene for clues. Another bodyguard, named Don, offered to act as a distraction while the rest of us would gather as much information as possible from the police.

"I will confess the crime," he said, "which will bring everyone's attention to me while you look for the real culprit."

I shook my head. That was the craziest idea I'd ever heard. "The bombing will probably be labeled a terrorist act in no time. You don't want your name tarnished in front of the entire world. There will be reporters everywhere looking for a good story to tell. You wouldn't survive a day in that madness. No. We must make ourselves invisible."

Karl was about to reply when the passenger side of our van was hit by a dark red Toyota. I had just enough time to look out the window and realize we were heading straight into the railing of the Delaware Memorial Bridge.

Chapter IV

THE FACT THAT I HAD BEEN SUCCESSFUL during my
two first semesters was quite encouraging, but it also meant that
I had lost memories of all the material covered since. And most
importantly, memories with my family, friends, and boyfriend.

Moreover, I'd have to wake up soon if I didn't want to
miss the opportunity to travel with Wyatt. We'd planned to visit
England shortly after I got my degree. If that were delayed, he'd
have time to find a job and everything else would have to wait.

"I can sense your emotions, Amya," my mother said with
a hint of excitement in her voice. "Don't worry. Everything will
be all right. We'll figure things out when you come back to us.
The important thing is that you're better now. The fact that I can
feel emotions emanating from you means that you are one step
closer to recovery."

There was a long pause, in which I just wanted to open
my eyes and throw myself into my mother's arms. The silence

was interrupted by someone at the door.

"Hello, Sylvia," said a man. A man whose voice I would recognize amongst thousands; a man whom I'd missed very much. The man I loved. "Mind if I join?" Wyatt said. "I haven't seen her for a week. How is she?"

I heard my mother stand up and walk toward the door to greet him. "Wyatt. I am really glad to see you. After all this time. I was just about to ask Amya if you'd been visiting."

"Ask her? Is she awake?" He sounded agitated.

Mom came back to my side and held my hand. "I am afraid she isn't yet; however, I can feel her emotions changing quickly when I speak to her. I assume she is somehow conscious." She patted the back of my right hand.

"How can she be conscious?" Wyatt's voice was a little pitchy, a sign that he was tired. He cleared his throat. "I wish I'd been here to notice the signs." He grasped my left hand and gave it a soft kiss. "I wish I hadn't left her side…" There was so much love and tenderness in his voice that it made me shiver. *Literally* shiver.

I miss you, too, I wanted to cry.

As if my mom could read my mind—and she actually could—she said, "I'll leave you two alone. I need to go back to work anyway." She kissed my forehead. "It was nice to see you again, Wyatt," Mom added before leaving.

My boyfriend waited for the door to be fully shut before he slipped his fingers between mine. At first, he seemed hesitant, but the now-familiar purple spot appeared as my body filled with warmth and love. And this time, the Sojourn felt complete; everything I said, thought or did came from Wyatt's mind, as I became my boyfriend.

***

Let me show you something. A memory that will never leave my side.

Both Amya and I are in my bedroom, studying. A few days ago, I redecorated it, as I knew that she wouldn't like the black walls and ceiling I had from my childhood. I've always needed complete darkness to fall asleep and I have a soft spot for darker shades.

Now, my walls are creamy beige with only a black stripe a little higher than midway between the floor and ceiling. A small window next to my bed allows the natural light in, although it is covered by thick curtains.

Sitting at my wooden desk situated across the window, Amya is frowning at her essay, probably about to ask me a question. Her curly black hair cover her shoulders, which is a sign that she is cold, again.

I can't help but smile. Studying Jane Eyre *had never been much fun—until I met her.*

"Hey, what did Dr. Rubby mean when—" she says as her gaze finds mine. Then her eyebrows raise as she realizes that I was staring at her. "What? Is something stuck in my hair? I hate it when I drop food in there" she says, shaking her head and examining a few locks.

"No, you're perfect." And I mean it. Today, she decided to apply mascara and mark her lower eyelashes with black pen, making her light green eyes even more radiant.

Her wrinkled nose and mild frown tell me she is not happy with the compliment. She told me not long ago that she was raised believing that outside beauty is a waste of energy, and was pushed toward developing many talents such as ballet, piano, violin, reading, and horse riding. She was told so many times that inner beauty is the only thing that matters that she has started to believe it too. But I try to remind her how lucky she is to be beautiful. Models would kill for her curved nose, full lips, and small waist.

"If I say thank you, will you please change the subject?" Amya finally answers. I must admit, not being able to compliment your girlfriend can be annoying sometimes.

"As you wish, princess."

"Then thank you," she mutters, looking exasperated, although anyone who knows her well would see an inch of a smile forming on the right corner of her mouth.

Before I can stop the words spilling from my mouth, I blurt, "No problem. I love you."

Idiot! What the heck is going on with your tiny little bird brain? *I should have never said that, but again, I mean it. Isn't the truth inevitable? I love her even though we only met two months ago. And I love her even though my family forbids it.*

While her jaw finds the floor and her eyes grow gigantic, I try to think of something to distract her. Think fast! *I scream at my brain.* "Hey, you don't have to say anything, you know. I didn't mean to tell you. I don't even—I mean—I don't really mean it. It just came out wrong." *Seeing that she is not about to answer, I add,* "Actually, just forget the last minute or two, and let's talk about Jane—"

"Do you realize how cute you are right now?" *She is smiling at last.*

"Nah, let's just forget about that and—"

"I love you, too," *she declares, her eyes shining like a hundred suns. That's when I realize that those four words just made my life simultaneously better and a lot more difficult.*

But there is no time to think of it, as Amya leaves my desk and jumps on the bed, instantly pushing her mouth hard against mine. Did she just say that to make me happy? Does she really love me? *I fear that she'll Sojourn and see what I am thinking, but then I remember the silver necklace I am wearing—the one sprayed with vanilla she offered me last month. My inner demons set aside, I can enjoy the rest of our evening together.*

***

I came back to my own body with a strong feeling of euphoria.

"I don't even know if you can Sojourn right now. But if you did, I hope you remember that night." He paused. "Whoa! Your eyelids are shaking like crazy, princess. I miss you, too. I wanted you to remember our first time together, how happy we were."

My heart was beating so fast that I hadn't noticed my body's reaction. I did remember that night. It had been my first time *ever*, but nonetheless amazing. I had never been so close to anyone in my entire life. Both mentally and physically. The way he had kissed me and the patterns his hands had made on my body...

My reverie was interrupted when Wyatt's phone rang. His ringtone was *Treasure* by Bruno Mars. I know it is cheesy, but this song was playing during our first kiss.

"Damn," he said before picking up. "Wyatt," he answered. "Yes. I was delayed." His interlocutor sounded angry. It was difficult to hear anything, but I was able to make out the words "red" and "Jeffrey". "No need to worry. I've got this," he said before hanging up.

I longed for him to show me the rest of our first night spent together, so that I could see how he had experienced it, but a wave of fatigue made me want to nap for a while. Wyatt's comforting fingers brushed my cheeks and then my lips, like a lullaby allowing me to sleep. I wanted to stay awake for him, but my body felt too heavy: heavier than when I had woken up earlier. I hoped it was possible to sleep while in a coma, as my mind drifted into nothingness.

"I miss you, Amya. Believe me, I do…" was the last thing I heard.

Chapter V

Ian Cohen

WHAT THE HELL WAS THAT? I WONDERED as I was dragged out of the van by the feet. I could hear people whispering around me and feel blood streaming down my face.

"Let go of me," I said in a faint voice.

My head was spinning but I nonetheless kicked whoever was helping me out of the car and got on my two feet. Everyone's face was distorted in a dizzying way and the bridge seemed to twist on itself. I thought I was going to be sick.

"Hey, man. I'm just trying to help," the short guy with dirt in his hair told me.

"Don't."

"I lost control of my car," he said. "I'm so sorry."

He made a few steps in my direction and I charged at him, my fist finding his nose in a hard blow. A woman screamed.

"Hey! What do you think you're doing?" the guy said.

I replied with a second blow, this time next to his left eye. My sight cleared and I noticed that his nose was intact and he was smiling. I didn't have time to understand what was happening before his fist found my face, sending me onto the hard concrete.

"Stop!" an older man shouted. "The police are on their way. Now get yourself together, both of you." He made a step in the direction of my van, but the guy who'd gotten me out of the car blocked his path.

"Get up," he ordered me.

I didn't think twice before I pulled myself up again and blindly attacked him, my head in his ribs. I had done that before in combat classes and never had I crashed into such a hard stomach. It was like I'd shoved my head into cement. And the guy didn't even budge.

It was only after he pushed me away that I realized the knuckles on my right hand were bleeding. Not from the accident, but from the blow with the guy's face. I looked up and he was laughing.

The people around had recoiled from us, taking pictures of the scene with their cell phones. I couldn't see any of the other Protectors, and when I peeked at our van, the guy in front of me back-kicked my shoulder, throwing me onto a spectator.

"Stop it!" someone shouted.

"Shut up," the guy snapped. "Now, get up," he told me.

I didn't understand. The madness inside me grew

stronger. He'd crashed our car and now he was trying to prove he was the strongest. And he sure as hell was enjoying himself. All I was thinking about was how to make him pay for the accident as well as for his arrogance.

I got up and pushed away the woman I'd fallen on top of. Then I turned to my opponent. "Get lost, man. Stop showing off," I said, not certain how he'd react. I couldn't let him win, but I couldn't look weak in front of everyone either. I turned to the crowd. "There's nothing to see here. Go on with your life. Come on, leave!"

When no one was moving, I grabbed my fake FBI badge from my pocket and put it on display so that everyone would see it.

After a moment of doubt, all of them retreated into their cars and drove away. We were standing on the left side of the road, so there was enough space for vehicles to easily pass by without hurting any of us. Though I wouldn't have minded if one of them ran into my adversary.

"FBI my ass," the guy spat after everyone was gone. "Get up and make a man out of yourself."

That was exactly what my twin sister said when we were kids. We used to fight. Not like a normal brother-sister fight, though. It was more like real combat, to prove to the other who was the strongest, the highest in our family hierarchy. She kept reminding me she was born a minute and a half earlier, which, she said, made her my superior. She was also superior in a way that my parents loved her the most.

I slapped myself in the face to get my thoughts together, spat the metallic-tasting blood from my mouth, and before I knew it, I was back on my two feet, running at the short, crazy guy, just like I used to run at my sister when she got me mad. His smile widened and he rushed toward me too. It all seemed to happen in slow motion. I dreaded the imminent blow, but I knew there was no going back. I realized only too late what he had in mind when he abruptly stopped, bent over sideways and thrust me into the air with his shoulder, throwing me off completely.

Next thing I knew, he was on top of me, one hand on my right arm and the other pushing my face to the ground.

"Look at them," he said, talking about the other Protectors in the car. They weren't dead. They weren't even injured, except for a few scratches to the head. None of them could get out of the car, though. "I know what you want, Ian."

"How do you know my name?" I asked through his fingers.

"It doesn't matter. I know you crave power. Power over them all. Over the Protectors. And I can give it to you."

Surprised, I struggled to break free, but it was like fighting against chain links: tiresome and hopeless.

"What are you talking about? Get off of me!"

His grip on my face and arm tightened as he laughed. "You definitely need to control your anger. Just let me help you."

Regardless of his arrogant attitude, this guy seemed to know his adversary very well. I was curious about his sources and intentions. "How?" I asked.

My rival let go of my face and smirked. Who was he? And how did he know so much about me?

"You are going to do exactly as I say. In exchange, I'll make sure you become the leader of the Protectors. Do you understand what I'm saying?"

Confused, I nodded. I could now hear sirens from not so far away. The police were finally arriving.

"Take this," the guy said, hiding a small device in my FBI gear. "I'll call you for more instructions. If you tell anyone about this…" He smiled. "I know you won't. Ian, this is your chance to be recognized for what you're worth. Don't waste it." He peeked at the Protectors struggling to get out of the car and added, "They can't know about this. And I'm not even sorry."

"Sorry for what?"

I'd just understood what was happening when his metal-like fist found my face again and everything went black.

Chapter VI

I WAS LEAVING THE UNIVERSITY Center for Jews, where I just met with Samera. She wanted to show me her new hair color and it didn't surprise me when I saw it was red. Not auburn, not orange-brown, but red *red*. As she bounced around, more excited than ever, her straight, flamboyant hair made her black skin even darker. It was like she'd caught on fire. I felt a twinge of jealousy; I'd never been able to dye my hair. No matter how much product the hairdresser tried on me, it remained as black as a raven's feathers.

I closed the door of the building, inhaled a cool breeze of April, and started heading toward my dorm, when I heard two men's voices deep in conversation.

"But she's always with her," the second complained. "He never leaves her side, either."

I recognized the voice from somewhere, but couldn't put my finger on who it was.

"He's gone for two days. Take advantage of the situation instead of whining." The first man could barely keep himself from shouting. "You already failed to—"

"I know," the first interrupted. "It won't happen again, I promise. She won't get away this time."

It occurred to me that they were talking about someone I knew. I wasn't sure why I had this feeling, but I still decided to move closer in order to see the men's faces.

The night was extremely dark due to the lack of any constellation in the cloudy sky. Anyone with a bit of intelligence would have hidden inside, waiting for the big fat cloud transporting water to pass, but curiosity won over sanity. I walked to the next corner of the building and was about to have a good look at the two strangers, when I stumbled over my own foot and collapsed on the ground.

"Ow!" I squeaked. My hands and knees had miraculously cushioned the fall; only my mouth decided to give away my position.

Everything fell silent. I laid still for a few seconds, waiting to see if the men had heard me.

"If it's her, I swear I'll—" the angry man began.

"She's still supposed to be—"

"I don't care what you suppose. Find her and fix this or *I* will."

I managed to clumsily get back on my feet and tried not to panic. Were they talking about me? Even if they weren't, I'd heard enough to know they wanted to hurt a student.

Think, Amya. When I was fifteen, my parents had forced me to take a karate class. The instructor once said that when you are confronted with a difficult situation, you can either fight or flee. Considering that I was alone against two men; that it was really dark; and mostly that I was absolutely terrified, my choice was quite easy. *Run.*

I ran as fast as I could, acknowledging for the first time the pain in both my knees.

"Hey, wait!" the man who was now behind me shouted. A part of my brain knew who it was, but I felt as if the other part blocked the information from me. The only knowledge leaking was this: I had to get as far away from that man as it was humanly possible, or I would not only put myself in great danger but also the people I loved.

As if things weren't stressful enough already, the deluge began. It was not so bad at first because I thought that the warm storm would make it harder for my pursuer to know where I was going; I was having a hard time keeping my eyes open, constantly attacked by a thousand drops, but then, I heard the thuds my feet produced on the pavement.

A few thin trees appeared in my sight and my legs immediately led me behind one of them. I hoped that my dark brown T-shirt would act as a good enough camouflage. *Now blend with the shadow of the tree,* I told myself, like I was a chameleon. I needed some time to think of an escape plan.

"Amya! Stop, please," the man shouted. He was getting closer.

And that's when it hit me. A strange feeling of *déjà vu*. I had been in that situation before. I had been running away from that man, whoever he was, and I hadn't been able to escape.

The dream. The one I had before I woke up at the hospital.

If it's just a nightmare, it will soon be over, I reassured myself.

I took several deep breaths, trying to calm my thoughts. I had nothing to worry about anymore.

"Amya?" the man cried. "Where are you?"

He was so close that I could see his shadow against the 1903 Hall building.

"Amya, show yourself. I'm not here to hurt you. You know I would never do that."

I closed my eyes, trying to wake up. I pinched myself. I bit my tongue. I moved an invisible wand like in Harry Potter. But nothing happened. Not a single thing!

The man had stopped running, as if he knew I wasn't far. My heart pumped in my ears. *Do something. Anything.*

I suddenly heard a dog barking closeby and almost cried out of surprise. My pursuer must have heard it too, because he immediately started running to where the sound had come from.

Saved by a dog, I now had two options. *One, I stay here for a little longer and risk being found by the man as soon as he comes back. Two, I try to reach my dorm before he notices anything.*

I had a choice to make and I had to make it fast. Even though I couldn't remember who this man was or what he wanted, I knew I needed to stay out of his reach to keep some people safe, so this time, flight wasn't the weak alternative. Without thinking any further, I peeked behind the tree to make sure that the man was out of sight, and I started to run again. This time, however, I didn't look back. Ignoring my painful knees, my headache, and the world spinning around me, I raced to Lauritzen Hall.

I kept my pace as my body threatened to collapse. My legs now trembled and I feared I would faint or throw up, but I had to keep going.

I was so close.

When I finally reached the wooden door, like a strand of sunshine peeking through the heavy rain, I took a last glance behind me and, more automatically than by will, as my knees and weakened lungs hurt badly, climbed the stairs three by three.

You're safe now, I repeated and repeated until I stood in front of my room, keys already in hand.

I unlocked, opened, slammed and locked again the door in four vivid movements. Then, I stood still in the complete darkness, taking deep breaths and allowing my eyes to adjust. After only a few heartbeats, I could discern my single bed facing the left wall. The window, standing right above the middle of the bed, was covered by thick blue curtains. I felt safe.

As I was about to take off my shoes, my eyes discerned a black silhouette stepping out from behind the wall that hid my working desk.

"Amya, Amya. Did you really think you could outrun me? You forgot something; I know where you live." The silhouette stepped out of the shadows, looking dangerously gorgeous, and grabbed my wrist.

***

I came to at the sound of my heartbeat echoed by the monitor next to me, and was welcomed to the real world by the exquisite scent of lilies.

Again.

I wasn't surprised at all when several nurses came rushing into my room, bickering about what had agitated the "poor inert girl." I had a nickname now. *Great.* I would have preferred Sleeping Beauty or Sleepy Head anytime, but I couldn't really tell them that, now could I?

At least you're safe, I reassured myself.

While the nurses argued about what had caused my heartbeat to increase that much, I reflected on that repetitive dream of mine.

It felt so real.

I'd read somewhere that people in your dreams are sometimes a substitute for someone else you know. Who was I afraid of? No one I remembered. But again, I'd lost the memories of eleven months of my life. Who knows what had happened since then?

My dreams could also be a side effect of a drug I was given at the hospital. I'd never been able to take aspirins, even for big headaches or fever. The medicine here certainly was ten times stronger.

"Surely she had a bad dream, again," a nurse concluded. "I'll inform Dr. Bennett; she hasn't had one in two weeks."

Shock, confusion, and terror stewed in my veins. I'd been out for two weeks? That meant we were no longer in September. I had lost my chances of getting back to University for the first semester. How was I getting better if I was unable to stay conscious? How would I ever wake up?

I felt like I would explode if I didn't calm down. *Breathe*, I told myself, even though I had no desire for serenity. I felt useless and rejected. Hopeless and tired. The whole world seemed to have forgotten about me. *Poor inert girl*; that's exactly what I was for everyone now. And all I'd managed to do was to pass out for *two freaking weeks*!

"Her sister is visiting today," said another nurse. "We'll notify her as well."

The rest of them acquiesced and before the door closed

behind them, I heard, "Oh, here she is already. Good morning Delilah."

The nurse said something else to my sister, probably about my nightmares.

"Thanks, Mona." Delilah said. She closed the door and sat to my left. Apparently, the chair hadn't moved for two weeks either. "Morning A," she said cheerfully. "I brought today's newspapers."

My sister was speaking to me as if I were awake. She had gotten used to my state as much as anyone else in this hospital. It was like she didn't care. It hurt.

"They say in here that Europe's homicide rate has increased by fifteen percent in the last year. *The authorities are looking for the cause of this phenomenon. There is no sign of a terrorist organization; homicides seemed to be orchestrated by a massive amount of people at a time. Federal agents in Italy admit to arresting one hundred and twenty-four people in the last week. They are building a new prison in Turin due to a lack of space in the already existing ones.*

"It goes on and on like this for three pages. Every country in Europe is under high surveillance. Some of my friends think that the Mafia is responsible. Erik is certain that a bunch of Mafias allied together and are trying to start the Third World War."

I let the words sink in. Things were definitely catastrophic.

"Here's what I think: everyone is freaking out for nothing," she continued. "It's all happening thousands of miles away from here and there's no way this craziness is going to cross the Atlantic. Plus, I was in England all summer and saw nothing suspicious. I'm sure European governments are making stuff up to scare everyone. They'll eventually come up with a 'solution' and become everyone's heroes."

She wasn't making any sense. Delilah was still young and thought that everyone was nice, pink, and creamy. She had turned seventeen in August, but still had the imagination of a seven-year-old. Following her dream of becoming an artist, Delilah had been recruited by a talent agent at the age of ten. She had a great voice, but my parents were not thrilled by the idea of sending their youngest daughter into the crazed world of music.

After she'd turned sixteen, Delilah decided to leave the house and focus on improving her vocal and dance skills, which forced her to take a part-time job in a restaurant. I was confident that she'd get what she wanted sooner or later, as she wasn't the type to give up on things she truly craved. She was the most stubborn person I knew, which was her best quality and worst flaw.

"Anyway, enough with the boring stuff," she said. "I've got some boy problems to share and you have to help me."

How can I possibly help you? I wanted to say, although I was more interested in learning more about a possible Third

World War.

As if sensing my challenge, she added, "Yeah, I know you're asleep and all—and by the way, I'd appreciate if you could just come back and stop being the center of everyone's attention. Mom and Dad can't do anything without mentioning your name: 'I hope she'll come back' here, 'I really miss her' there. It's positively annoying. *I* used to be the problem to solve in the family. *I* used to make our parents panic and deprive them of sleep every time I clandestinely left the house at night. Now I'm the one taking care of them. I even had to come back home for a while. Ugh." She paused, probably nostalgic.

I was getting a little worried for my parents. They didn't deserve the stress I was causing them. They already had enough on their shoulders, juggling their jobs and personal time together.

Add to that being nursed by Delilah, I mused. I wouldn't be so enthusiastic either if I were them.

Okay, enough with the mental bitching.

"He's sooo perfect!" my sister burst.

My little sister was in love. That was something I would have never thought possible for a while. She'd had boyfriends, but had never been serious with any of them.

"He has the most gorgeous face and the sexiest body. He's also really rich and super nice. And his family LOVES me."

Her phone buzzed twice and she paused before adding,

"Seems like he wants to keep our relationship secret for a little longer." She was definitely upset. Who was stupid enough to boss my sister around? *An amateur, obviously. He won't last long,* I anticipated.

"On the other hand, I'm sure you won't tell him that you know." She chuckled. "That's if you can hear me, which I honestly doubt."

Her attitude bothered me. *I'm in a coma, not deaf,* I wanted to yell. Her nonchalance hurt my feelings, though she had a point; I would definitely not be able to tell anyone about her secret lover.

"I'm not sure if I should tell you," she teased, which sent oxygen to my already burning curiosity. Why all the secrecy?

I must admit that we'd never shared the best sibling relationship, especially since I'd started university. I had become so busy with school that I'd set my own family aside for a while. My sister and I talked on the phone maybe once a month, no more. But I still loved her. We had so many priceless memories together that I didn't see how we could ever be estranged.

An urge of knowledge grew within me; I had to know who this mysterious guy was. I focused on her; on how she'd described her new boyfriend; on how she'd reacted to his text message; on her immediate thoughts.

I grew warm and at ease, like when you're sitting in front of a fireplace, reading a good book. My muscles relaxed and my mind cleared.

Even though I wasn't physically in contact with Delilah, the purple spot appeared; however, instead of moving forward until it filled my sight, it transformed into an image. At first I couldn't quite comprehend what it was. It resembled a beige balloon surrounded by the sand. Then, the balloon grew eyes. And soon enough, the circular shape was furnished with human features, and the sand transformed into soft and long sandy-blond hair. I immediately recognized the man my sister was in love with. Her new boyfriend.

Wyatt.

Chapter VII

"IT'S YOUR EX-BOYFRIEND, Wyatt," she confirmed. "You have to understand; you've been here for months, so we thought you'd be okay with it. If you ever wake up, that is."

That I'd be OKAY? If I EVER woke up?

HOW could she ever think I'd be fine with the idea of her with…? BLERCH! The mere image filled my mouth with bile.

Rage, betrayal, and hatred choked me and left a taste of iron that clawed its way up my throat. I felt nauseous. *What is she thinking? What in the world does she think she's doing with MY BOYFRIEND?*

Saliva was not welcome in my mouth anymore; it tasted too acrid. Its bitterness seemed to fill my muscles, tendons, and bones, like I was burning from the inside-out. The now thick and blazing air in the room made my body sweat, as if I was standing right next to the sun. Waves of emotions, swirling and raging through my mind, were slowly getting me seasick. I wanted to get out to compose myself, but the image of my sister with Wyatt kept coming back, which tied me up to an endless rollercoaster of hysteria.

I imagined doing things to both of them. Things to make them regret their treachery. Things I never thought myself capable of wishing on anyone, let alone on the people I loved. Nevertheless, things I would have gladly done to put my mind at peace.

Somehow, in this outburst of mad feelings, I felt Delilah retire in the corner of the room. I could *feel* her anxiety and terror. Her shame and regret. I could discern her voice repeating to herself that she should've kept her mouth shut.

Too late! I wanted to scream. My body was getting hotter by the second, though my heartbeat was even, which kept our situation unknown to the nurses.

"Amya…" Delilah said. "I understand that you're not thrilled by the news, and I apologize for breaking it to you. I honestly thought you two were over." She sounded genuinely sorry.

I don't care! She wasn't apologizing for hooking up with my boyfriend. She was just sorry she'd told me!

Kill her! A voice inside my head suggested. Madness really was controlling me now. *Wake up and beat her up. Wyatt won't like her anymore if her face is bruised and bloody.*

The idea seemed more and more appropriate for the

situation. Wyatt wouldn't date a girl with missing teeth and swollen eyes. Then he would run right back to me.

Go get her! The same voice encouraged.

"Your skin is red, Amya. Please try to calm down." It was Delilah again.

How dare she give you orders? After what she's done.

I thought I'd drowned in my own madness when the door opened.

"Hey Deli! How're you doing, girl? Long time no see." It was Samera. She seemed gleeful.

Knock my sister down for me, would you? I mentally requested.

But she couldn't hear me.

Samera had probably just noticed me in the room, because her next words were: "Holy moly—crap! What happened?"

"Nothing," Delilah answered, which convinced me that she was the stupidest girl alive. "I think she got mad at something I said. But I don't understand how…"

She's lying! She knows perfectly what happened! SHE is the cause.

"You must have done or said something…"

Tell her you stole my boyfriend, you bitch!

"I—I…" was all that came out of Delilah's mouth.

"All right. Can you please wait outside? At least until Amya recovers her natural colors." Samera paused while Delilah walked toward the door. "And Amya, you need to settle down. Now. You can't see yourself, but I'm telling you… it's not pretty. There's even a big vein popping out of your forehead."

As soon as my sister left the room, the air around me changed: a cold breeze soothed my skin and quickly made its way to my head. Then it was like someone dropped ice water on me. My previous emotions suffocated and promptly died out.

The threat is gone, I thought.

"Whoa, it worked. Good. Now, I need to make a call. Can I leave the room for two minutes without you catching fire?" Samera's high spirit was back, but I could still discern concern in her voice. "I'll take your silence as a yes," she said and left.

Now that my tantrum was finished, it was good to hear my best friend's voice.

What was that all about anyway? I'd never felt so outraged and out of control in my entire life. It was like I'd been possessed by insanity itself. What had Delilah said earlier? Had my skin been red for real?

It was so confusing. How had I seen Wyatt's face in the first place? Delilah didn't touch me, and without skin-to-skin contact, a Sojourn isn't possible.

Thinking back on it, I was still mad at both my sister and Wyatt; however, I was able to keep my calm and think rationally. I'd been gone for a total of five months. Surely Wyatt had missed me and waited for a while, but I couldn't ask him to wait forever.

Still, he could have chosen someone else. Even if you normally don't decide who you fall in love with.

Was he in love with her? Ugh. The images forming in my head made my stomach twirl. And the way Delilah had talked about Wyatt before mentioning his name told me she really loved him.

They had only met once during a family dinner and my sister had seemed so shy and distant, which was contrary to her normal behavior.

Maybe they saw each other behind my back. Maybe they've been going out for longer than...

That's paranoia, a voice inside my head told me. It was weird; the voice sounded like mine, but more expressive; as if I had two inner personalities.

That's it. I'm going crazy.

The door opened, interrupting my newly building anxiety.

"This being done, you and I have to talk," Samera told me. "Well, I'll do the talking and you the listening." She paused, all serious.

I wasn't used to that side of her. She'd always been the lighthearted one, always bringing a smile to people's faces and laughing at anything. Being serious and boring was my specialty.

"You need to come back," she continued. "Not in a

month, not in a week. *Now*. We need you back here."

I want to! Believe me, I do, I wanted to scream, but my lips were sealed.

"Try something for me, would you?" she asked.

She didn't have time to finish before the door clicked open and someone walking slowly and probably with a stick entered the room.

"Samera, dear," my grandmother said. "Thank you for calling me. What happened exactly?"

I did not pay attention to Samera's account of my earlier outburst. My grandmother was here!

I hadn't seen her in ages. The last time I could recall was a couple of weeks before I started university. Even that memory was blurry. Trying to remember, I focused on her apartment in Baltimore: the orange furniture and the dozens of paintings, photos, and clocks on the walls. We'd been working on my special gift... yet that's not why I'd paid her a visit.

I remembered being scared. But of what?

By then I was able to control my Sojourns. There was something else, though. Something special about the Sojourns that I didn't understand. Something the rest of my family couldn't do, not even Grandma... something dangerous.

"Look at her right hand!" Samera exclaimed, which made me lose my grip on the memory. "Her fingers moved! I saw it, I swear."

Her enthusiasm was contagious. A sudden thrill passed

through my body and made me shudder.

I actually *felt* the goose bumps *lift* the hair on my arms. Did that mean I was getting better?

I wish.

"Did you see that?" Samera cooed. She was beyond excited, now. "That's what I was trying to tell Amya before you arrived," Samera told my grandmother. "There is no doubt she can hear us now; the incident with Delilah wouldn't have happened otherwise. That means she's literally gaining back control of her senses. C'mon Amya, keep trying."

I am! I just didn't know how.

"Amya, darling," Grandma said. "All you need is two cupfuls of will, a half-cup of tenacity, and a tablespoon of support."

Grandma's favorite hobby was cooking. She always had the best recipes for everything: cakes, stews, soups, pies, and often life, too.

If she believed in me and thought I was ready, I owed it to her to at least try something.

Taking a deep breath, I focused on my fingers. No, only on my right pinky. *Take small steps,* I told myself. I pictured my pinky moving freely, without the tense feeling inhabiting my body.

Go, go! You can do it! Go, go! A voice inside my head cheered. The same one who'd wanted me to kill my sister earlier.

Don't push her, another voice said. *Even though she can't hear you, you know how your emotions influence her, particularly at the moment.*

That last voice sounded older. It spoke very slowly.

Hello? Who's there? Gosh, am I going crazy again? I asked.

Do you think she's talking to us? The first voice said.

Of course not. It is impossible, the second, older voice answered.

Not that impossible, I guess, I carefully replied.

Silence.

Yay! You can hear us! That is sooo great! I'm Amya, your Red-self, and she is Amya, your Blue-self, the younger voice said. *It's so nice to finally talk to you!*

Red? Blue? I considered the idea. *What are you talking about? God, I've got a triple personality disorder. I should be sent to an asylum.*

Red, Amya lost part of her memory, like we had before we were able to converse together. She probably doesn't remember what Dimensions are. Don't scare her just yet.

Right, Red said.

Amya, we should not be the ones to tell you. The fact that you can hear us is already dangerous enough. Try to wake up. Samera and your grandmother will explain everything.

How do you know they're at the hospital with me? What's going on? Who are you guys?

We should at least tell her something, the youngest said.

All right. I am your Blue-self from the Blue Dimension and the other voice you hear is your Red-self from the Red Dimension. We've been hearing your thoughts ever since you became conscious. But you're not supposed to hear us. *Your soul must still be too close to our Dimensions.*

I didn't know what to say. This made no sense at all. *I've never heard of Dimensions and I have no idea what you're talking about.*

All I wanted was to wake up and stop hearing voices.

Pushing my thoughts toward my family and friends, I imagined seeing them again, being able to talk to them. I pictured their faces: Mom, Dad, Samera, Xander, and Grandma. I purposely avoided thinking of Delilah and Wyatt, as I wanted to recover my sanity, not lose it completely.

They were all surrounding me, smiling and encouraging me to follow them. I tried to touch my mother's hand. I tried to grab Xander's elbow, but they were still too far. Out of my reach.

I'm completely useless. The only thing I managed to achieve so far is talk to imaginary voices.

We're still here, you know. And we're not a product of your imagination. You'd know if you paid a little attention to what Blue said.

Blue? Aren't you both called Amya? How could it get more confusing?

Since we all have the same name, we're calling each other by our Dimension, Blue said. *Look, we have neither the time nor the appropriate knowledge to explain to you what Dimensions are. All you need to know is that your soul is probably wandering between the four Dimensions. It's the only explanation as to why you'd be able to hear us.*

Why would my soul be wandering?

You were able to Sojourn without touching your sister, right?

You should've never done that, especially considering your present state, Red interrupted.

Why? I don't even know how I did it.

You projected your soul into your sister's head.

Right then, everything clicked together. *And I'm the only one in my family to have this ability! I remember now!* It was like the memory had been triggered by Blue's words.

That's why I had visited my grandmother the last time I saw her. We'd worked on the Sojourns, to hone my new skill. I didn't need to touch people to Sojourn anymore; I could project my soul.

You're the only one with that cool power? Whoa, that is awesome, Red said.

It really is amazing, Blue continued. *However, it seems to me that it is a dangerous thing to do when in a coma. I believe that your soul did not have enough time to come back to your own body because you experienced strong emotions.*

Rage.

Exactly. The power of those emotions must have brought your soul closer to the Red Dimension, which is all about passion, energy and immediacy.

You talk about Dimensions like they are different worlds. I don't understand, I said.

One question at a time, Amya, Blue stated. *Samera and your grandmother will explain everything when you wake up. Right now, you are still wandering in between Dimensions, which would explain the fact that you can hear and speak to us. I studied the interaction between individuals in different Dimensions and I've never heard of anything like this. It could be dangerous.*

Why do I have Red and Blue selves?

You are made of Blue and Red. Isn't it obvious? That was Red. I was getting used to the differences of tone in their voice. Blue was calm and patient, while Red's tone was dry and abrupt.

Samera and your grandmo—

I know, I know. They'll answer all my questions when I wake up. But just tell me: is it why I see a purple spot right before a Sojourn?

Very good. My Blue-self sounded pleased at my inquiry. *I personally never experienced a Sojourn, but it would make sense since the two colors mixed together represent you in the Dimension of Amani.*

And why did Delilah say my skin was red earlier?

I was more and more curious about this Dimension thing, even though I barely understood what it meant.

As I said, Blue continued, *your soul wandered too close to the Red Dimension when you realized that your sister was dating your ex-boyfriend.*

Boyfriend. He didn't break up with me, I corrected.

My point is—Blue ignored my comment—*that, as you realized they were a couple, you became influenced by your Red-self alone*—

And I was really pissed! Red said.

Her anger overwhelmed you in your Dimension—*Amani.*

I let their words sink in. It all made sense, even though I still wasn't completely certain if I was—or not—imagining the conversation. Glad to finally obtain some plausible answers, there was one more question I needed to ask.

This is all a nice story, but how do I go back to my body?

Chapter VIII

TRULY, I HAVE NO IDEA.

Thanks, Blue. That helps a lot.

Here's what I know, Blue continued. *Your soul was created in Amani. Therefore, it will eventually have to go back where it belongs, especially if your body is there.*

Her words made me shiver. *Eventually?*

However, if you wake up, Blue continued, as if she was talking to herself, *your soul will have no other choice than to go back. Or not. This is far too complex.* She paused. *Unless... Unless you become conscious of your environment again. Gain back your senses. All of them. That way, your body would need your soul to comprehend everything that's happening to it. Right now, you can hear, feel, and smell, is that right?*

Yes. And taste. Well, kind of.

Sight! You're only missing your sight! Red exclaimed.

Yes... Blue pondered. *But what if your whole body—*

including all your senses—was appealed to?

What do you mean?

Do you remember, when you projected your soul before being in a coma, if it worked when people touched or talked to you? Did it block your soul in any way from leaving your body?

I've never tried that. Not that I remember, anyway.

There's a first time to everything! Red said, more cheerful than ever.

Try to appeal to all your senses at once.

Maybe they were right. Maybe becoming conscious of my surroundings would call my soul back into my body. And then, just maybe it would help me wake up.

C'mon Amya! Not that I've got other things to do than to sleep for the rest of my life... but that's exactly what it is.

Red, I said, *why don't you wake up if you're in such a hurry? And I hadn't thought of it before, but are you two in a coma as well?*

Yep! Our life in our Dimension isn't like yours, but if something radical happens to you—like, I don't know, if you die or get your legs chopped off—it'll happen to us, too.

Great. So, your lives depend on me. No pressure at all.

Pushing aside the realization of a new burden, I focused on the task at hand. Red and Blue stopped talking to let me concentrate on Samera and my grandmother. They were now chatting about *haute cuisine*. Grandma was explaining to Samera how to make macarons.

"But every time I try, they burn," my best friend complained.

Grandma laughed slightly and kept telling her that cooks need to be patient and learn from their mistakes.

Still listening to their conversation, I tried to smell the lilies in my room. I'd gotten accustomed to the scent, which made me forget they were even there. It was fresh and soothing and reminded me of my parents' house. They grew many types of flowers in the garden and often left the windows open.

Having nothing to chew on, my mouth didn't taste anything. With a bit of imagination, however, I could picture myself eating one of Grandma's apple pies. It was a bit spicy— as she loved adding a little more cinnamon than the recipe required, but the main flavor was sweet and warm.

I couldn't see how I was lying in the hospital bed, but the dry feel of the sheets under my hands told me both arms lay alongside my waist. A stronger pressure over my torso also revealed that the sheets stopped a little under my neck.

I had a hard time picturing myself in that position, though. Was my hair tied up? Were my cheeks flushed? What color was my hospital gown? Blue? Yellow?

"You're right, Magda, it's getting late," Samera said, which piqued my curiosity.

Were they leaving?

"I will go back to the hotel, Amya dearest. We can try again tomorrow. Your grandma still needs her beauty sleep."

Grandma was leaving! She sounded so tired. "Sweet dreams."

No, wait!!

"I'll be back tomorrow," Samera said. "I just thought that since you'd reacted earlier… Oh, well. I have a family gathering tomorrow afternoon, but I'll come as soon as it ends."

"Will you escort me to my hotel, Samera?" Grandma asked.

Don't give up on me! I wanted to scream. They expected me to fight and I couldn't. I didn't know how.

Don't leave me alone. I didn't want to sleep for two more weeks like the last time I'd been conscious. Five months in a coma was more than enough.

"My hotel is very close to the hospital," my grandmother said. "I want to be ready at any time my little angel wakes up. Sylvia and Kellen are gone on a business trip for only three days, but we never know what will happen."

Mom and Dad were gone? Even *they* had given up on me.

Panic transformed into an urge to prove myself, as I heard Samera and Grandma slowly head for the door.

I concentrated on everything I'd done before realizing the departure of my two visitors. Hearing their feet leaving my side; smelling the lilies; tasting absolutely nothing; and seeing absolutely nothing; and feeling only the dry sheets under my comatose body!

And NOTHING happened.

How can I be so weak?

One is not weak. Only their will is, Blue mused.

But I want to wake up! I cried with all the strength I had left. *I want to see my family and friends again! I NEED to go back!*

The clothes on my body tightened, as if to strangle me. It was like the fabric wanted to keep me from any movement—had I been able to move. It became hard to breathe, but I struggled and kept trying to get away. I would not become the "poor inert girl whose soul hadn't had the strength to come back."

Keep fighting, some voice said. I couldn't be sure if it was Red or Blue. *It's difficult but not impossible.*

The world spun around me, as I tried to grip reality. I was getting dizzy and couldn't hear the beeping of the heart monitor anymore.

Am I going to pass out?

Technically, you passed out months ago.

Shut up! You're not helping! I shouted at whoever was playing smart ass. *I'm still conscious and I intend to keep it that way!*

The mere effort I'd made to reply was one struggle too many. Disoriented, I was caught in a spiral of colors, every one brighter than the other, not knowing how to stop the spinning. The convulsing.

The circular rainbow finally disappeared, leaving me in complete darkness, breathing deeply and noisily.

"Amya?"

Darkness transformed into a dark shade of brown, which became lighter and lighter with every breath. A burning pain started on top of my hand, but immediately faded when I broke away. Someone gasped.

"Amya," I heard again. "It's me, Samera."

The burning sensation came back, but this time on my arm. I wanted to move again, but then I realized that it was Samera's fingers. She was touching me. Coming back to my senses was a little more painful than I thought. I didn't move, though, and after a few seconds, the blazing sensitivity of my skin died out.

Looking for my best friend's hand, I moved my fingers along hers.

"Oy, Magda! She's back! She really is!" she said.

"I am so proud of you, Amya," my grandmother stated. "Your soul is coming back from a long Sojourn; your body might not be very comfortable at first, but I'm certain it will ease up as you go."

My grandmother's voice was gentle and patient. I tried to open my eyes to see her, but every time my eyelids lifted a little, a bright and silver light—much too dazzling for my taste— blinded me and forced my eyes to close again.

"Take your time, little angel," grandmother said.

"Close. Light," my lips spoke before I could even process the thought.

My throat felt dry and bitter, as if I hadn't opened my mouth for years. I wondered if they'd brushed my teeth in the last two months.

"Oh. Sorry," Samera said as she made her way to the door, where, I assumed, the switch was.

But she was instantly stopped by my grandmother. "She needs to adapt to her environment, not the other way around," she explained.

I grunted.

"As difficult as it is right now, Amya," Grandma continued, "you're almost there. We will let you rest as soon as you are awake and sound." She paused. "I remember the day of your first steps like it was yesterday. Your parents and I went for a walk. It was the whitest day of winter. Your father had been carrying you for a while when you began struggling to break free. Kellen decided to set you on your two feet and see what would happen.

"The first thing you did was fall on your backside; however, you quickly climbed your way up, grabbing at your father's pants. Then, you turned around and started putting one foot in front of the other... until you stepped on your own shoe and fell on your face and knees.

"Having barely thirteen months, you cried for your mother's help, but I got to you first. I looked into your fair green eyes and said: You fell, Amya. And it might hurt right now, but this feeling will soon be replaced by one of pride as you will get back on your feet and walk some more.

"Maybe that day was the first time you ever experienced helplessness, but believe me, today isn't the last. Weak or strong, everyone falls at least a thousand times throughout their life. It is in what they learn from their fall and how steady they become that you recognize the strongest of all."

Her words gave me a new boost of courage. I hadn't made all these efforts to give up that easily. I yearned to open my eyes, and I was going to, even if it meant that I had to look at the blazing light one more time. As my grandmother said, my eyes would adapt and the pain would cease. I had to get back on my two feet.

Using my eyelashes as protection at first, my sight gradually cleared and shapes began to form in front of me. There were two shapes, one taller than the other. They seemed dark against the white ceiling and walls. My eyes paused on the smallest form, slowly transforming into my grandmother.

"Welcome back," she said, smiling mostly with her eyes.

The more I stared at her, the more I recognized her familiar features. She had the whitest hair, whiter than the walls behind her; only a few black stripes were still striving against her age. She wore her usual thick glasses, which hid most of her bulbous nose and almond-shaped green eyes. Just then did I notice how tired she looked. She wore heavy blue rings under her eyes, which seemed bulky and worn-out. I felt responsible for the new wrinkles on top of her mouth and forehead. Her affectionate expression couldn't hide how worried she'd been in the last five months.

With my eyes now accustomed to the dim light and with the pain gone, I took a closer look around. The second shape, my best friend, smiled at me with her big white teeth.

"You cut your hair," I said as I realized that instead of touching her waist, it merely patted her shoulders. My voice sounded so fragile, I thought for an instant that I'd turned into a mouse.

"I was wondering if you'd noticed," she said, her smile widening to her ears.

Samera shook her head, which brought her straight locks in front of her big brown eyes. And she smiled again, waiting for a compliment.

"It looks great."

"Thanks! Anyway, I'm glad you're back. I was beginning to worry about you."

"Beginning?"

"Well, you know what I mean."

I did. Samera wasn't the best at expressing her feelings. Actually, she probably was one of the worst.

"I missed you, too," I told her and squeezed her hand.

Then I closed my eyes, enjoying the sensation of my muscles coming back to life. Limb by limb, I recovered my mobility. Limb by limb, I recovered from a long journey.

Which reminds me that I still have no idea what brought

me here in the first place.

I opened my eyes again, but this time, I didn't fear the unwelcome light; I was eager for answers.

"What happened to me?" I whispered a little louder than I'd expected.

Samera looked at me dubiously. "You were in a coma, remember?"

I half-rolled my eyes and ignored the question. "How?"

"That we don't know. Xander and I found you unconscious in your room at Princeton mid-April, right after the finals. The door was open. There was no trace of alcohol or drugs or even violence for that matter. When we got to the hospital, they said you were in a coma."

It didn't make any sense.

My grandmother must have perceived how upset I was because she added, "We are still looking for the cause of your condition, however. Or the culprit."

Her last words echoed in my head. "Could someone have something to do with this? Surely, I would have had some kind of physical damage if that were the case."

"We don't know, Amya." Grandma looked tired. "We will let you rest, now." She kissed my forehead. "We will be back tomorrow."

"Yeah, don't worry 'bout that for now," Samera said. "You're safe here. We'll figure things out. And don't you dare be unconscious again tomorrow or I'll kick your—"

"I'm certain Amya is only going to get better from now on," Grandma interrupted and winked at me. "Sweet dreams, angel."

"Night, Amya. See you tomorrow!"

Samera opened the door for my grandmother and quickly followed behind.

"Good night," I murmured, still thinking about our conversation.

I was finally awake but all I wanted to do was to take a long nap. My eyelids felt so heavy. After deciding that I wouldn't uncover the truth on my own, I closed my eyes and fell asleep.

Chapter IX

WHEN I WOKE UP FROM A DREAMLESS NIGHT, I felt really grateful to be conscious and sane again. My eyes opened and I immediately noticed the window on the left wall. The sky outside was a mixture of pink, purple and orange; the colors intertwined around each other, as if trying to make one.

Someone must have left the window open; a mild breeze brushed my cheek, which made me close my eyes again and take a deep breath.

Now that I'm awake, everything will go back to normal.

Feeling already better than I did the previous day, I decided to have a look around the room. Next to the window were two jars of lilies and a pink rose. They looked freshly plucked and smelled like heaven.

On my left was the machine that gathered all the tubes connected to my body. I wondered about their use. The only one I was familiar with was the heart monitor.

There were two chairs in the room; one to my left and one in front of the bed, close to a small desk—which, to my disappointment, didn't exhibit any food or water. I was getting a little hungry and my mouth tasted like lemon and rotten potato chips. However, I was uncertain how my stomach would react to actual food and liquid after being on a forced holiday for five months.

Once the idea of screaming at the nurse to bring me something to eat was dismissed, I did a retrospective of yesterday's events.

I declined the first thought that came to my mind—Delilah and Wyatt together—simply because I couldn't do anything about it on my own. I'd have to eventually talk to them, although *eventually* might take a while.

Blue and Red were my next inner inquiry. Were they real? If so, what about Dimensions? I thought about asking my grandmother or Samera later, but doubted my credibility, having just barely recovered from a coma. I planned on going back to school after leaving the hospital, not being sent to a mental institution.

I remembered Grandma saying something about Dimensions and colors: how if you own the three primary colors—blue, red, and yellow—plus black and white, you can create any existing color. Moreover, I'd eavesdropped on my mother and grandmother once. The latter was asking for the former's help. She also said that it was my mother's duty to help her and mentioned something about Dimensions. It didn't take long before Mom got angry and stormed out of the house, leaving my grandmother dumbstruck.

Two quick knocks on my door startled my speculations.

"Are you awake, Amya?" asked a man with a British accent.

"Um, yes," I answered, not liking the idea of being interrupted.

The door opened only to let emerge a tall man wearing thin glasses, a long white scrub and a pair of yellow and purple converse shoes. The odd combination made me giggle a little, but I immediately composed myself, not wanting to be disrespectful.

As for my doctor, it was difficult to guess his age. His hair was nearly all white, though his features were wrinkle-free. In the end, I decided that he was around thirty-five, as men often grow white hair at a young age.

He looked at his feet and smiled. "They are cozy," he said.

I smiled back as he carried the chair in front of my bed to my right and sat on it.

"I am Dr. Cole Bennett. You were assigned to my care on April 20th, after Mr. Macfrey and Miss Cohen brought you here. I was informed yesterday by your grandmother that you were awake; however, the nurses found you sound asleep when she came to disconnect some of your tubes." He looked at me over his glasses.

"I was tired, I guess."

"Indeed, indeed," he mused. "How are you feeling today?"

How *was* I feeling? Confused? Hungry? Thirsty? Tensed? All of the above?

"Better than yesterday," I chose.

"Very well." Dr. Bennett wrote something in a small pocket pad I hadn't noticed before. "We removed the tube transferring the solute yesterday, so you might feel thirsty in the next couple of hours. A nurse will bring you food and water as soon as we are certain that your condition is stable." He paused. "Are you able to move, besides your head?"

I was surprised I hadn't tried to move earlier. After doing a few circles with my wrists and shoulders, I decided that even though my muscles were sore, I would try to sit on my bed.

"My muscles ache a little, but other than that, number one," I said as my enthusiasm filled my eyes.

Slowly, I lifted my head and shoulders and was about to set my elbows under my shoulder blades, when I felt a strong pain like a knife piercing my internal organs.

"Ow," I shrieked.

"Slow down," Dr. Bennett said. "You need to let your body adapt, as it's been motionless for five months. Take small steps, would you?"

"Yes, sir," I muttered.

I hated the idea of being glued to my bed. Plus, I was starting to feel a pressure on my bladder.

Shoot. How will I be able to go to the bathroom?

After clearing my throat, I asked, "Dr. Bennett, how can I, hum, attend to personal business… over there?" I nodded toward the bathroom, warmth rising in my cheeks.

"Please, call me Cole," he said. "You do not need to use the bathroom until we remove the catheter from your bladder, which will be done later today."

"Oh." *That's embarrassing.*

"It was either that or a diaper," he joked, trying to alleviate the conversation. "It is likely that you feel a constant need to go *over there*," he indicated the bathroom with his chin, mimicking what I'd just done.

He smiled, which morphed his eyes into two half-moons, and wrote something else into his notepad. Then, his hands reached for a small flashlight in his scrub pocket, probably to examine my pupils' response. I instantaneously thought of how I'd reacted to the dim light of the room the previous night, and shrunk away from him.

"It is not going to hurt you, Amya. I need to make sure that you are in complete control of your brain." He paused, as if assessing whether he could continue his train of thoughts. "When—" he frowned, "—when you arrived at the hospital in July, a nurse tested your pupils, the same way I am about to… but they were of equal size and both reacted to the light."

Cole looked at me expectantly.

"Isn't that supposed to be a good sign?"

"That your pupils are responsive is good," he replied. I exhaled the breath I'd been unconsciously holding. "That your pupils are responsive while in a coma is… unconventional. You see, we tested you on many drugs, but none of the results came out positive, which makes me believe that *perhaps* you were not in a coma."

"I don't take drugs," I said as fast as possible, and a little louder than I intended.

"I believe you, Amya. What I am saying is that at least one of your pupils should have reacted abnormally, whether it was a result from drugs, a lack of oxygen, a head trauma, or so on. In your case, nothing indicated that you were in a coma. You could have been asleep and your eyes would've reacted the same way."

I remained silent.

"We—and I speak for all doctors working in this hospital and its surroundings—have no bloody idea what caused you to sleep for so long," Cole continued. "Furthermore, you went through an empty wake-sleep cycle."

Having no clue what he was talking about, I remained silent, again.

"Were you aware of having visitors? Were you, in a certain way, conscious?

"I sort of was. But only twice including yesterday."

I looked down at my hands, playing with the sheets, wondering if I could trust him. For one, I hadn't known Dr. Bennett—Cole for more than ten minutes, but somehow, I felt like he was trustworthy—for most of the truth, anyway.

I told him about the dreams I'd had and how lost I'd felt waking up without being able to open my eyes or move in any way. I talked about my visitors and how tired I'd felt at the end of the first day, before falling asleep for two more weeks. I obviously left off the parts with the Sojourns because most people are afraid of anything out of the ordinary. Cole kept silent and often nodded and squinted.

When the altered truth was told, I felt hopeful that my doctor would be able to find answers for me.

"Would you mind telling me what you remember of the night before the incident?"

"I wouldn't mind, but I can't remember a thing." It was the truth, except that I had a feeling my dreams were somehow related to that night. "The first time I was conscious, my mother said that I would be able to return to Princeton for my third semester as soon as I woke up. The thing is, I don't even remember finishing my first semester. You said I was admitted here in April. Well, the last memory I have is going out with my boyfriend. In November."

Cole had been writing in his pad, though he stopped when I finished my sentence and lifted his startled eyes to meet mine.

"You suffer from amnesia?"

I thought about it for a second. It was like I was remembering bits and pieces at a time. My sixteenth birthday. My ability to Sojourn. But there was still such a big gap. So much information missing to be able to connect the dots and see the full picture.

"Yes, I suppose I do."

"What were your dreams about?"

"In both, I was chased by a man. The weird thing is that in the middle of the second dream, I realized that I'd dreamt of the situation before, so I made different choices. The man still found me in the end, though."

"Can you recall his face? Some of his features, maybe? Was he tall? Where were you? Why were you running away?"

"I don't know! Why is this important? They meant nothing," I lied, as I tried to remember what my pursuer looked like. But the image was blurry.

"Sometimes," Cole said, ignoring my impatience, "memories take the form of dreams. Surely, if both dreams were similar and occurred before consciousness, they might have a specific meaning. Perhaps your brain is trying to tell you something."

"My brain can't talk."

"Exactly. It can only show you… Now, I'm not here to judge you, so would you please tell me what you remember?"

He thought I was embarrassed by the dreams. I wasn't. I

was scared. Scared that he might be right. But if I wanted answers, he had to know the truth. Therefore, I told him everything that had happened in the first and second dreams, carefully recalling my thoughts and feelings during both. When I finished—a little out of breath—his eyes moved fast, as if trying to solve a math problem. And then, they found mine.

"This person, the man you are describing, do you remember anything about him?"

"No, I'm sorry. Oh! Well, I know his voice sounded familiar."

My ears and the back of my neck felt extremely warm, although I shivered at the idea that maybe—just maybe, someone I knew was responsible for all this.

"Do you have enemies? Anyone who would want to hurt you?" Cole asked.

I immediately thought of the man who'd been at my bedside the first time I came to my senses. The man who'd mysteriously disappeared, probably jumping out of the window or something. I couldn't be sure. What if he knew about my ability? What if what he'd showed me was pure fiction—just a diversion while finishing what he'd started? While injecting something into the solute, which eventually made me fall right back into a coma?

My heart rate sped up; I thought it would rip off my rib cage.

Hearing the beeping of the heart monitor, Cole put his

reassuring hand on my arm and smiled. "It's all right, Amya," he said. "You are safe here. It is only a theory, but you must tell me everything. Who is it? Who do you think did this to you?"

"When I first woke up, there was a man sitting next to my bed, holding my hand. But I never knew who it was. He was whispering the whole time, so I couldn't recognize his voice, but—" *Oh my God, the nurses.* "The nurses saw him! Ask them. Ask the nurses who was at my bedside the first day I had a nightmare."

"All right. That is a good start."

I took a deep breath and closed my eyes. We were finally going to know what had happened to me.

"I will let you rest, Amya," Cole said as he rose from his chair. "Please let me know if you remember anything else."

He said farewell and left me alone with my fears, hopes, and speculations. It made so much sense now. Well, most of it did. The man chasing me on campus and the man holding my hand at the hospital were the same. But who was he? A classmate? An old friend? A professor? And why had he been so gentle with me? Why had he called for help? Maybe he wanted me unconscious but not dead.

I also kept in mind what Cole had said about me not being in a real coma this whole time. But again, the drug used by the unknown man could be untraceable to a drug test.

Dots were starting to connect.

Chapter X

I MUST HAVE DOZED OFF FOR A WHILE, because I nearly jumped six feet high when I heard two unsure knocks on my door. I immediately hid under my sheets, even though I knew it didn't shield me from any danger. My mind couldn't get around the possibility of the mysterious man coming for another visit. What would he do to me?

"Amya? You awake?" Samera whispered, which erased any kind of unreasonable ideas. I'd forgotten she was supposed to come back today.

I pushed the sheets away from my face and said, "Come on in."

"Thank goodness you're still conscious! What's up? You look awful."

"I *feel* awful. I'm glad you're back, though. We have so much to talk about." My stomach growled. "But first, do you have something to eat, by any chance? Anything, really. I'm so hungry!"

My best friend smiled. "It's funny that you ask. I brought a granola bar, in case they were starving you here." She winked. "I can also call Magdalen. If you want, she can stop at the grocery store on her way here. She had a couple of errands to run anyway."

"No it's fine." I thought of how tired my grandmother looked the previous day. She didn't need anything else to worry about. "I'll be fine with the bar, thanks."

It was a maple brown sugar *Natural Valley*. Yum! After ripping off the bag at lightning speed, I devoured one in less than four bites and kept the second for later, providing the hospital staff forgot to bring me substantial food. Samera looked at me as if I were a lion devouring a zebra.

"Any*how*," she said, "what's going on with you? Why were your sheets pulled over your head when I came in?"

Afraid she'd call me paranoid, I decided to start with my own question.

"Do you know anything about Dimensions?"

"Yes," she carefully replied. "Don't you?"

Shocked—and a little relieved—I shook my head. "Am I supposed to?"

"You're not joking, now are you? Jeez, the doctor just told me you suffered from amnesia, but I didn't think it was that bad."

She was silent for a moment.

"What is it?" I asked.

"The thing is… I never had to explain it to you. Your grandma did. Plus, you've known for so long now that it's just odd that you don't remember."

"Everything feels odd these days." From the constant fear of falling back into a coma to the fuzzy feeling of millions of ants shifting in my legs. "Could you please help me sit? If it takes forever to explain, I'd rather be comfortable."

Samera lifted my head and shoulders, while I put my hands on either side of my hips and pushed, in order to lean my back against the wall. The pain in my stomach wasn't as sharp as the previous time I'd tried, which gave me hope for the rest of my body. *I might be able to walk soon.*

"Wait!" Samera said before pushing a red button on the side of my bed.

I fell back and let the upper half of the bed squeak its way open, until I was in a comfortable sitting position.

"Should've thought of that before," I said, as I enjoyed the way my body responded, the ants dissipating. "Feels gooood."

My hips still hurt a bit, but my legs and torso seemed to grow longer and stronger at every breath, like my body was slowly coming back to life. "I'm all ears, now."

"All right. I still don't know where to begin—Oh! Wait." Samera looked into her fake Chanel purse and came up with a pen and an old receipt. "Might be easier with this." She drew a five-pointed star on the back of the receipt. "There are four Dimensions. One," she indicated the head. "Two," she pointed to the bottom-left leg. "Three," she pointed to the bottom-right leg. "And four," she circled the center of the star. "We are here, in Amani," she said, her pen still central."

"Dimensions are like parallel universes. The first is called Blue, because people there live on water and are very eco-friendly. Our Blue-selves are also really calm—slow, actually. You'll see, when we go back. The average age is forty.

"The second is the Yellow Dimension, mostly because it is always sunny during the day, except in the Crags, but no one ever goes there. Anyway, the age average in Yellow is seven, so you won't be surprised if I tell you that its citizens favor pleasure, amusement, and creativity over everything else.

"The third—and my favorite Dimension is—"

"Red," I said, without thinking.

"That's right. How did you—" Her eyes widen. "Can you remember now?"

The excitement radiating from her made me smile. It was amazing how her mood could change so radically in only a few seconds. She was all business-like and then poof! Transformed into a child at Christmas—or Hanukkah to be exact.

It was with a good amount of guilt that I answered, "No, I don't. I just… it's complicated."

Now that I knew the Dimensions were real, could I confide in my best friend about the voices of Blue and Red?

Probably, although I still didn't think it was the right time.

"Tell me!" she begged.

"I don't want to interrupt you," I said. "We'll talk about it later, okay?"

I would be able to assess if hearing their voices in my head was plausible or not after more information on Dimensions. Her suspicious eyes stared at me before she agreed. "Fine, but you're not getting away with this."

"I assumed." I smiled, hiding my uneasiness. Was she going to believe me if I told the truth?

"Okay, so the Red Dimension isn't named after anything in particular, except that red is the color of passion, which describes pretty well our Red-selves. My ancestors said that our Dimension, Amani, is composed of the three primary colors (blue, yellow and red), plus black and white. It means that Amani is influenced by all three Dimensions, plus Heaven," she pointed at the right arm of the star she'd drawn, "and Hell," she indicated the left arm. "Heaven and Hell aren't Dimensions, though. We can't actually Travel there, but both still influence Amani."

"What do you mean by influence?" I remembered Red and Blue telling me that they couldn't wake up from their coma unless *I* did.

"Well, that's the scary part, for me at least. People living in Amani, like you and me, are influenced by the other Dimensions in a way that if they experience a strong emotion or any kind of trauma, we'll feel it too. It mostly happens with our Red-selves, as their mood keeps changing, not always for the best." When she realized I didn't quite understand, she added, "You know how sometimes you feel angry at nothing in particular or happy or sad for no reason? It simply means that you're being influenced by one of your selves who's experiencing that strong emotion.

"Or when you're drunk, your brain doesn't have the ability to differentiate your feelings from your selves', which leads you to act impulsively when influenced by your Red-self; like a child, when influenced by your Yellow-self; or to do everything slowly and act like Einstein, when influenced by your Blue-self. Same thing applies for other types of drugs."

I was overwhelmed by all the new information, but my curiosity won over.

"Why do you prefer the Red Dimension?" I asked, smiling as Samera's eyes lit up.

"Our Red-selves are so passionate about everything they do, and full of energy. It's like the world belongs to them every minute of every day. So inspiring. If they feel like dancing, they'll dance. If they feel like building a new house, nothing will stop them. They don't care about others' opinions, unless they're passionate about their appearance or being right. Everyone acts *now* and never thinks back on what they did. If it was all right. If they should have made another decision. It's the best, really. Plus, they all have big apartments or houses, and streets gleam with lights everywhere you go."

No wonder she liked that Dimension so much: she'd fit in perfectly.

"Our Red-selves are just like you. Is that what you mean?" I taunted.

She laughed. "I do have a Red-self, but so do you."

I already knew that, as I'd talked to her. Now was probably a good time to confide in my best friend.

"Samera, if I tell you something, can you promise you won't freak out?"

"You just learned about Dimensions, Amya—for the second time, but still. You should be the one freaking out right now."

"I was able to talk to Red and—well, to my Red and Blue-selves, before I woke up yesterday…" I explained everything in details; how they'd sounded the same, though so different in their way of expressing themselves. I could now better understand why they had such different personalities.

"Hm. I've never heard of this before. And you say that it was caused by your Sojourn? We'll need to ask Magda."

She looked abashed, leaning forward, her chin against her hand. I couldn't help myself from grinning.

"What?" she asked as soon as she caught sight of my amusement.

"Nothing. I haven't seen you this confused since our math class with Mr. Kerby," I said.

She burst out laughing, remembering how lost she was when it came to algebra.

After talking about our sweet years in high school, another question came up to me. "Samera, how is it that I didn't talk to my Yellow-self?"

Red had said that I was made of Blue and Red. Why not Yellow?

"Do you really consider yourself creative and entertaining?" I shook my head. "Exactly. Not everyone is composed of the three Dimensions. I know your grandmother and Xander are... but other than that," she squinted. "No, that's it. Most people are made of two and it is extremely rare to be made of only one. Well, most children only have a Yellow-self; though as they grow older, their personality changes, and so does their influence from other Dimensions. Some, like you, lose their Yellow-self completely."

"What happens to the children in Yellow? Do they carry on either way?"

"No. They, um, die."

"What? How? Why?" I had killed someone. "Don't they just disappear or fade away or something?"

"It's not how it works, Amya. Let's take you for example. You were born with a Yellow-self, although the older you got, the more it faded away—or died if you wish—leaving space for a Blue and a Red-self. When you ceased being creative and... and—"

"Fun?" I said, knowing that Samera would never say that about me.

"Sort of. When you were no longer influenced by your Yellow-self, she simply died. Her heart stopped beating. Nothing painful."

As hard as Samera was trying to cheer me up, the idea of killing someone was sickening. Red and Blue had sounded so real. So human. Like me. Children in Yellow were probably as real and alive as I was—until they died because someone in Amani lost their inner youth.

"Could we talk about something less depressing?" Samera said.

Not listening to her, I kept going. "So they don't have their say in anything. They live merely for the sake of their Amani-self?"

"I guess not. All right. You influence them for the big things, like if you die, they die, too. But they have an impact on your behavior. They define who you are, though it is your choice how many Dimensions you wanna be influenced by. Get it? It's like a rotation. You make your own choice as to how you live your life; what kind of personality you have, etc. Then, the selves you create from that choice might influence your emotions and how you react to certain situations.

"If Samera in the Red Dimension gets really mad at something, I might feel it, but I chose to be influenced by my Red-self by being passionate and because of my strong character. The more you resemble one Dimension, the more they can influence you."

I was torn between feeling relieved and scared. Back when I had been mad at Delilah, when my Red-self had taken over almost completely, I wasn't in control of my emotions. I wasn't able to think straight because of her influence. I could have hurt my little sister. Over a guy.

"Amya?" Samera said, startling my growing panic.

"Huh?"

"You're not listening to me. Magdalen is downstairs. I'll go make sure she's all right. In the meantime," she looked for something in her purse, "you could make yourself a little more… decent. No offense, but you're as pale as a ghost. Here."

She handed me some mascara and skin powder.

"You know that my skin is whiter than yours," I said.

Thanks to my grandmother's Hispanic origins, I had a natural tan, but nothing compared to Samera's chocolate complexion.

"Well, just pinch your cheeks or something; we're getting company!"

She practically ran out of my room, leaving me perplexed.

I applied Samera's mascara carefully—though having no mirror made the task almost impossible—and finally decided that a little powder on my cheeks wouldn't do me any harm; I'd seen models on TV wearing much darker shades under their cheekbones.

I was just starting to wonder whom Samera had been talking about when I heard my best friend in the hallway, asking my grandmother's opinion about her new purse.

"Are you certain you don't want me to wait outside?" a man's voice said.

The same voice who'd cried for help the first time I'd been conscious; the same voice I had impersonated in the meadow during the Sojourn; and probably the man who'd been chasing me in my dreams.

My mysterious visitor was coming back and I had no way out.

Chapter XI

"GOOD GOD, AMYA! Did you have a fight with my mascara?" Samera said as soon as she saw me.

"I—" was the only thing I managed to say before my gaze fell on Xander.

Or was it some twin he'd never mentioned? The guy standing in the doorframe had the same features as my friend, but somehow, he looked completely different. His pale blue eyes were apprehensive and wary and his mouth was set in a straight line, hiding the once-beautiful full lower lip I remembered staring at in sixth grade. Xander also looked taller and much more muscular than before. What had happened to him in five months? No wonder I hadn't recognized his voice two weeks back, it had probably changed like the rest of his body.

"Hey," Xander hesitantly said.

I noticed how fast he was breathing; his jaw was tight and his hands formed fists that appeared as solid as rocks. Just then, I didn't quite feel safe and I suddenly was really grateful that my best friend and grandmother were around, though it didn't keep my eyes from looking for emergency exits, in case something happened.

I was about to panic when he turned his back on me and murmured something to Samera. She nodded once, looking apologetic, just before he stormed out of the room.

And I could breathe again.

What was that all about? Did he still hold me responsible for his sister's death? Or had something happened in the last months that I couldn't remember?

All that matters is that he's gone. There must be a reason for his behavior. Xander is not dangerous. He'd never hurt anyone.

My grandmother and Samera—completely oblivious to my anxiety—sat on either side of my bed. I stared a few seconds at my best friend, thinking she'd explain Xander's strange behavior, but she shrugged.

"Xander is really tired, Amya," my grandmother finally said. "He has a lot on his mind right now."

"Did I do something or say something to make him angry?"

Samera shook her head reluctantly.

There was an awkward silence in which my two visitors looked very uncomfortable, and then Samera spoke. "We have some big news, Amya," she said, pretending like everything was fine. "But first, Magda wants to tell you a little story. My family's story."

Seeing as I would not get my answer promptly, I faked a smile and said, "You already told me that your grandmother, Adina, had blond hair and blue eyes and that you owe you're natural tan to her husband, Uri Hendrick."

"Not *that* story," Samera interrupted. "Well, you used to know the other one, too, but you happen to have forgotten. It's also about my grandmother, Adina Cohen, the first Jew in my family line to marry a gentile man, add to that that he was African-American." She laughed. "Even for conformist Jews, marrying outside of the community isn't encouraged."

"Go ahead, then."

Grandma looked right into my eyes, frowned, and said, "Does the title 'The Protectors of Amani' mean anything to you?"

I shook my head.

"Then we shall begin at the commencement. Samera's ancestors were very powerful Shamans with a specific power; they could travel from Dimension to Dimension. The majority created an alliance and swore to protect their own Dimension, Amani.

"From the time when they arrived in America, during the eighteenth century, and the Second World War, Dimensions were known to everyone, as Samera's family—the Cohens— decided to entertain people with their ability in order to fund their organization. Jews were not fully accepted in New York and they needed money for weapons and new technologies. Excursions were organized to allow citizens to visit the Dimensions, although they were very expensive.

"Throughout the years, the Cohens spread out around the globe to have a greater control on and to protect our Dimension—and to make more money. Unfortunately, with the rising of industrialization, the Protectors of Amani became entrepreneurs. They did not advocate protection as much as entertainment and capital. They became greedy, and—since they were the only family with the ability to Travel—famous and undoubtedly wealthy."

"So why doesn't anyone know about the Dimensions now?" I asked, looking directly at Samera. I had lost the memory of ninety-nine percent of the past eleven months, but I was certain I'd never heard of parallel worlds before today.

My best friend looked at her feet. "Magda will explain everything."

Grandma's eyes grew sad. "In 1933, the chancellor of Germany, Adolph Hitler, asked his good friend, Edel Cohen, to be taken on a private visit of the three other Dimensions. Mr. Hitler did not personally believe in the existence of Dimensions. He thought that the Cohens were illusionists. Therefore, you will understand how surprised he was when he saw what hid under the curtains."

Samera laughed slightly. "Sorry, but everyone is

surprised by what's behind the curtains. Even *I* was, the first time I Traveled, even though I'd known about the Dimensions ever since I was six."

"Curtains?" I asked.

"Yeah. Honestly, Dimensions are exactly like four sets of curtains, stacked vertically together." She drew her hand in the air. "Where you feel air, I feel curtains, if I focus on them."

Samera's hand got a grip on something invisible. "The first is Blue," she said, distorting my view of the window. It seemed to fold on itself. "The second is Yellow." The window folded a little more tightly. "And Red's the last."

It didn't look like a fragment of glass encircled by a wall anymore. Pieces of the sky were piled vertically together, creating an eerie sight. Samera was right, it was like an image of a window was projected on a green-screen curtain.

She was still holding the Dimensions together when a bird flew outside, sometimes disappearing in the creases of the curtain, sometimes bending into weird shapes; and then, it sporadically flew away.

"This is incredible," I said faintly. My brain could hardly perceive the miracle in front of my eyes and speak at the same time.

After a moment of silence, in which Samera's fingers let go of the invisible curtains, she looked at my grandmother and said, "I just thought that Amya would understand better with a visual effect." She meekly grinned.

Grandma nodded and smiled. "She will have all the visual effect she needs when you two visit your mother in a couple of days. Where were we?" She paused. "Oh. Of course, you must imagine how astonished Mr. Hitler was when he met with his Red-self. Then, he asked a lot of questions to Edel, about how he was able to Travel. Not knowing what Mr. Hitler would do next, Edel explained that only his family had that ability. That his God, *HaShem*—and you must understand that, like every Jew I know, Edel was very proud of his religion—gave his family the highest gift of all. Had he kept this information secret, a substantial amount of people could have been saved.

"Back in Amani, Hitler was angry that such a wonderful and powerful gift had been given to only one family. He assumed that since Edel kept talking about the generosity of *his* God, only Jews were given the possibility to Travel freely between Dimensions. Jews were special in a way he could never be and that wasn't fair. Jealousy eclipsed his friendship with Edel and led him to murder his friend. Later on, Hitler thought that by eradicating every Jew on Earth, no Protector would survive and thus, their society and economy would be balanced again. No more injustice.

"After the Second World War ended," Grandma continued, "the surviving Protectors of Amani decided to demolish the popular knowledge of the Dimensions. They made a general announcement in every country and said that

Dimensions were not real, that they had invented a drug creating powerful illusions. It took several years for people to believe in the Cohen's sudden change of heart, and some are still skeptical."

"But the Dimensions must remain a secret well-guarded," Samera said. "If we want to avoid another war... Well," she paused and peeked at Grandma. "Chances are we found a new way to—"

"I don't think we should talk about that just yet," my grandmother interrupted. Samera shrugged. "From that moment on," Grandma continued, "The Protectors tightened their rules and priorities. And that is why the knowledge of the Dimensions is lost today."

"But it's a good thing, as we don't want to be famous anymore," Samera said. "Besides, there's so much to do. We help the government, always trying to make peace in between countries."

I was curious about the information they were intentionally keeping from me, but decided not to push too hard. They said they would tell me in due course. "How long have you known?" I asked my best friend instead.

I recalled the day she made me swear to stay out of her head, never to use my ability on her. That was her big secret.

"All my life. But I was forbidden to talk about it... until you told me about your Sojourns. Then I tried to convince my family that *your* family could be helpful to our task. They were only able to have a meeting thirteen months ago, in which they discussed whether or not you, your mom, and Magda would be good Protectors.

"Things have changed. It's getting harder for us to make peace with everyone. Every country wants more and more power. Especially these last few months… Anyway, when the decision was made, Sylvia, Magda, and yourself were contacted by my mom. It was a few days before we started university. Only your mother declined the invitation."

I gasped. I had absolutely no recollection of any of this. It wasn't like the time my mother's words had triggered the memory of my sixteenth birthday. There was nothing left. No image, no flash… nothing.

"I know it's a lot to take in right now, but I'm sure you'll remember when we Travel together, and everything will be back to normal," Samera said. "Well, almost everything."
She looked at my grandmother. "Can I tell her now, or do you prefer—"

"Tell me what?"

"Do as you wish, Samera," Grandma said. "Just make sure you don't scare—"

"I guess you don't remember, but things haven't been all nice and peaceful in Europe during the last year and we think that a bunch of my mother's cousins and their employees in Europe have gone rogue and are trying to start the Third World War," Samera said, without so much as breathing. "So we need you to Sojourn in their heads to find out who's working against us."

Chapter XII

SAMERA'S WORDS SOUNDED LIKE A BOMB to my ears. She kept talking but I could only see her lips moving. The shock of her revelation had rendered me deaf.

After the Holocaust story—after everything Samera and Grandma had just dropped on me, they expected me—a nineteen-year-old girl—to help them end a new war—possibly the World War Three? No. Just, no. I'd just woken up from a coma and I still had no idea what had caused it; I wanted to go back to College; and most of all, I had no memory of how to control the Sojourn. I was the wrong person, worthless to their cause.

Samera must have noticed my reaction because she stopped talking and looked apologetic.

Probably sensing my growing distress, Grandma squeezed my hand. "What Miss Cohen is trying to say is that her family would like you to work with them, but only when you're feeling better. I would have gladly helped; however, your ability would be more discreet as you do not need to touch people to Sojourn. Samera's mother, Michelle, does not want her people to panic until we uncover the truth."

"I can't control the Sojourns anymore," I blurted.

Doing what they were asking of me would require a lot of preparation. Otherwise, the Protectors would realize that I'd been Sojourning in their heads and would only have to think of something else to lead me astray. In that case, I'd be completely useless.

"What do you mean, Amya?" my grandmother said.

"I forgot a lot of things during my time spent at the hospital. It may be because I have a minor concussion or something. I don't know. Some memories come back to me once in a while, but *that*, the memory of how to control my ability, it's just gone. And I fear that I'll Sojourn every time I touch someone."

"We can train for a few days before you fly to Europe," Grandma said, as if I'd already agreed to go.

"Of course!" Samera added. "You're allowed to get in shape before leaving. As long as we don't delay too much. I've heard it is getting pretty bad, mostly in Italy. How many days do you need?"

"I—I don't know. I mean, I don't remember how long it took the first time."

I didn't know what to answer. Were they really relying

on me? Me? I could barely remember the previous year and they thought I was ready for an important mission. In Europe, what's more!

"I know this might be a little unexpected, Amya," Grandma said. "But you worked for the Protectors before. They will take good care of you. Don't worry, angel. Plus, you will master your powers in less time than it takes to boil water. It's like making chicken noodle soup; it can never be forgotten."

I was about to give up and tell them that I couldn't do it. Too much pressure. Too great expectations. I couldn't bare to let them down. But a knock on the door interrupted me.

Please don't be Xander. I was anxious enough as it was.

Without waiting for an answer, a nurse came in with a tray full of food: rice, two chicken-wraps, a cup of what looked like orange juice, and a piece of raspberry cake. She nodded to everyone in the room and left.

"Okay, I'm soooo hungry right now," Samera said, salivating over my meal.

"We will come back later this afternoon, Amya," Grandma said. She looked as hungry as my best friend.

"Yeah, let's grab a bite before I devour Amya's plate. Hmm, chicken."

Too mesmerized by the food in front of me, I didn't see them rise and leave.

However, as soon as the door closed behind them, I

dismissed my growing anxiety, I dismissed my questions about the imminent war and I surrendered to my empty stomach.

***

And the last bite of cake. Hm.

Certain that my stomach was full, I fell in a sort of trance—pensive trance to be exact. The previous day, I had believed that waking up would be the last of my struggles before things went back to normal. My prevision couldn't have been more inaccurate. During my five months in a coma, I had lost the memory of almost a year of my life *plus* information on Samera's family and my ability to Sojourn. The only events I remembered clearly were ones with Wyatt, but even those memories stopped in November. It didn't make sense.

But who was I to complain? Delilah had been wrong: Europe was going mad. According to Samera, incidents triggering a war had started almost a year ago. How had I forgotten such important information?

I closed my eyes and focused on—

"Oh. I truly am sorry for waking you," Cole murmured, putting an end to my train of thought. He waited for me to open my eyes. "The nurses need to remove your catheter so you can freely attend your business in there."

I had no time to answer that two nurses came in, did what they had to do—which wasn't all that comfortable—and left immediately. In the end, they'd not only removed the catheter, but also all the other tubes connecting my body to the machine. I was free for movement.

"Thanks, I guess," I muttered.

My doctor laughed, knowing all too well how awkward I felt. His eyes were smaller and looked much more worn out than they had this morning, and his head seemed too heavy on his neck, as if threatening to fall if he wasn't careful. I wondered if he did night shifts. I knew from Samera's experience that working at night could be a real pain in the—

"I've been thinking about what we discussed this morning," Dr. Bennett said. He squinted, looking even more exhausted. "I've been doing some research in the field of special *skills* certain people have…"

Dr. Bennett looked at me through his glasses. Did he know about my family? Or Samera's? Had he been eavesdropping on our conversation?

I thought about my grandmother's story, how Hitler had reacted to his friend's confession. What would happen if Cole was the same? What if he wanted to eradicate Samera's family—or worse, control them?

Not knowing how to react, I leaned away from my doctor and was glad to feel more ease and fluency in my muscles. Too absorbed in his own thoughts, Cole did not notice the sudden change of atmosphere.

Good, I thought. *I will deny everything.*

"Have you known your friend Xander for a long time?" he asked, taking me aback.

What? That was unexpected.

"Xander? Hm, since high school, why?"

Cole looked away and frowned. "I see. Have you any idea where he lived before attending this high school of yours? Have you met his parents? What do they do for a living? Any siblings?"

"Why are you asking me all this?"

"I questioned the nurse who was taking care of you on September 15th, the first day you had a nightmare. She described the visitor you were talking about exactly like your friend Xander. The one who was here earlier."

I knew it! It'd been him all along! His voice. His different attitude. He'd probably injected some drug into my solute to keep me in a coma.

But why?

And how could Grandma and Samera be oblivious to his intentions?

"His father owns a restaurant and his mother died of cancer a couple of years ago. His father is Swedish and his mom was born in New York. They visit Europe every year and his father's been travelling around the globe ever since his wife and daughter died."

"Swedish? They visit Europe every year? How interesting. Have you heard about what is going on in Europe? Of course you have not…"

I had, but I was interested in hearing what Dr. Bennett had to say about it.

"I do not want to alarm you, Miss Priam," Cole continued, "but I believe you ought to know where I am going with these questions. Innumerable people are going nuts in Europe, either killing others or themselves. Earlier today, reporters proclaimed that many countries were about to be put in quarantine. They are mostly talking about Italy. That means there will be no more communication available; no trip to Italy, no more phone calls. The country will be completely cut out from the outside world."

How had the situation degenerate so fast? "What does this have to do with Xander?"

"Perhaps nothing. Perhaps everything. I have reasons to believe that Europeans are possessed by evil spirits. A friend of mine living in England told me that most murderers are going mad, even in prisons. They claim to be controlled by something, someone. Some don't even remember murdering their family and friends… Do you understand what I am saying?"

"You think Xander is possessed?"

He squinted his eyes. "All I am saying is that you should be careful. If he went to Europe during the last year, he might have caught whatever is creating this madness."

"Xander would never hurt me, Dr. Bennett," I asserted with more assurance than I really had, recalling how he'd looked at me earlier and how his voice sounded exactly like my mysterious visitor.

"Your friend might not be in complete control of his body, Amya. All those murderers in Europe… they were different before it all started." He looked at his hands. "They were good people…"

I frowned. My doctor appeared even more tired now. Wrinkles had formed on his forehead and between his brows. "What is it?" I inquired. "What are you not telling me?"

Water filed his eyes, but he swallowed the unwelcome emotion. "I am only telling you this because I want you to understand how dangerous Europe has become." He stared at me for a moment and then added, "My father was arrested last night for the murder of his wife… my dear mother." He paused and swallowed once more but this time with difficulty. When he continued, his voice was shaking. "You should know, Amya, my father is—was a good man. He had never laid hands on anyone before yesterday."

"I'm so sorry…" was all I could respond. Then something occurred to me. "Are you going back to England? For the funeral?"

Cole shook his head. "There will be no funeral for too many people have died this week. I wasn't even allowed to call my father. What I am trying to tell you is that you don't seem to understand how bad the situation is. If countries start putting other countries in quarantine and the sickness propagates around the globe, we're buggered. There will be a war. And a war triggered by madness is not likely to end well. Just promise me you'll be careful."

We heard the door open and both turned our gaze to the newcomer.

Chapter XIII

IT WAS SAMERA.

"Don't look so surprised. I told you I'd come back soon." She glimpsed at the clock on her cellphone. "Oy! It's almost three. Sorry, I got caught up and I can't stay for long." Then she noticed Cole in the room. "Oh! Hi, Dr. Bennett. I didn't want to interrupt, but may I please have a word with Amya?"

"Of course you may. We were done, anyway." Cole eyed me knowingly. "Remember what I told you."

And he left right away.

Turning to my best friend, I said, "You're not staying? I wouldn't mind some company, you know. Especially after what Cole just told me."

Samera halted for a second but quickly dismissed my sentence. Something else was on her mind. "Your grandmother's apartment was robbed, so she needs to get back

ASAP. Xander and I will drive her home."

"Is everything okay? Do you know if the robbers took anything? And why is Xander helping you? Does he know about the Dimensions?" I whispered the last word, in case Dr. Bennett was listening.

"Magda's neighbours said they saw somebody enter her apartment an hour ago and they called the police. So far, nothing was taken." She answered a text message before she went on. "As for Xander, he's known for a while, Amya. We used to Travel during weekends before you met Wyatt."

"Your mom allowed this?"

"A little while after I told you, we thought it was unfair to leave him out of it. He'd grown suspicious that something wasn't right and I begged my mother to give him a chance. Fortunately, she had only made a few calls when she had the idea of making him my bodyguard. He trained with a martial arts instructor for months and swore his oath around the Christmas holidays. He's been even more important since your incident. Mom became really paranoid."

Speaking of Xander, I figured it was the right time to talk about my concerns.

"Can I ask you a question?"

"Of course. I'll have to leave soon, though," Samera said.

"Did something happen between me and Xander during the last year?"

Her eyes grew bigger. "What do you mean?"

"I don't know. He seemed really angry at me earlier and I don't feel all that comfortable with him around. I don't know why. Is it possible that—I mean—I suspect him to be responsible for my being in a coma."

Samera burst out laughing.

"Oy, Amya," she said between her laughs. "I can't believe—my ears—right now."

I exhaled sharply. "I knew I shouldn't have told you. I'm serious. I had a dream and I think he was chasing me on campus."

"Stop right there," she suddenly said, now serious. "You have no idea how wrong you are, Amya. Xander would never, *evvvver* hurt you. I don't know what they've been feeding you here, but you need to realize that you're not looking in the right direction. We'll find out who did this to you. I promise. But don't waste your time accusing your friends."

Maybe she was right. Maybe I'd come to a conclusion too fast. "I'm sorry," I said.

Even if I still suspected something was off.

"I really have to go now. I'll see you later."

"Tell Grandma I apologize for not being there for her."

She was almost at the door when she turned around, holding something purple with a sticker of Tinker Bell on it. My old cell phone.

"Here. I thought it'd be useful if you need anything.

Your new one was crushed the night of your incident, but I updated the phone numbers on this one. Your parents activated it for when you woke up. You can call them if you want. They're on their way back from their trip. They were so excited when Magda called yesterday to announce you were awake."

"Thanks," I said. "I'm really sorry, okay?"

She smiled. "You are very welcome. See ya!"

And she was gone.

I thought back on our conversation and decided to believe her. Xander was her bodyguard—and had probably been mine too when I Traveled with them.

It still didn't explain why he'd appeared so mad at me.

I'll ask him the next time we see each other.

In order to shake my ideas a bit, I stretched my legs and rotated my ankles ten times each. It was only when I tried to reach the ceiling with my hands that I felt a funny pressure at the bottom of my belly.

My bladder was full.

Shoot. I contemplated the option to push the red button next to my bed, which would alert the nurse, but my pride greatly won over my fear to move. The best option was to try to walk, and only use the red button as the last resort.

I can do it. It's only about eight feet away, I cheered myself.

My first step was to shove my legs on the right side of the bed, which reminded me that my muscles had melted during my journey in a coma. It hurt—a lot. I then set my arms on either side of my hips and pushed upward while contracting my abs—now non-existent—until I found a sitting position facing the door.

Next step: stand on my two legs. *Go.* I gripped the side of the bed in an attempt to transfer all my weight on my feet already touching the gray floor. The word *attempt* was maybe a little too optimistic, since as soon as I let go of my bed, my legs started shaking and hurting so badly that I immediately collapsed on the floor.

I still wasn't helpless enough to press the red button, now looking at me with flirty eyes. I was going to crawl my way to the bathroom. Trying to ignore how dirty the floor was, I started moving one limb at a time, and then two to progress a little faster. Without a doubt, I looked like a fish stranded on the shore, trying to wriggle its way back into the ocean.

I had just passed across one of the chairs and was only three feet away from the intended door when I almost crashed into someone's black sneakers. They had a yellow stripe on the exterior side.

That is definitely not Cole, I thought.

I looked up, only to see two beautiful and compassionate blue eyes staring down at me, as if I were a lost puppy.

"Where do you think you're going?" Xander asked, as he offered his hand to help me onto my feet.

Why was he in my room? Should I believe Samera and

trust him? Or—

"Just be careful," Cole had said.

But Xander was my friend.

I accepted his hand and he gently pulled me up, but as soon as my weight was back on my legs, they started shaking again and I would have probably crumbled down were it not for my friend's strong arms.

"Easy there," he said.

His two arms were under mine as our bodies got closer. We were only two inches apart and my heart was racing against itself. I could feel his minty breath on my nose and his fingers carefully supporting my elbows.

"I don't think that your present shape allows you to escape from here anytime soon," he said, followed by a friendly smile.

"I'm not running away," I answered, my voice trembling much like the rest of my body. I didn't want to tell him why I'd been crawling on the floor, but he was my last hope, so I pointed my chin at the bathroom.

"I see. May I escort you to your next destination, then?"

There was no mockery in his voice, but remembering his earlier behavior, I remained cold and distant when I said, "Yes, please."

That is when he surprised me. He swiftly slid one hand behind my back and another under my knee pits and lifted me off the floor. Then, he walked toward my "destination" as the ants, previously in my legs, made their way to my belly. He finally set me down in front of the toilet.

"I cannot be of much help from here, but you can try to support your weight using the sink," he said.

He stayed a few more seconds, to make sure that I wouldn't collapse. As soon as he had left and closed the door, I attended to my business and tried to wash my hands, supporting my weight on one arm at a time.

It is only when I saw myself in the mirror that I almost succumbed. I was barely recognizable, transparent, almost fading. I wore purple bags under my eyes and my lips were as dry as the humidity level during mid-April in New York. No fresh air, no exercise, and no real food for months was definitely not good for my system.

I believed that my reflection could only get better, so I tried to wash Samera's powder off my cheeks and mascara off my eyelids. Sadly, it only made me look paler.

All right, there's nothing I can do, anyway.

Taking a deep breath, I bent toward the door and opened it to signal to Xander that I was done. He was still waiting, leaning against the wall in front of me.

He stepped forward as to lift me up and carry me to my bed, but I stopped him at once.

I can walk on my own, my pride cried.

"I'm fine," I said.

Still vigilant, Xander smiled and left me some space.

Step by step, I balanced my weight from legs to arms and decided that my lower body was steadier and ready for a short walk, so I let go of the sink and moved my left foot in front of the other. So far so good, my right foot joined the left one and I repeated this motion until my legs started shaking and Xander came to my rescue again.

I braced myself for an "I told you so" because I knew I deserved it.

"That's an improvement," he said. "Tomorrow, you'll be running down the stairs as if nothing ever happened." There was pride in his eyes.

His chest pressed against my back as his two hands supported my elbows and we walked clumsily to the mattress. It was only after I was comfortably laid down that he sat on the chair to my right.

"I'm not angry with you," he said.

Samera must have told him about my suspicions. Surprised and embarrassed, I couldn't repress a laugh but soon became serious. His pale blue eyes were so deep, I believed I would get lost in them.

"I don't want to talk about it," he continued. "All you need to know for now is that you did nothing wrong. We're still friends and I'll do everything I can to protect you…" He muttered something I couldn't understand and shook his head.

On the one hand, I was grateful for his honesty and glad that he wasn't mad at me. We'd been really good friends ever since we'd bonded over our mutual love for the movie *Casablanca* during a boring party in high school. I'd had a crush on him for a long time after that but he had made it clear that we would never be more than friends.

On the other hand, I still didn't understand why he'd seemed so stiff and bitter this morning. If I wasn't the cause, then who was?

As if sensing my concern, Xander took my right hand and started moving his thumb on my knuckles... the same way my mysterious visitor had a few weeks back.

My heartbeat increased and I instantly removed my hand. He'd been honest with me. Now it was my turn to return the favor.

"Did you visit me two weeks ago?"

"What do you mean?"

"Were you sitting right here," I pointed to the chair on my left, "two weeks ago, just before my mother entered the room?"

His eyes grew wary. Was it really him?

"Why do you ask?"

I had to get it out.

"Did you inject something into my solute to keep me in a coma?"

My heartbeat was going too fast, now. Xander's body was tense and he didn't seem to know how to answer.

"Are you insane?" he said.

"Was it you?"

"Yes it was me! But I didn't inject anything into your solute. What are you talking about?"

Oh my goodness... "Leave."

"What? Amya, what are you talking about?"

I was so scared, my entire body started to shudder. It was him.

"LEAVE."

"But I didn't—please just explain to me what happened. Were you conscious?"

I didn't want to hear any more. Too frightened by what he might do, I searched for the red button next to my bed.

"Amya, what are you—"

"LEAVE. NOW!"

Chapter XIV

THE SECOND AFTER HE WAS GONE, tears ran down my cheeks like a waterfall. I couldn't contain my emotions. It wasn't all about Xander; I just couldn't take it anymore. All the lies and secrets.

Xander admitted he was my mysterious visitor, but denied having anything to do with my state. Could I trust him? And all the talk about the Third World War. What about Cole and his theory of people being possessed? Was Xander possessed?

I laughed at myself. The idea was ridiculous.

But I didn't feel safe at the hospital anymore. What if Xander decided that I was better off in a coma? He said he would protect me but from what? And at what cost?

Another complication came to my mind. How long would I need to gain back control over the Sojourns? It was all too much...Would I be equal to the challenge?

I didn't have time to think this through before the door slammed open and Wyatt's gaze fell on me. I quickly dried my eyes, not wanting to alarm him.

"You're…"

"Awake? Yes," I said with a shy smile.

I forgot all about my previous concerns and the fact that he was dating my sister. He was here, at last. I'd missed him so much.

Without waiting another second, he ran into my arms and started kissing every inch of my face.

"How did this happen? And when? Oh. I missed you," he said in between kisses.

"I missed you, too," I whispered.

It was a relief for me to see how much he still cared. His reaction meant so much more than Delilah's words.

When he finally stopped, leaving me breathless, he sat on the side of the bed and held my left hand between his. We both smiled at each other like two idiots.

"I was so scared you were going to remain a veggie for the rest of your life," Wyatt said, patting my palm.

"Me too, believe me." I paused. "I was conscious, by the way, two weeks ago. And I was able to Sojourn…"

His smile reached his ears. It had always been so easy to talk to him, even before we'd started going out together. He had a soothing voice and spoke to me smoothly, like everything was normal. It was a huge change from the last twenty-four hours.

"Thank God. I thought you were only having a nightmare." He smiled. "I remember that evening like it was yesterday."

"Me, too," I said, as I realized that our first night together was the only thing I remembered of the last few months. I could recall every part of the evening, but I had no clue as to when it had happened.

"How are you?" he inquired.

"I feel… okay, I guess. How about you? What have you been up to in the last five months?"

Just then I feared that he might bring up his relationship with Delilah and I didn't want that. I just wished things would go back to normal.

"I took some time off school to travel. Been all around Europe with my family. It was nice. I learned a lot."

Europe? With all that was happening over there, I was surprised he'd even want to go. Hadn't he seen anything? Crimes and madness? Hadn't Delilah spend the summer in England too? Surely either would have known it was dangerous to leave America.

"How was Europe? Haven't you heard about the war?" I asked.

"How do you know? When did you wake up exactly?"

"Yesterday. But that's not the point. Why did you endanger yourself by going to Europe? You could have been killed!"

Wyatt crossed his arms in front of him. "Who talked to you about Europe? Have you seen Delilah?"

Shocked, questions piled in front of my eyes and I didn't know where to begin. Had he been to Europe *with* my sister? When it had been *our* plan to go together after College. When we'd planed everything for when the two of us had enough money. My sister had told me that his boyfriend's family loved her. Had they all been to Europe together?

"Did you go to England, by any chance?" I asked, a sarcastic tone to my voice.

Taken aback, he leaned further into his chair. "Uh, yes."

"Did you happen to see my sister there?" *Please say no.*

I mean, yes, I wanted things to go back to normal, but if they'd been to England together… It might just be too much to forgive.

"How do you know she was in England? So, you did speak to her. She told me she hadn't visited you in weeks." He muttered the last part.

Were they still a couple? Why wasn't he answering any of my questions?

"Did you go together to England? Did you really visit my dream country with my *sister*?"

"Wait," he said, raising his hands in the air. "Did you just Sojourn into my head? How do you know all of this?"

Suddenly, I didn't care whether any of them had witnessed the beginning of the war. I didn't even care if one of

125

them had been injured. I was mad at Wyatt for lying to me and saying he'd missed me, and I was utterly furious at myself for being so naïve.

"I didn't Sojourn, Wyatt. Why do you think I did? Are you thinking about her right now?" He remained silent, which triggered the most resentful emotion inside of me. "What should I make of that, Wyatt? I knew something had happened between you and Deli, but this? Going to England was *our* big plan. *We* were supposed to go *together*. What happened? Did you even miss me at all?"

"Of course I did! I missed you, princess." He tried to caress my cheek, but I pushed him away. "I—It's just that—It's complicated."

"Right. Well, let me make this clear to you," I said, as tears started to make their way down my cheeks again. "I love you, okay? But there's no way you're getting both of us. I understand that I was gone for five months and you needed someone—or whatever. But I'm back now, so you have to make up your mind."

"Oh, Amya. I wish it were that easy." His tone became more serious, darker.

"It is. Just choose—" *Me.*

"I can't do that, princess. I love both of you."

"You *love* her?"

"Sort of… It's—"

"Complicated?"

"Look—"

"No. I've been wanting to see you ever since I woke up in this stupid hospital and you're telling me that you *love* my sister? I give up, Wyatt. I'm out."

"You don't have that choice, Amya. You never had." His Australian accent was discernable now.

"What do you mean? Of course I can choose. And I choose to get out of this game of yours."

"You can't just break up with me this time," he said, as his jaw tightened and his pupils dilated until his blue eyes were as black as his t-shirt.

Then, an image of my dreams came back to me, like the missing piece of a jigsaw puzzle.

Wyatt. Black eyes. The rain.

I knew what had happened.

Wyatt was a Rascal.

Chapter XV

I REMEMBERED THE DAY—on the 17th of October—when Wyatt had asked me to join his group and become a Rascal as well. I'd said no, obviously, but he didn't want to listen, so I broke up with him.

We were over. Done. But I also remembered how much of a stalker he had become. I could feel his eyes on me everywhere I went… except—except when I Traveled with Samera and Xander. I was safe in the other Dimensions. Xander had become my bodyguard more than Samera's.

That night on campus, though—on April 20th—I had just finished my finals and I hadn't seen Wyatt since I'd broken up with him, so we all thought that he'd dropped out of college and gone away. That night, I'd allowed myself to visit Samera without Xander. Without his protection.

It was Wyatt I'd heard in the alley. He had come to take me away. To keep me close to him, no matter what I wanted.

And that was exactly what he was going to do, all over again.

My growing fears were interrupted by Wyatt's phone.

Bruno Mars's song was so inappropriate right now.

"No. No, no, no, no…" I said, looking around for a way out.

He frowned and answered his phone.

"Yes," he said.

I had to get out of the room. Now.

"Okay, I'll be right there," he answered his interlocutor.

After putting his phone back into his pocket, he took a deep breath, and when his eyes fell back on me, there was no more regret, no more affection. There was only hunger and darkness.

"I did not come to argue with you, princess. It was nice to be able to talk and all, but this can't last forever. You need to go back to sleep."

And I knew exactly how he planned on doing that. He was going to feed on my energy, the way he had on campus two months ago.

I tried not to panic and started to feel around myself for an object I could use against him. Anything that would give me time to try and get out of the room and seek some help.

The red button.

My right hand reached for it, but Wyatt was faster. He grabbed my wrist.

"Don't make it more difficult than it has to be. If you alarm the nurse, I'll have to take care of her, too. Don't worry. You won't feel anything. You'll simply doze off until…"

"I won't let you do this to me again."

My right hand was trapped but my left still patted around for something… until my fingers found my cell phone in the bed sheets.

Of course, my phone!

However relieved I was, I kept a neutral expression; Wyatt couldn't know I had a phone.

"Again?" he said. "What do you mean, again?"

I opened the lid of the phone and spoke at the same time, in case it would be noisy. "I know it was you five months ago. It took me a long time, but I remember now."

"It's impossible. Meo removed your memories. You can't—"

Meo, Wyatt's best bud, was also a Rascal, but instead of feeding on energy and strength like my boyf—ex-boyfriend—he fed on people's memories.

And apparently, he'd fed on my reminiscence of the last eleven months of my life, leaving only the good and happy memories with Wyatt. It all made sense, even though the fact that I remembered spending time with Wyatt in November was odd since I'd ended things between us in October.

Luckily, Samera's number was the third on my contact list under BFF, so I was able to locate her in less time than it took Wyatt to get up and pace around the room.

"How can it be? Unless Meo did a poor job—and I doubt it because he really doesn't like you—I don't see how you could recollect information that he drained from you. He'll have to come back once you're asleep."

Wyatt stepped forward and grabbed my wrist again.

Immediately, my newly recovered strength started to fade away and my eyelids threatened to close on themselves. It was the same sensation I had had two weeks back. The puzzle was complete: Xander hadn't injected anything into my solute. I thought the solute had taken some time to be effective, but it'd been Wyatt this whole time. As soon as he'd caressed me—a gesture I'd believed amiable—he'd started feeding on my energy.

No. NO! This can't be happening. I can't go back.
I won't go back.

I tilted my head to my left and pretended I'd already fallen asleep; but squinted slightly in order to see my phone screen. No more time to waste, I texted:

SOS WYATT

And then I waited. There was nothing else I could do; running was out of the question, as I already felt my limbs getting numb and stiff, and I couldn't cry for help or the nurse would face the same fate. All I could do was hope. Hope that Samera would be able to notify a doctor or the police before I lost consciousness.

Wyatt, on his side, was enjoying his feeding. His breath thickened and his grip tightened on my arm. I dared to peek through my eyelashes, only to see that he had closed his eyes.

I could hit him. He'd never see it coming.

But the mere thought of lifting my hand was tiring.

Are you kiddin' me? God, this girl can't stay conscious for more than forty-eight hours, a voice said.

What do you think happened?

Red? Blue? I asked. *Are we already asleep?*

The pressure Wyatt's grip inflicted on my arm was still palpable and I could—although with great difficulty—still open my eyes.

No; however, I feel very tired and had to lay down on my couch, Blue said. *What is going on?*

I just fainted in the middle of the street, thanks to you, Red said. *And believe me, no one will pick me up. No way, José.*

I'm so sorry...

"Psst!"

What? I asked, as I realized that I couldn't feel nor hear Wyatt anymore.

"Psst, Amya!"

What do you guys want? I can't fight him.

I didn't say anything, Red said.

Neither did I, Blue added.

"Amya," someone murmured.

"Who's this?" I asked out loud, still confused. *Don't tell me I have a Yellow-self now.*

"AMYA!"

OPEN YOUR EYES, Red and Blue said at the same time.

Chapter XVI

Ian Cohen

WE NEVER FOUND OUT who had set off the bombs in Washington. After the car accident, I woke up at the Headquarters infirmary, a bandage to my head and several people at my bedside. Karl told me he had lost control of the van and we had crashed straight into the bridge. He said that somehow, I'd been projected out of the car and they'd found me a few minutes later, unconscious with blood all over myself. But I knew better. How was it that he didn't remember trying to get out of the car? He didn't even speak of the fight I'd had with the crazy short guy.

Karl told me that they had immediately come back to the Headquarters and sent me to Dr. Goldbridge, in case I had a concussion. And that was it. No question asked. Nothing. I was certain that this guy, whoever he was, had set off the bombs to lure me out of the Headquarters. But why me?

That was two weeks ago.

***

"Stop sending me presents," I told Amanda. "I don't want any of it."

She looked hurt. It was the sixth time this week she was bringing me either coffee, chocolate, or flowers.

"I thought you liked tulips," she whispered.

"Where did you get that stupid idea?"

She looked down. "The photo on your desk. I'm sorry. I really thought you'd like them." Still staring at her feet, she threw the flowers into the trash can next to my desk and finally left me alone.

Tulips weren't my favorites; they were my sister's. Or they had been my sister's, before the accident at the lake. I kept a photo of the both of us from when we were five on my desk to remind me that in life, you have to seize what you want before somebody else takes it from you. We're all alone on this planet. Everyone puts themselves first so you might as well do the same.

My thoughts were interrupted by a mild vibration in my sock. The device I'd been given by the short guy two weeks ago was finally proving to work. I still wasn't convinced that trusting him was a good idea, but I couldn't turn my back on such a great offer. Within seconds, I was in the men's bathroom, taking the device to my ear.

"Ian speaking."

"No way. I really thought I was calling your grandfather." Silence. "Now, let's be serious for a second. You need to get better—better enough to convince your leader to send you on a mission, if the need comes up."

"Why? And what tells me you're not going to kill me if I help you?"

"I'll kill you if I want to." He laughed. "But for now, I want you to be ready. If things go wrong here, three kids—including your boss's daughter—are going to come to your Headquarters, and that's not likely to please my boss. If that happens, I'll need you to kill two of them. Only spare the one with the black hair. Her name is Amya."

"How do you want me to kill those kids? Do you know how many Protectors there are at the Headquarters? Someone will see me."

"I don't care how you manage it, as long as it's done."

I could hear people fighting on the other side of the line.

"Who are you?" I asked.

"I gotta go. We'll talk later."

"No! You tell me who you are or I won't help you and I'll alert the Protectors of your plan." Would he call my bluff?

He remained silent for a moment. I wasn't sure why but I knew he needed my help as much as I needed his. It was only fair to know who I was dealing with.

"Meo. My name is Meo." I heard a *bang* close to where he was standing.

"What's going on?" I inquired.

"Gotta go. Get better."

He hung up, leaving me in a mixture of excitement and nervousness. What he was asking from me was almost impossible to pull off. It was hard enough to get close to Michelle alone; her daughter was ten times less accessible. Everybody loved her. And why did I need to save Amya? I remembered her from when she'd worked for us last year, but she'd been in a coma for months now. Who was the other kid? Who was it I needed to kill?

My new task requires assistance, I thought.

Once I had the device hidden back in my sock, I took out my cell phone and texted Jim to meet me in the men's bathroom. Two minutes later, the door opened.

"Ian? What are you doing here?" Karl inquired, finding me leaning over the sink. "Your co-workers reported that you'd been gone for half an hour."

Co-workers meant Amanda.

"I—I..." What was I doing here? What would a guy like me be doing in the bathroom at four thirty in the afternoon? "I think I ate bad shrimp for lunch."

"Do you need anything? I think Michelle won't mind if you go home early, especially since... She still blames me for the accident."

"I'm fine," I said. I had to make them believe I was well enough for field-related work again. "In fact, I feel much better. Would you mind if I used your gym downstairs later? I feel a little rusty at combat."

"Are you certain you're ready for this? Dr. Goldbridge said you had a pretty bad concussion—"

"It was two weeks ago!" I replied a little too harshly. "I know I'm ready, sir."

I tried to look ashamed of my outburst but all I wanted to do was get rid of him. Karl was Michelle's favorite both because he was her husband and because she trusted him the most. The fact that he had recently converted into Judaism helped quite a lot as well. Maybe that's what I needed to do next. Because even though I was Michelle's right arm, I knew it would be Karl's duty—not mine—to become the leader of the Protectors if she were to die, at least until a new leader was voted in. Becoming a Jew would certainly give me points in the eyes of my family members. But that would only come in as the last resort. I didn't want to give my sister, Jemina, the satisfaction to have won after all this time.

"Fine," he said. "But I'll come with you. I want to help you get back into good shape."

I was about to refuse his help when the door of the bathroom opened again. Jim had arrived. In the split second that Karl looked in his direction, I nodded my head toward a toilet cabin for Jim to walk into. Karl couldn't know I'd beckoned Jim here or he would suspect something was going on.

Jim walked past us. "Karl. Ian," he said before he closed the door of the toilet cabin behind him.

"All right. I'll see you at five at the gym?" Karl said.

Worried he was already suspecting something, I nodded once in agreement. Besides, if he saw me in training, my chances of proving to Michelle that I was better had just increased tenfold.

When I was certain Karl was gone for good, I called Jim out of his cabin.

"I need you to do me a favor," I stated.

"Anything."

Jim was getting old. I believed he'd turned sixty last year. He had been working for the Protectors all his life as a weapon technician. He'd once told me that he'd been promised a promotion one day. They had trained him as a bodyguard. They'd promised Jim he'd be one soon. But that day had never come.

I smiled at him. "I want you to keep an eye on Michelle. If she receives a call from her daughter, you need to come to me. If Samera arrives at the HQ, you need to come to me. If—"

"If anything happens regarding her daughter, I'll let you know."

"Good. And when you do, I need you to get me out of the Headquarters without anyone else knowing. Michelle's daughter will be murdered today."

Chapter XVII

I DID OPEN MY EYES. I scarcely opened them enough to see Samera's head floating in the distorted air next to the window.

Am I already dreaming? Or dead maybe?

"Amya! Jeez, I thought you were unconscious, again. Hurry!" my best friend said.

"What the—"

"Questions later. Now come up here before Xander can't restrain your crazy ex-boyfriend anymore."

She opened the curtains a little more and waved me in.

Xander was here? My eyes opened completely and I angled my head in order to see the other side of the room. There were two shapes moving in harmony, as if dancing. I frowned, certain I'd been lost in a dream, but the more I squinted, the clearer the shapes became.

Wyatt was struggling against a man whom I would have never recognized, were it not for Samera's last insight on the scene. Xander was like a taller American version of Jet Li: blocking every blow and attacking his opponent in a way I'd only seen in movies. At some point, I could have sworn he was flying. But although he threw harder punches and moved faster than Wyatt, my friend became more feeble at every blow.

Wyatt was feeding on his strength.

"Amya, focus! We have to get outta here," Samera cried, which caught Wyatt's attention.

He was furious. His black eyes shifted fast between me and my best friend, while Xander tried to keep him at a certain distance from us. I wondered how long he could hold him up.

A wave of adrenaline supplied my muscles with all the strength I needed to find a sitting position. I lifted my back using my elbows anchored in the mattress, and contracted my abs, but as soon as I was perpendicular to the bed, I felt myself falling backward.

"Oh, for Pete's sake," Samera muttered before grasping at my shoulders to keep me straight. She'd let go of the curtains and was now bending to be of equal height with me. Looking directly into my eyes, she said, "Can you stand and walk? No. This is not a question, Amya. You *have to* walk into the curtain I am about to open for you. Okay? One more effort and we're out and safe."

I couldn't answer. My head was throbbing and I didn't think I'd be able to move, anyway. It was probably just a question of time before I fainted.

"Amya! You listening? I can't carry you or we'll both collapse on the floor. You need to put in some effort. Now, on three." She set her arm under my armpit. "One." She looked at me, and then at Xander. I braced myself. It was going to hurt. "Two." She reached for the curtains. "Three!"

I felt her arm pushing me upward and my legs immediately started to tremble from the weight. I grunted, but kept fighting the urge to give up.

"Xander!" Samera shouted, not paying attention to the endless blue sky behind the curtain.

My heart beat faster with anticipation. I'd Traveled before, but those memories had been taken from me, so this felt like my first time.

There was a big *bang* and I had just enough time to see that Xander had hit Wyatt with a chair before the former pushed us into the open curtain.

Then we fell... and Samera cursed.

Was something wrong?

We fell some more... and I dared to look under my feet, just before we hit...

Water.

On the bright side, it was cool, refreshing and filled with zillions of small fish that I couldn't name. On the downside, I was too tired to swim, so I instantly started to sink, much like an anchor. My legs and arms were like large, cooked spaghetti noodles, while the rest of my body just felt numb.

The more I sank, the bigger the fish appeared to be. Sharks, whales, and other cetaceans I didn't know. But they did not attack; they simply circled me, one after the other.

Somehow, I felt calm, as my eyes shifted onto the two blurry silhouettes of Samera and Xander. They seemed agitated, probably looking for me, and completely oblivious that I was drowning right under their feet. One at a time, they dove into the water, but I was getting deeper and deeper, and the turquoise water around me was much darker now. I'd become invisible to their human eyes.

I was going to die.

At least it's a pretty place to die, I thought. My lungs wanted to burst open and the throbbing in my head was so strong that I was certain I'd explode before long.

I'm so tired. I should sleep a little. I'll take care of... whatever tomorrow. It can wait, I convinced myself.

The last thing I saw before I blacked out was a blue whale's mouth opening and engulfing my body.

***

"Gosh, I hope she's not dead," Samera said.

"Her heart's still beating; she'll be fine," Xander replied.

"Wake her up!"

"What do you think I'm trying to do?

"Can I help?"

"Sure."

"What do you want me to do? Hold her head? Massage her throat?"

"Stop talking, it'll be enough. Twenty-seven, twenty-eight, twenty-nine, thirty!"

Then, someone pinched my nose and released air into my mouth, which inflated my abdomen, again and again. My friend was about to put his mouth on mine once more, when I vomited close to an entire gallon of water. The pain in my throat was almost unbearable and I was having a hard time breathing.

"Alright, that's gross, but you're *alive!*" Samera cried, as she threw her arms around me and held my hair while I finished. "You scared the hell out of me, girl. You were supposed to grab my hand when we jumped."

"I don't think she knew we were about to land in the ocean," Xander said.

"Where's Grandma?" I whispered. I didn't know why but my grandmother was the first thing I thought of. Wasn't Samera supposed to drive her home?

"I didn't know either," Sam told Xander. "I panicked and opened the first curtain my fingers could grab, and Wyatt was already behind you, so there was no time to change my mind."

I popped my eyes open and turned around, but my best friend did not notice.

"Where's my grandmother?"

"We traded her to your parents. They were very close to the hospital when I received your text. We told them you'd be waiting for their arrival as soon as Magda's house was taken care of. The police were already there, so they didn't argue. Might be a little mad, though, when they come back to the hospital and realize you're gone." She turned back to Xander. "Besides, you should be thankful. If I'd picked the Yellow Dimension, we might have fallen on a tree or in the Crags. Now *that* would have been a disaster."

"Oh, thank you for nearly killing us, then."

I hoped my grandmother was all right and I longed to see my parents.

The white, silvery sand was so warm against my bare skin that I decided to plunge my hands and cover my legs completely in it. When Samera and Xander argued, nothing could be done. It was only after my ankles were completely concealed that I realized my hospital gown was soaking wet and the sun made it almost transparent. The only solution that came to my mind was to rub some sand on it and pray for the best.

"Hey," Xander said to me, turning away from Samera. "How are you feeling?"

"How do you think she feels? She nearly died," Samera answered for me.

"According to your account, we all came very close to dying today."

"Well,—"

"Hey guys," I interrupted. "I'm fine, really. Thanks to—wait. Did I see a blue whale in the water, or was it just my imagination?"

"It was Bait," Samera said, smiling. "She saved you."

"Bait?"

"Yeah, our friend Bait. Oh, how I wish you'd remember some things."

"Yeah, it would make everything much easier," Xander added.

Samera looked at Xander with an expression I'd rarely seen on her: sadness. Then she said, "We used to play with Bait all the time during weekends. Animals in Blue live in harmony with humans. All of them."

"Okay, well thanks, Bait," I said, clueless. My head was still spinning and I felt like a child.

"Hey, you're sitting on your own!" Samera cheered. "That's a great improvement."

I hadn't realized it, but I had been supporting the weight of my back on my hands for a couple of minutes now. Great improvement indeed.

"Could you help me get to the water, though? I'd like to wash my mouth."

"Uh, sure, anything," my best friend said, as she and Xander carried me to the turquoise water.

It was incredible how the sky blended perfectly with the

ocean, as if they were the same element. Once in, I was able to move and walk freely, washing my hair and brushing my teeth with my fingers. I washed away the stress from the hospital and allowed myself to float on my back. The water seeping through my hair and loosening my muscles made me happy. I felt relaxed for the first time since waking up. The realization that Wyatt was responsible for everything was still a shock, though my few memories of the last year made it more bearable. Deep down I knew I didn't love him anymore.

"Are you all right?" Samera inquired.

She was standing close, the water not higher than her knees. Instead of giving her an answer, I moved my feet to splash water into her face and started laughing.

"Hey!" she cried, throwing a handful of water on me.

Xander laughed and submerged Samera at the same time as the latter pushed him into the ocean.

We played for a while, forgetting the world and mostly the fact that we'd have to report to Samera's mother and my parents soon. Surely the hospital would call someone and tell them I had disappeared. Literally. But for a couple of minutes, we were happy and careless like in the old days.

When we finally stopped, I was able, like my two friends, to drag my way onto the beach and rest on the hot sand.

"That was fun," I whispered.

"It really was," Xander said, looking at me.

I was about to apologize for not trusting him at the

hospital, when my eyes caught the sight of a wound on his shoulder.

"You're bleeding!" I said, with an emphasis on the last word; on the one hand because I had just noticed it, and on the other because I suddenly forced myself into a sitting position.

He examined his arm and shrugged. "Your lovely ex bit me."

Oh no...

"Jeez, Xander!" Samera exclaimed.

"Don't worry, it all got cleaned up in the ocean."

Bits of information on Rascals came back to me in a spurt of images. Wyatt, a guy tied up to a chair, and a lot of blood. Wyatt had once showed me what happened when he bit someone. He'd forced me to witness the long and painful process.

It can't... no. Not Xander.

"Xander," I said, not knowing how to break it to him. It was all my fault. "Wyatt did not bite you to defend himself."

Stay calm.

"*I* was defending myself. He was attacking."

"Exactly, but it's not what you think. It's really bad."

"Bad how?" Samera asked.

"Amya, what do you mean?"

I took a deep breath. "I don't know if I told you guys before that Wyatt is a Rascal."

"You bet he is," Xander answered.

"No, not the adjective. The noun."

"You've never mentioned this before," Samera said. "What's a Rascal, exactly?"

"Rascals feed on people's humanity. For example, Wyatt feeds from strength and energy, which is why it was so difficult for me to wake up from my coma. I think he visited me at intervals and fed on my strength so that I'd remain asleep, too feeble to wake up. His friend, Meo, feeds on memory, which is why I've forgotten the last couple of months of my life. There are probably others, but I've never met them."

I waited a few seconds to make sure my friends were following. Seeing the surprised looks on their faces, I continued. "Last October, before the incident, Wyatt demanded that I join his group and that I become a Rascal, but I said no. That is why I broke up with him and why he started following me everywhere. I couldn't see him but I could feel his presence. I can't remember why I never told you this, but it probably was for a good reason. Or maybe the memories had already been drained out of me…

"Anyway, Rascals all have their specialties, but there is one thing they have in common. When they bite someone—"

"I'm going to die, aren't I?" Xander asked.

"Wait, no!" Samera cried. "That can't be happening. Amya, tell me this isn't happening."

I looked at Xander and then Samera. Both looked so helpless, I didn't know what to say.

"You're not going to die, Xander," I stated.

They both exhaled and threw their heads backward. "Girl, you took your time to answer," Samera said. "Don't do this to me again." She turned to Xander. "You're fine. Oh, I'm glad you're not going to die."

"Me, too," he answered, putting a hand on her shoulder.

"Guys, Xander isn't going to die," I said, facing my friends. "But when Wyatt bit you, his teeth ousted venom into your blood. The process takes about twelve hours…"

"What process? What are you saying?" Samera inquired, shaking her head.

I couldn't face their gazes. It was too much, so I looked at my feet. "You have twelve hours before you'll turn into a Rascal."

Chapter XVIII

"NO. NO, NO, NO, NO, NO, NO…" SAMERA repeated.

"What happens then?" Xander said, trying to keep his calm.

"Honestly, I've only seen it happen once. You'll experience a growing headache, and then… well, the guy didn't look so well toward the end."

"Then?"

"Then, I don't know. You'll be a Rascal. The guy I saw immediately started working for Wyatt's 'family.' I can't quite recall what they were doing, though."

"Is there a cure?"

"A CURE!" Samera exclaimed. "Of course, there must be a cure!"

"I have no idea," I answered. The mere idea of losing my friend to a bunch of monsters created tornados in my stomach. "We should start looking for it right away."

"What if I become dangerous to you two?" Xander said, looking straight into my eyes.

"I don't think you will, not until you're fully transformed," I replied.

"All right, all right," Samera pondered, rubbing her hands together. "Where can we find a cure?"

"We should start by looking for the information of whether or not there is a cure."

"Amya is right," Xander agreed. "Do you think the Protectors know about Rascals?"

"If they did, I would," Samera said, insulted. "I was raised in that world and I've never heard of them."

"What about the library?"

"What library?" I said. Anything related to a library gave me a little bit of hope. Most miracles happen in libraries.

"The one at the Headquarters?" my best friend inquired.

"Why not?"

"It's worth a shot."

"Guys, what are you talking about?" I asked. What exactly was the Headquarters?

Samera shook her head in exasperation. "The library at the Protectors of Amani. The one we've always wanted to visit. Rings a bell?"

"No, but it sounds great. Let's go."

"Hold on for a second," Xander said. "How are we going to get to New York? We can't Travel back into Amani or Wyatt might find us. And the curtains at the HQ can only be opened from the inside."

"And I'm not letting my car into the hospital's parking lot," Samera stated. "God knows what would happen to it."

"Well, we could use Benny to get to your car, and then drive to the HQ in Amani," Xander proposed. "This time, however, I drive."

"Who's Benny?"

Samera smiled. "Great idea! We just need to know which direction the parking lot is."

"Who's Benny?"

They both looked at me. Samera was about to answer my question when Xander grimaced and clutched his head. "Argh!"

"What is it?" both Samera and I asked.

"I guess the start of a long and painful transformation." He walked to the boundary between the water and the sand, and then dropped.

"Xander!" I shouted before I got on my two feet and joined him, followed by Samera.

"Is everything all right?"

He shook his head and cried out.

We had to find a cure. Xander couldn't become a monster. There had to be some kind of solution.

Samera tried to help him to his feet, although he fought against it. "C'mon," she said. "No time to waste. We gotta go."

"Leave me alone!" he cried, pushing her away.

My first instinct was to indeed leave him alone for a moment, giving him time to adjust to the pain, but then I remembered how my mom used to hold me after I'd had a nightmare or when I was crying because I'd fallen off my bicycle when I was a child, and I felt the urge to do the same for my friend. My legs, now feeling a lot stronger than before, walked to his side, and I bent down. Hesitation made me pause for a moment, but when I finally put my hand on his back, his whole body relaxed, his shaky breath slowed, and he lifted his eyes to meet mine.

As I gazed at his scared features, I felt a rush in my stomach and saw a purple spot coming right at me. Then everything went black before I was thrown into the familiar meadow.

***

"Oh. Xander, look at this!" Amya says, agitating her hand to beckon me to her. "Bait is here."

I run to meet her on the beach and acknowledge the blue whale as it jumps on the open sea. Amya is clapping her hands and laughing. It's the happiest I've seen her in a while.

***

"Stop," Xander said as he gently removed my hand from his back. "Please don't."

But I didn't want to interrupt the Sojourn. I wanted to know more and more about that memory of his. That memory of us. The same one he'd shown me when I was still at the hospital. An urge for knowledge grew within me. I had the right to recollect the lost memories Meo had stolen from me.

Xander grabbed a silver chain from his pocket and put it around his neck, all the while looking directly into my eyes. I knew what it was.

I'd offered silver necklaces sprayed with vanilla to Samera and Xander as soon as I'd acknowledged that the essence blocked my ability. It was only a way to show them that I didn't want to invade their private thoughts. I'd soon learned how to control the Sojourns, but I guess Xander didn't trust me anymore. With good reason.

"I'm sorry," I said, ashamed, even though I still yearned for more.

"Can I have a word with you?" Xander said.

He stood and started walking away from me. I couldn't be sure whether he looked angry or in pain, and Samera only shrugged, probably more bewildered than I was since she didn't know I'd just Sojourned into our friend's head.

"I'll be right back," I told her before I hurried to Xander.

We walked in silence for a couple of minutes, looking at

the endless beach and enjoying the sun beaming on our skin. I still felt uncomfortable with the transparency of my hospital gown, but the sand stains helped cover my most private parts.

I was trying to amplify the dress so that it wouldn't stick on my skin as much, when Xander turned around, as if to say something, and stopped. He looked at me from head to toe and seemed to realize that I wasn't dressed very appropriately for a walk on the beach—to say the least.

"Would you like my shirt?"

He was wearing a damaged wine-red shirt over a white T-shirt. Even his jeans had been torn apart during the fight against Wyatt. Because he was a foot taller than my 5'2" self, his red shirt would fit me like a dress.

I looked down at myself and then at his shirt and replied, "If you don't mind."

In spite of the holes on the sleeves and back, Xander's shirt covered half my thighs up to my shoulders, which was a big improvement from my previous apparel. I could move more freely and less self-consciously.

"Thanks," I told him, trying not to look at the muscles shaped by his wet t-shirt. "Hm, how's your head?"

"Better. If the pain isn't constant, the transformation shouldn't be too difficult."

It was obvious that he didn't mean it.

I faked a smile, knowing all too well that the twinges would only increase with time, in strength as well as in length.

But I didn't want to scare him. "We'll find a cure."

There was a moment of silence.

"Look," he said, scratching the back of his head, "it's not that I don't want you to Sojourn, Amya, but there are things that I'd rather you remember on your own. I can tell you this, though: After you broke up with Wyatt, you told Samera and me that you were scared of him, but failed to mention that he was a Rascal. Seriously, we could have done a much better job of protecting you."

"Meo had probably already erased that memory from my brain."

"Maybe. Anyway, we Traveled in the other Dimensions after class, every weekend and basically every spare time we had, to make sure you felt safe and happy. I even told my dad that I'd been accepted to a special culinary class in Italy, so I'd have some time off the restaurant to protect you. I could feel that something was off. But then you started worrying that someone was following you on campus and you almost dropped out of university for that.

"That night," he paused. "You called me because Samera wanted you to come over to the Jewish Center on campus, but you still didn't feel safe enough to go on your own. I was busy covering a shift at Hippy's for a friend, so I asked you to wait, that I'd be there as soon as possible. But you didn't wait, Amya."

"I'm sorry," I said, without thinking.

"No. Look, I need to apologize to you. I swore nothing would ever happen to you. I also made a vow to Mrs. Cohen that I'd protect both you and Samera, and I failed. I should have known that there was more to your story than a simple break-up."

"It's not your fault."

"When I saw you awake at the hospital, I was so angry at myself for allowing someone to do this to you that I snapped. I couldn't look at you. I couldn't even look at myself, for God's sake. The incident weighted too much on my conscience… And I never put anything into your solute, I swear."

"I know that, now, and I'm so sorry for—"

"Don't be. I tried to visit you as much as possible. That day, the one when you were conscious but asleep, Samera was waiting on the other side of the curtain, in Red. I wanted to see if you could hear me or Sojourn. I was trying to show you how much I—we—missed you. When I heard your mother in the hallway, I couldn't face her, so I just Traveled back to the Red Dimension."

His behavior made sense, although he wasn't the one to blame. From his account of the night of the incident, it was all my fault.

"I want to show you something," Xander told me, before he took my hand and led me to the other side of a bunch of palm trees in the middle of the beach.

"What is it?" I asked just before my gaze fell upon the

most extraordinary view I'd ever seen.

The beach led to a dozen bridges seemingly made of wooden knots and braids, and those linked to a hundred or thousand tree houses emerging from the ocean. They weren't ordinary tree houses like you build as a kid; it was almost like every tree had distorted and evolved into a house shape, closing on top to produce a decent roof. The further the houses were from the beach, the bigger, and they continued farther than my eyes could see. Plus, I could discern several people in boats, going from one house to another. No one was close enough to the sand to see us, though. How hadn't I noticed them earlier?

"Our Blue-selves live on water, since continents and oceans are reversed from Amani. You'd have to see how big some of these houses are. I'm talking about two to three floors high and as large as mansions."

"Why doesn't anyone live on solid ground? There seems to be forests and lands," I said, nodding toward the mountains chock-full of trees behind us.

"No one ever adventures into the forests—the same applies to the Caves in Red or the Crags in Yellow. Before a person dies in these three Dimensions, they turn all zombie-like and unconsciously walk to these places and never come back."

"Samera told me that their heart just stopped beating, that it wasn't painful for them."

Xander looked away. "Maybe that's what happens once they're in. I don't know. We should go back now."

"Yeah."

"Hey, you guys," Samera said, running in our direction. "Not that I don't like sunbathing on warm sand and counting the crabs on the shore, but we should definitely start heading to the HQ, if we don't want to waste any time." She paused. "Am I interrupting something, or…"

"No," Xander replied quickly. "You're right. We should go."

"All right," Samera said, facing me. "Ready to meet Benny?"

She drew the curtains and gestured Xander and me in. I took a last, longing look at my surroundings and stepped forward.

Chapter XIX

THE YELLOW DIMENSION was nothing like Blue, aside from the warmth and sun radiating all around us. We ended up in front of a twenty-foot-tall waterfall, surrounded by trees with red, orange, purple, yellow, or green leaves. There were also a couple of white trees, resembling white cherry blossoms from New York, but those were rare amongst the colorful ones and their leaves were much bigger.

I didn't have time to admire the rainbow created by the waterfall before Samera grabbed my hand and we started walking toward what seemed like a white tent. And I realized that there were many of those around us, shaped like big, fat, puffy clouds.

"Let's scout for a Benny," she said.

And I still didn't know what she was talking about.

We faced the entrance of the nearest tent, through which we heard Celtic music, when Samera turned around and told me,

"They are kids, so don't expect civility." And she pushed the swinging door open.

Inside were children from the age of three to fourteen, dancing around and clapping their hands together. The oldest were singing and playing wooden instruments I'd never seen before. As soon as they saw us, they shouted something in another language and created a large group hug around us.

"Talee," Samera translated. "It means 'adults' in Takku, the children's language."

"Welcome, welcome. Welcome, welcome," they sang.

Someone threw dead leaves over our heads, while others went back to their little party.

"Excuse me," Samera said, trying to grab one of them, but they moved too fast and seemed to be playing tag with her. "HEY!" she shouted.

The whole party abruptly stopped and looked abashed. Some, the youngest, even started sobbing.

"I'm sorry to bother you," she continued. "But we'd like to borrow a Benny. Please."

"Benny, Benny. Benny, Benny!" they repeatedly sang, while leading us to the opposite door.

Outside, half the children from the tent circled around us and danced, all the while showing us the way to a nearby tent. The other half stayed in and kept on singing in Takku.

"Here's the tent of the Benny," one of the kids said.

She had red hair and a dozen freckles around her nose.

She reminded me of a ten-year-old version of Nevada. Xander must have noticed, too, as he looked very uncomfortable.

"But first," the girl continued. "You must answer my question." She smiled. "Which one of you is the most ticklish?"

My eyes immediately diverted to Samera's. When we were younger, she'd often threatened me with tickles to win an argument. She knew very well that I couldn't resist laughing and going crazy. Every time.

"Amya," she admitted, her smile as wide as her face. "Her," she nodded toward me.

The half-dozen children all came rushing to me and I froze, helpless. Surely, they weren't really going to do it.

But they did. Each one of them tickled either my armpits, ribs, legs, and some even tried my neck. I was utterly helpless as I began laughing and laughing, trying to push them away, but it only made me kneel on the ground and gave them more room for the tickles.

"Guys!" I said, trying to breathe. "Guys, I can't—" I couldn't stop laughing. "I can't breathe. Please."

Meanwhile, all I could hear was children laughing and singing in their language, which didn't seem to hold many words or syllables. It probably took less than a minute, but seemed like forever before Xander and Samera came out of the tent with a Benny.

A giraffe.

And then, every child kissed my cheek and ran back into

their tent, leaving me on the ground, smiling, light-headed, and completely out of breath.

The giraffe wore a sort of large, rectangular saddle from neck to bottom, to even out the angle of its back. It knelt down and shook its head three times, which encouraged Samera and Xander to mount it.

"Come on," Xander reassured me. The fact that I'd never, ever heard of people mounting a giraffe added up the pile of reasons why I didn't want to mount it.

I got up. "What's its name?" I asked.

"Benny."

I stared at its long neck. "I thought Benny was a word meaning giraffe."

"Exactly. That's why all giraffes are called Benny. They all have the same name," Samera told me.

"It doesn't make any sense."

"I know, but no one cares here. Hop on, girl, and buckle up, because Bennies don't have long legs for nothing."

Against all reason, I used the step on the saddle to mount, and sat next to Xander at the rear. I took a deep breath and fastened the closest thing I found to a seat belt: a rope.

"Daa," Samera said to Benny, who in turn raised to its full height and started walking.

"Kaya!" Samera added a moment later.

And Benny started galloping.

Fast.

Mostly using her head to propel her body even faster.

Which, if you do the math correctly, left us in a shaking and dizzying roller coaster.

"How—long—will we—stay on this—thing?" I asked, trying not to sound too upset.

"It shouldn't take—more than—thirty minutes," Samera answered. "If we're—heading in—the right direction—that is. Still—faster than walking. Es—pecially with—you."

She was right. My legs had recovered enough strength to support my weight, but I didn't know how far and fast I could walk.

We passed a group of kids plucking out leaves from a white tree, and a gathering of… It was hard to put a name on these creatures. Or were they birds? I did a double take, just in case my sight had been clouded by the stress of riding a giraffe, but they looked the same: baby gorillas with owl wings.

"Banimos," Xander said, looking at the strange species. "They carry—the peliolites, the leaves from the—white trees, and—use them to—build tents."

He later told me that the leaves from the white trees were waterproof. During our little ride, we came across two other types of—I soon learned the names of these weird animals— critter. There were Ocelitos, baby cheetahs with eagle wings, who transported things like food and sometimes even babies, when all the Bennies were busy; and a Frapidor, which often hid under trees. A Frapidor had a rabbit's body, a pig's nose, and bat's wings.

"They dig out—all kinds of food—like mushrooms, roots, and plants—for the kids. And—when the Frapidors—or any other critter—get old, our Yellow-selves—eat them."

Benny also galloped around high, dark, wall-like rocks named Crags. It was there, Xander told me, that children in Yellow went to die and disappear.

Less than thirty minutes later, we reached yet another bubbly white tent—probably the hundredth we'd seen so far. Xander said it was the only type of dwelling the children were able to build, using the wood for support and thick white waterproof leaves of peliolites to cover from the sun and occasional rain during the night.

It was my turn to climb off the giraffe, welcoming Xander's help, when six red fireworks set off high up in the sky. I was the only one who reacted, though. Even Benny remained calm.

"What's going on?"

Samera smiled. "Their way to keep up with time, as they don't have clocks. Every hour, a different color of fireworks bursts in the sky. Some natural wonder that happens only in Yellow. Red is the six o'clock one. If you don't want to learn the colors by heart, just count the number of explosions."

I was still in awe at how fascinating the Yellow Dimension was when Samera peeked into Amani and beckoned me and Xander in. "We're right on-spot. I can even see my car."

"We're leaving Benny on its own?"

"She'll be fine. Don't worry."

"It's a she?" I said, before I stepped into the ordinary world… into the hospital's parking lot, which, to my great disappointment, didn't hold any critters or colorful trees. Nor could I smell the beach or feel the warmth of the sun on my pale skin. The sky was gray, threatening an eventual precipitation, and the wind was cold and raw.

"Right this way," Samera said, just before Xander collapsed on the concrete and grasped his head tightly.

"I'm fine," he said, immediately rising up, even though his face clearly indicated that he was in pain. "Let's get going."

He was walking again, but it was obvious that his head was pushing his limits. His eyes even appeared a little darker than their usual bright, brazed color. And I knew that only Rascal's eyes turned to black when they were angry or upset. No matter how amazed I was by the other Dimensions, my friend needed all my focus. We absolutely and imperatively had to find a cure.

When we finally reached Samera's car, a sapphire blue 1966 Ford Mustang, she decided to warn her mom of our arrival.

"I'll drive," Samera said, against Xander's protests.

He grunted but seemed to understand that it was safer for her to drive, in case his headache became insufferable.

I sat in the passenger's seat and tried to calm my thoughts. Wyatt could be anywhere looking for me and we didn't know if he'd call for backup. Xander was becoming stiffer and less patient by the minute. And it would only get worse.

"Mind if we listen to music?" I asked, when I figured out nothing else would distract me from my growing fears.

"Sure," Samera said before turning it on herself.

...Italy, France, Greece, Germany, Poland, and Finland are also part of the movement. Authorities do not know how to react. There are police officers as well as the army posted on every corner of these countries, waiting for directions...

"What movement?" I inquired.

...We will know more about this situation later today. Thank you for listening, and be safe.

Then the music of WABC radio started and we were introduced to a new song by Taylor Swift. We all knew that Europe was not in a good place right now and we feared a Third World War. Maybe a movement of peace had started and it would calm things down a bit.

"It's really happening, isn't it?" Samera pondered out loud.

"What's happening?" I asked. "The Third World War? Are they talking about a movement of peace?"

"Unfortunately, no," Xander replied. "It is a movement of hostility more than anything else. Many countries, including Italy, Greece, Poland, and Germany are threatened to be put in quarantine if they are unable to control their growing criminality rate. Today, we learned that those countries created a movement and they are planning on attacking the remaining European countries."

"But they stand no chance," Samera said. "There are approximately fifty countries in Europe. They would be greatly underpowered."

"That and they are already surrounded by armies. If they move as much as their pinky against a neighbor, they'll be put down immediately."

"Still, I hope they change their mind," Sam continued. "If that were to happen, if everyone starts attacking, it'll reach Asia, Australia and eventually America. No one will be safe."

"All that because of some disease rendering people insane."

I remained silent, trying to cope with the news. The situation was worse than I could have ever imagined. I noticed that Samera was chewing on her upper lip, which meant that she was anxious. Clearly, the war affected her the most since the Protectors in New York believed their family members in Europe responsible for it. But how was that possible? How could somebody with the incredible ability to Travel make others go nuts? And why would they even do it?

***

We stopped at a small shop in order to buy dry clothes and new shoes for me, and then took off for New York. Xander only had one migraine, but this time, he cried out of pain and banged his head on the back of my seat until it passed.

"Keep driving," he firmly said when Samera offered to stop for some fresh air.

And we carried on until we arrived in the Bronx. We must have been near the Headquarters because Samera decided to call her mother.

"Can you stay close to the entrance and open the gates as soon as you see my car? We'd rather not stay *à découvert* for too long. We can talk when we're there... No, not yet. Thanks." She hung up.

"A divers?" Xander said, puzzled.

"*À découvert,*" she replied. "It means to be in the open, in French."

I'd almost forgotten how proud Samera was to study French. She'd always wanted to be a French teacher growing up, even though she'd probably have to follow in her mother's footsteps as the head of the Protectors of Amani.

"I think we're being followed," Samera said before she put the pedal to the metal.

Chapter XX

"WHAT IN THE WORLD do you think you're doing?" Xander uttered. "Let me drive. Now."

"Of course, I'm just going to stop the car, ask those guys to wait so we can exchange our seats and then—"

"Just—argh! Be careful," he said as he gently squeezed my shoulder.

I looked in the side mirror and saw a dark blue Ford SUV two cars behind. I wondered if the fact that they were still following us, even after Samera had accelerated, was just a coincidence. Maybe we were heading the same way.

She attempted an immediate U-turn and almost crashed into a golden Toyota Echo, which in turn hit a stop sign.

"Sorry!" I cried, even though I knew the driver couldn't hear me. I really hoped they weren't hurt.

"They better not hurt my baby," Samera said, patting the wheel.

The SUV was much faster and didn't care whose car they wrecked. They were back in our lane in no time, which eliminated the coincidence theory. Who were they? And what did they want?

"Do you think it's Wyatt?" I asked.

"Let's not wait to find out," Xander answered. "Although I wouldn't mind having a little chat with him after what he's done."

"Guys. I don't know what to do," Samera said. She managed to shift in between cars and accelerate, but it wasn't enough. Our pursuers were right behind us.

"Turn here!" Xander shouted, as we were about to stop on a red light.

"But it's red!"

"NOW!"

I gripped at my seat as Samera complied. Our pursuers, however, were quick enough to mimic our stunt and, before any of us knew what was happening, they positioned the SUV in the lane to our right. A man with a brown ponytail emerged from the back sliding door and pulled mine open.

"Hey, what the—" I said as I tried to hold the handle closer.

"You're coming with me," he told me, forcing the door open completely.

He was held by a rope attached to his waist and, once he'd transferred in our car—he was literally hunched in the doorframe, almost kneeling on my seat—he began to wrap it around my waist as well. But Xander didn't let him. He punched the man in the face. I thought it would be enough for Ponytail to lose his grip on me, but it only distracted him for a second.

"His skull's like a brick wall, dammit," Xander said.

"Do something!" Samera cried as she let go of the wheel with her right hand and plucked her fingers into our opponent's eyes.

But Ponytail wasn't surprised for long and hit Samera on the cheek, which rendered her unconscious. Her foot fell on the accelerator and we were heading directly into a building, when Xander took control of the wheel and managed to push Samera aside, face to the door and feet away from the gas pedal.

Ponytail resumed circling my waist with a rope and I was left dumbstruck. I didn't want to be taken. What if Wyatt was behind this? Of course Wyatt was behind this. I didn't want to go back to nothingness and lose all my memories again. I had to do something.

I kept struggling like a fish out of the water and punching my assailant as hard as I could. Even though my knuckles gradually became red and a little bloody, I didn't stop, which slowed Ponytail's motions.

"Stay still, would you?" he said, touching my face, which sent an electric shock through my body.

How was I going to win over that guy? He was probably a Rascal, which made the task impossible. I was weak and tired.

I couldn't win that battle. I couldn't do anything.

"Amya!" Xander cried. "Amya, what are you doing?"

I was letting Ponytail win. I had given up.

"What's taking so long?" I heard a man shout from inside the SUV. It was Wyatt.

I was about to be delivered like a fresh piece of zebra to a hungry lion and I was too feeble to defend myself. The battle was over. I would never be able to find a cure for Xander or even to help stop the war. Wyatt had won again.

Then it struck me. I knew what Ponytail was doing. He was feeding from something important. I could feel it. Ponytail was eating away my faith and hope.

"Almost done here," he answered.

He started to lift my back, as if to carry me into the SUV, Wyatt was on the other side, stretching his arms to receive his price.

"Amya, there's a truck about a hundred feet ahead," Xander noticed. "We have to do something. Amya! No!"

Xander swerved the car as much as he could to throw my opponent off balance, while the latter struggled not to fall off the Mustang. The sudden commotion made him lose his grip on me and I fell back on my seat. But I was now tied to him. If he fell, I would too. And Xander soon realized that, so he stopped what he was doing and looked at me, helpless.

By the time Ponytail recovered his bearings, I had a plan.

"I think I'm going to be sick," I said, as I started to hunt around my assailant's body to find a way out. He was blocking the door, after all. "Move aside."

"No. No, you won't," Ponytail said, remaining firmly in place, but looking for a bag so I wouldn't be sick on him.

What he didn't realize was that his distracted gaze gave me the opportunity to untangle the rope around my waist while faking complete panic. He'd only managed to circle me twice with it and hadn't even tied a knot. After that first task was completed, I faked vomiting on the carpet beneath my feet as my hands brushed open the glove compartment. There, next to a flashlight, was a small tool box, in case of emergencies.

"This is just disgusting. Wyatt will owe me," Ponytail said, averting his eyes, which gave me enough time to open the tool box and find a cutter.

"Amya, are you alright?" Xander asked.

"What's taking so long?" Wyatt shouted from the SUV.

That's my opening, I realized. Ponytail was about to answer, when I grabbed the cutter and stabbed it into his neck. He screamed out his pain and slapped my cheek with the back of his hand. Xander, realizing what had just happened, swerved the Mustang onto the SUV, sending unstable Ponytail out of our car and into the street. The driver of the SUV didn't have enough time to recover his trail before they crashed into the truck Xander had previously noticed, hurling Ponytail on the pavement, his limbs like a puppet's.

The Mustang quickly found its way on to the nearest

street to our left, turned right—and right again, until we were no longer near the accident.

I killed someone, I repeated in my head, trying to swallow unwelcome tears burning into my eyes. I had killed someone. I had ended the life of a person… The image of the cutter in Ponytail's neck produced a cold, raw shiver down my spine. I didn't even know his name. I didn't know where he was from or if he had a family… So I just stared outside and prayed for the rebel tear running down my cheek to remain unnoticed by my friends.

We stopped and dragged Samera out of the car on the sidewalk.

"Sam," Xander whispered while shaking her shoulders. "Sam!" he said, much louder.

A couple walking nearby came rushing, but I told them that we had things under control.

"She drank a little too much," I said, which made them laugh and carry on their way.

After a moment, Samera's eyes slowly opened and, as if she'd just woken up from a wonderful dream, she started grinning.

"Hey," she said. "Why are you guys looking at me like that?"

Xander and I were speechless. Maybe she was dreaming.

"How do you feel?" Xander asked.

"Stupid headache… but it's all right. Everything is…

oh!" she exclaimed and rose into a sitting position, her smile transforming into an anxious frown. "Jeez, how did you get rid of him? It was like in a movie. Oy! And the SUV. Was it Wyatt? Who else was there? Is my car okay?"

Her right eye was a little swollen and, even through her dark skin, we could discern tints of green and purple slowly coming out. She probably had a concussion.

"We have to get you to a hospital," I said.

"We can't go back," Xander stated. "Dr. Goldbridge will take care of her at the HQ."

After Samera was comfortably settled in the back seat, we drove off to the Protector's Headquarters, hoping Mrs. Cohen wouldn't freak out. As for me, I tried to push aside the concern and remorse I felt toward Ponytail. Even though he'd been trying to deliver me back to Wyatt, he hadn't done anything to me himself—aside from the slap.

Xander must have felt that something was wrong. "Are you all right?" he asked me.

I shrugged. "I don't know. I didn't want to kill him."

"I know. I'm sorry you had to do that, but it was either him or you. I really thought we were going to lose you again." He gently squeezed my left arm.

I didn't answer. Instead, I looked down at my hands, only to realize how bloody they were, and I wondered if some of that blood was Ponytail's.

"You did the right thing, Amya," Xander stated.

"Honestly, Amya," Samera said, after we told her what had happened. "Don't feel bad for that guy. He wasn't really human. I mean, did you notice how hard his body was?"

We agreed on telling Mrs. Cohen about the accident only after we'd gotten our information. Otherwise, she might lock us up in the HQ until we'd recovered completely or until Wyatt and the others were apprehended, which meant we wouldn't have time to put an end to Xander's transformation.

The car slowed down on Broadway, in front of the Van Cortlandt Park entrance.

"Here we are, at last," Samera said.

"A park?" How could the Protectors work in a park?

"You'll see."

I followed them to a nearby tree, trying to understand where we were going. There weren't many pedestrians around, only a woman walking her poodle, probably to the dog park, and a man jogging with his earphones on. The air was chilly—the wind carrying an early-winter smell—however, I didn't have time to get too cold before a tree split in two, revealing a narrow stairway.

"Is that the gate you were talking about? What if people see it?" I said, looking nervously around.

"There are cameras everywhere. Mom would never open it if someone was in the area."

"That was fast. Michelle is very efficient," Xander said, impressed.

"Like mother like daughter."

I was expecting to go down in the dark, but the stairway revealed itself to be illuminated by several lightbulbs that were the size of my hands. Once at the bottom, Samera used a key card to open the steel door and ushered Xander and me inside.

"Welcome back to the Headquarters," she said.

The walls, ceiling, and floor were equally white and bright, and were lighted by the same kind of lightbulbs we'd seen in the stairway. The walls were equipped with fake stripped windows full of light, to compensate for the lack of natural brightness. It was almost dizzying to keep my eyes open and I had to squint for a while before my pupils acclimated to the glow.

"You'll get used to it," Xander reassured me.

"You *were* used to it," Samera added, reminding me that I'd been here before.

I heard the tapping of high heels coming from another room right in front of us and recognized Mrs. Cohen as soon as she opened the only door leading to the entrance we were standing in. Next to Mrs. Cohen were my mother, father, and sister.

"Mom! Dad!" I said, running right into their welcoming arms.

"Sweetheart, where have you been?" Dad asked.

"We were so worried," Mom added.

They broke our embrace and frowned at me. Samera,

Xander, and I had agreed on telling nobody about the Rascals until we had gathered enough information on them, but right now, all I wanted was to tell everyone the truth. Even to my sister who was looking at me like she was too shy to give me a hug. No words came out of my mouth, so I simply shook my head at my parents.

"What happened to your cheek?" my mother asked me. "Your father and I were so, so worried."

"Samera," Mrs. Cohen said. "Did you have an accident? Look at your eye."

Neither I nor Xander knew what to respond. We should have told Mrs. Cohen about Samera's concussion, but the latter spoke before any of us could say anything.

"Can we speak in private?" Samera asked her mother.

Mrs. Cohen was dressed in the same style and color I had always seen her wear: a light brown dress and office shirt. Her hair hadn't changed from the last time I'd seen her, either; she wore her straight bangs above her eyebrows and the remainder of her locks was neatly tied up in a low pony-tail, which created the illusion that her brown eyes were even bigger than they already were.

"I am very happy to see you all," she said, flashing her big, bright teeth. "Especially you, Amya. But why are you two hurt? How in heaven did you get here? I want to know everything."

Again, I was compelled to tell her everything, but

Samera was faster and requested that we speak in her office. Mrs. Cohen looked questioningly at her daughter, but nonetheless guided us into the room she and my family had just emerged from.

As we left the entryway, Delilah came closer to me. "Amya," she whispered, but I ignored her. We walked in a long, white hallway resembling the previous room. "Amya, I'm so sorry. I should've known you and Wyatt were still together. He told me you two were through."

Yep, you should have, I wanted to say, but kept quiet because I had actually broken up with Wyatt way before she mentioned their relationship. There were more important matters to take care of for the moment, although she ought to know how dangerous he was. I planned on telling my parents that she shouldn't be allowed to see him anymore.

She closed the space between us and walked to my right. "I broke up with him," she murmured a little louder.

"What?"

She smiled, triumphant. "I broke up with Wyatt. He didn't take it nicely, but we're over."

I took her hand, making sure my parents could hear me. "Just be careful, okay? He doesn't take break-ups lightly."

Would Wyatt go after her as well? Would he drain her of her strength, like he'd done to me? I didn't think so. I didn't think he'd revealed to her his secret, or she would've told me. As long as she kept away from him, she was safe.

On the other end of the hallway stood two large French doors, and promptly after Mrs. Cohen opened them, just about a hundred heads lifted from their computers and greeted us with warm smiles and nods. Everyone was seemingly dressed like Samera's mother and although they seemed to know me, I couldn't recognize any of them. I still grinned back, glad to be amongst friends.

"Come this way," Mrs. Cohen said after everyone had gone back to their screens.

We followed her into a medium-sized room: wide enough to lodge a large desk, a bookshelf, and three chairs, but too small for everyone to get into. My family agreed to wait outside. Besides, according to Samera, my mother had never wanted to work with the Protectors, and Dad and Deli weren't even supposed to be here.

"I'll tell you everything once we've found what we're looking for," I told them before closing the door behind me.

Xander offered to stand, allowing Mrs. Cohen, Samera, and me to sit. When I looked up to thank him, his temples were gorged with sweat and his breath was unsteady. The transformation was keeping its course and we hadn't yet found a cure.

"Now that we are alone, I want to know what happened," Mrs. Cohen told us. "How did you wake up, Amya? Do you know who did this to you? Why does everyone look injured? And why were you in such a hurry to get here?"

"We'll explain everything in time," Samera said. "But there's something we need to find out first."

"No. I am entitled to get some answers, here and now. Why do you sound so anxious? Did somebody follow you here?"

"No, Mom. We're pretty sure we were not followed, and—"

"Pretty sure? Samera, you know how important it is for this place to remain hidden from the public eye."

"Yes, Mom! But you don't understand. We don't have much time and it would take too long to explain everything. We need information on something."

Michelle frowned and considered her options. When she spoke again, her voice was all business-like. "Fine, but none of you is leaving until I get some answers." She looked at the three of us with severe features. Her gaze lingered on Xander for a moment, but he didn't let her question him.

"Do you know anything about Rascals?" he asked.

Mrs. Cohen was taken aback. "Rascals as in mythical creatures?"

"You know about them?" Samera exclaimed, insulted.

"I've read something once... But how is this relevant?"

"Where did you read about them?" Xander inquired. "Was it here? In the library? Which book was it?"

"It was years ago, I can't remember, truly. I've read most of the books we own in the library. It was requested to read them, for me to apply as the Protectors' leader in the US."

"This is hopeless," Xander said as he started to walk toward the door.

"No, wait!" I said, quickly grabbing hold of his arm. "Mrs. Cohen, where could we find this book?"

"Oh, Amya, you know you can call me Michelle. The book you are looking for should still be in the library, downstairs. May I ask what you need it for?"

Take a deep breath and say something that'll close the deal.

"Actually, Michelle, the inquiries you made are somehow linked to the information we need. Therefore, as long as we don't have the information, you'll only get half answers."

Resigned, she dialed something on her cell phone and asked for someone called Gareth Williams and someone else called Dr. Goldbridge. "Gareth is our new librarian," she said as she stood up. "He will help you find any information you need."

"We're allowed to visit the library? At last," Samera uttered.

"Yes, but you may not remain down there for too long. Some of my colleagues who work on that floor won't enjoy being bothered." She looked at her watch. "While we wait for Mr. Williams to arrive, I have asked that you allow Dr. Goldbridge to take a look at your bruises. Samera, Amya, Xander, sit."

We did as she bid and the doctor arrived two minutes

later. He examined Samera first and concluded that she had a concussion.

"You need to rest, young lady."

"I know, I know," she said, looking at her mother with pleading eyes. Michelle exhaled sharply and made it clear to her daughter that she wasn't happy with the situation.

Dr. Goldbridge shook his head and came near me. "What have we got here?"

"She just recovered from a coma," Michelle said. "Do you believe it's okay for her to be out of her bed so soon?"

"Hmm…" Dr. Goldbridge pondered. I took that opportunity to hide my bloody knuckles behind my back. "There is no sign of any permanent damage. I believe that since she does not show any symptoms besides fatigue, she can have a little fun—after what she's gone through." He smiled at me.

A little fun? He certainly didn't know what we were up to. After Dr. Goldbridge examined Xander, he came to the conclusion that our friend had a strong fever. "He should rest as well. Give him aspirins and a lot of water. Nothing else is wrong with this young man."

When the doctor was dismissed, we told Mrs. Cohen that we'd get some sleep later.

"You three are allowed to stay at the HQ for as long as you wish, until you recover all your strength." Michelle had just finished her sentence when we heard two quick knocks behind us. "Come in," she said. The door hesitantly opened, revealing a tall and skinny boy wearing a shirt way too big for him. He had messy brown hair and big gray eyes that instantly fell on Samera.

"Hello, new boy," she said with a smirk.

"Hi—hi," he managed to answer, his face as red as a strawberry. He rapidly shifted his gaze onto his boss. "Mrs. Cohen, you asked to see me?"

"I did," Michelle answered, oblivious to the boy's uneasiness. Poor guy, he must have been no older than seventeen years old. "This is Samera, my daughter; Amya; and Xander. Will you show them to the library and help them in any investigation they need to accomplish? I also want you to make sure that they come back here as soon as they are done." She turned to us. "He's still in training, but he knows his way around pretty well now."

"No problem, ma'am," the young librarian answered. He shifted his gaze back onto us, obviously avoiding Samera's eyes. "You may follow me."

Chapter XXI

Ian Cohen

"REPEAT TO ME EXACTLY why I couldn't kill them?" I asked Meo on the phone.

He called me before I was able to get my hands on any of the kids, asking me to spare their lives after all.

"Somebody else took care of the boy and Amya will soon realize that she isn't safe with her friends anymore. I won't be needing your services after all."

"What about our deal? Will you help me take control of the Protectors?"

I knew I sounded desperate, but I'd dreamed of the day that a solution would come up to me. It had, at last, except that in one phone call, all the hope I'd built was gone. Evaporated.

Meo was silent for a moment. I could only hear his slow breathing through the speaker.

"The deal is off. For now. Let me know if there's any development."

He hung up.

Without thinking, I snatched the hand soap dispenser from the wall and threw it at the mirror, which shattered into a hundred pieces. My heart beat accelerated and I thought I would lose control completely, when someone entered the bathroom.

"Hey, Ian. Are you all right?" the person inquired.

Had he heard my conversation? What if he told anyone? I didn't even look at his face. It didn't matter to me. Instead, I swiftly grabbed his shirt and threw him at the wall facing the door. *Throw the first hit*, Karl had told me during my training session earlier. The man I'd just attacked was already on his feet, arms stretched to prove he wanted me no harm. But I couldn't trust his gesture. I couldn't trust anyone.

"What's up, man? Pipe down," he said.

Karl had mentioned something else toward the end of today's session. *Don't be afraid. It's either him or you.*

I walked to the blurry face in front of me and hit him in the jaw, but he didn't let me back away so easily. His elbow found my neck in a sudden blow, sending electric jolts through my head. Then, I hit him again and again, but he was able to block most of my moves.

"Ian, stop for God's sake. Stop it! It's me…"

I didn't hear his name, as if my brain didn't want me to comprehend that information. I kept throwing punches at his stomach and his face, although his arms were in the way. I realized that my opponent was becoming weaker and weaker and he wasn't able to block as many blows anymore. My hands became swollen and bloody. This time, however, it wasn't my blood. It was his. When I thought he was feeble enough for me to slow down, I grabbed his shirt once more and threw a final punch at his nose.

But he blocked it instantly, held my fist in his large hand, and twisted my arm so that I was now facing the door, my back to him. I struggled and kicked backward with my feet, but he was stronger. He strangled me with his forearm and the world started spinning after only a few seconds. I had to break free. With the energy and alertness I had left, I looked around for an object to hit him with. The soap dispenser was out of my reach and I was in no way strong enough to rip out the water faucet from the countertop.

"Calm down, Ian. NOW. I don't want to hurt you."

Of course he wanted me to calm down—so he could strangle me more easily. But I wasn't going to let him, the same way I hadn't let Jemina hit me on my twelfth birthday. I'd had enough of her bully behaviors and had thrown her into the lake next to our house.

My eyes caught sight of a piece of the broken mirror. One of its corners was sharp enough to hurt my attacker. I feared I would lose consciousness before I was able to use it, but my elbow finally hit a soft spot in the man's stomach and his grip on me weakened enough, allowing me to grab the piece of mirror— my sleeve covering the inside of my hand in order to avoid any cut—and stab him in the chest.

I let go of the weapon and backed away, in case he would retaliate. My elbow and knuckles felt a little swollen and my neck hurt like hell, but, as my vision cleared, I was proud to see that my adversary looked much, much worse. His features were distorted into a grimace of pain and he had blood all over his face. His knees slowly bent, forcing him to slide into a sitting position, his back to the wall. Adrenaline was gradually clearing from my veins as my breathing resumed its normal pace. I leaned on the sink and looked at my broken reflection until my sight was back to normal.

Except for the renewed bruise on my cheek from two weeks ago, it didn't look like I'd just been in a fight. I smiled at myself and mostly at my victory. Then I looked back at the man dying on the bathroom floor and that is when I noticed the white hair and deep wrinkles surrounding his gentle features.

No.

I kneeled down in front of him and brushed the hair from his forehead. He had dark, brown, pleading eyes filled with tears, threatening to wash away the blood from his face.

Jim. No.

I wanted to grip his shirt and order him to stay alive. I wanted to scream at anyone for help. Most of all, I wanted to go back in time and recognize him earlier. But I could do none of that. If somebody saw me next to him, I would get thrown in jail—or worse. I would lose my name and all chances to become the leader of the Protectors of Amani. I had to flee the scene.

I swallowed back the guilt making my head hurt and took a last look at my only friend.

"I'm sorry," I said. "I have no choice."

Confusion and fear showed in his eyes when I tore the fabric of his sleeve and pushed it to his mouth. He tried to shake his head around, thinking that I was going to choke him, but as my left hand moved to his chest, he understood what I was about to do. I had no choice. If he survived, he might tell the Protectors I attacked him, or worse. He might tell them about my plan to become their leader. If he survived I wouldn't. *It's either him or you.* I pushed the cloth as hard as I could against his mouth and pulled the piece of mirror out of his chest.

Chapter XXII

WE FOLLOWED GARETH after we'd properly thanked Samera's mother for her cooperation. My family wasn't waiting outside when we left the office. According to Samera, they had been escorted to a waiting room, as none of them worked for the Protectors. They'd been blindfolded before entering the HQ, and had no clue as to what was going on here. When my grandmother and I had started to work for the Protectors, I had apparently told my mother that Michelle needed an editor for a book publishing company she was about to open. The Protectors were extremely vigilant when it came to strangers and letting out too much information.

We followed Gareth into another white and sparkling hallway, which led to a staircase. "The library is the last floor down," he said.

There were five staircases in total and I was already exhausted thinking that we would have to climb all the way back up later.

"Don't you have elevators?" Xander asked. Everyone except for Gareth seemed too weary to even think about making the first step down.

"That's like the first question I asked when they hired me. Unfortunately, the Protectors seem to value hard work in any form." Gareth looked genuinely apologetic.

Having no other choice, we descended one stair at a time, taking breaks in between staircases. Gareth looked a little worried, but we assured him that we were fine. Every time I gazed at Xander, his irises were a little darker, which informed me that his patience was at its limit. We needed to hurry.

One stair at a time we descended.

My legs were shaking.

But I tried to focus on our goal.

My heartbeat sped up.

There was no time to pass out.

One more stair.

When we finally reached the bottom floor, we faced an ancient bronze wooden door with an antique padlock. Gareth fetched the equally aged key in his jeans pocket and passed it in front of the lock. Just like a magnetic key card, the movement miraculously unlocked the door.

And that is when my jaw hit the floor. Being a bookworm, I enjoy the sight of any library, whether it's large or small or contains only a few good books. Yet, what my eyes perceived at this very moment was how I imagined Heaven to look.

Books were stacked on auburn shelves adorned with golden moldings, and the room was filled with statues and gargoyles everywhere. And all that on four humongous floors. The ceiling resembled a Michelangelo painting, depicting men and women from different countries interacting with angels and gods. Gareth said that there was a different image for each floor, respectively representing settings of the four Dimensions. The beauty of the paintings continued farther than my eyes could see. In the middle of it all were tables made of carved wood and dressed with golden lamps. And, as if to suit the ceiling, golden and sky-blue ornaments decorated the bookshelves.

I longed to go through each and every row to discover what genres they offered. I wanted to sit at a table all night and read as many books as I could. "This is where you work?" I whispered.

"Yep. Pretty cool, huh?" Gareth answered. "Wait, you've never been here before?"

Samera shook her head. "Mom never let us in."

"Can we stay here for, like, forever?" I inquired. I wasn't even kidding. "I want your job!"

There were actual cramps in my cheeks from smiling too much. I'd even forgotten all about my trembling legs and pounding headache.

We followed Gareth to the center of the library, where

there lay a ten-foot-long by ten-foot-large golden framed star painting on the floor. Each leg was different. It reminded me of the star Samera had drawn at the hospital to explain the different Dimensions.

"Is this—" I began.

"The Star of Amani," Samera and Gareth said at the same time. She smiled at him and added, "Amya, this is the Protectors of Amani's emblem."

"It represents the Four Dimensions, plus Heaven and Hell," Gareth explained.

The head depicted an upside-down tree that reached the middle of the star. The top-left arm was all black with a dark-blue hue; it looked like a cloudy night sky. The bottom-left arm was illustrated by a rainbow; the colors were so alluring, I could have stared at them all night. The bottom and top-right arms were the most luminous; the fire painted on the bottom arm made the floor look like it'd caught on fire, while the other was plain white with threads reaching the center of the star. What made the emblem even more remarkable was the lustrous golden frame. Next to it, the golden ornaments on the shelves looked used and bedraggled.

"The library was first built in 1936," Gareth began, while moving in another direction. "It was a secret underground space where the Protectors would meet and gather all the knowledge they could find about their era. After a little while, they thought it was a good idea to build a main center of operations. What you see here is the result of many years of accumulation of books, encyclopedias and documents from everywhere in North America."

"This is all really, *really* nice info, man," Xander muttered through his teeth, which made me take a good look at him. He wasn't just sweating anymore, his eyes were bloodshot and veins popped out of his arms, neck and forehead. Too amazed by the library, I hadn't paid attention to him and had almost forgotten what we came here for. "But where's the book on Rascals?"

"On what?"

I saw Xander approach the librarian in an offensive manner, but didn't let him get too close. I grabbed my friend's damp arm and told Gareth, "We—we're looking for a book on Rascals. You know, the mythical creatures?"

"Right, I'm sorry. I know you guys are probably not interested in—"

"We are," I interrupted. "We really are, but we're also really tired and we don't have much time to find what we need."

"Is he all right?" Gareth asked, nodding toward Xander. "Is it for a school project? I totally understand if you want to get a good mark, you know."

"Yes, exactly. A school project."

"Right," Samera said. "C'mon new guy, show us what you've got."

"Right this way." Gareth texted something on his phone

and walked toward yet more stairs. "I know you guys are a little tired, but my friends and I are going to a party tonight in Manhattan, if you want to join."

"Not tonight," Samera answered. "But maybe another time." She winked at him.

The librarian had just slowed his pace on the first floor, in front of a large bookshelf, when Xander dropped in a loud groan. Gareth stepped back, while Samera and I quickly knelt down at our friend's side. Then, no sound came out of Xander's mouth; it remained wide open in a silent agony, his hands tightly clasped on his temples.

I set my hand on his shoulder and told him that everything was going to be fine, that we were very close to finding a solution. A cure. Without further explanation, Gareth said, "I hope you find what you were looking for. I'll be at the main desk if you need me," before rushing downstairs.

Xander took a few steadying breaths and shook his head, as if trying to focus on something. He quickly jumped back on his two feet. "Let's find that book and get outta here."

"Are you all right?" I asked.

He grunted as a response and started looking through the shelf, which Samera and I did too, after anxiously looking at each other. "Let's do this," she mouthed.

We found books about every monster I could imagine, from sirens to the Minotaur. I hoped most of them weren't real. Actually, I hoped *none* of them were real. After gathering all the books we could find on mythical creatures, we met at the nearest table and started to read.

***

After about an hour, we had searched through each and every book on mythical creatures with no luck. Xander didn't waste time wondering what our next move was before he bounced off his chair and ran to the ground floor, Samera and I at his heels. We arrived just in time to witness Xander jerking poor Gareth off his chair, sending the latter's magazine on the carpet. Then, our friend lifted the frightened librarian off the floor and started yelling at him.

"Where is it? Where's the book on Rascals? *Where*?"

I approached the two really carefully. "Xander, maybe it's not here. Michelle said earlier that she read the book a long time ago."

"No! It has to be here!"

Gareth was shaking from head to toe. "I—I don't... let me—I'll see if..."

"WHAT?" Xander shouted.

"I—I'll see if—If we haven't... in the returned books— maybe..."

"Right. Good boy. Do that, would you?" Xander said,

allowing Gareth's feet to touch the floor again.

I feared that the librarian would run off and alarm the Protectors of our friend's behavior, but he hurried to a box filled with books and quickly examined each title.

"Here's another book on mythical creatures," Gareth said as quickly as he could and handed a black-covered book over to Xander, who in turn snatched it off his hands and started flipping through the pages.

He mumbled a couple of words and headlines until he found what he was looking for.

"So?" Samera inquired. "Read it to us."

Xander held his hand in the air while he read the entire page to himself. When he'd finished, his eyes raised to meet mine, his face as blank as a white sheet.

"What is it?" I asked. "You can tell us. What's the cure?" I waited for an answer, but he didn't budge. "Xander?"

Without warning, he lounged at Gareth, threw him on the nearest wall, and ran to the exit door. For the space of a heartbeat, I thought I would follow him, but when I looked at the unconscious librarian, my intuition told me he was badly hurt and needed medical attention. Several Protectors who'd been looking nervously at us during Xander's outburst came to Gareth's aid and started asking us questions, but neither Samera nor I wanted to tell the truth. Xander wasn't himself. He wouldn't have done that otherwise. But why had he run away?

Gareth came back to his senses only to be bothered with

his colleagues' inquiries.

"What happened?" they all repeated. "Are you all right?"

"Their friend happened," Gareth muttered.

Everyone stopped talking and looked at us disapprovingly. The Protectors helped Gareth up and said they were bringing him to Dr. Goldbridge. As much as I appreciated the librarian's help, I didn't think twice after he was out of sight before picking the book off the floor and reading the timetable.

"'Where Rascals come from,'" I read. "'How to recognize a Rascal'... I don't know where to look!" I flipped to the first page and started reading. "*Rascals were admitted into our Dimension three thousand years ago, during a time when Protectors could Travel in Heaven and Hell. Due to their human physicality, they found a way out of Hell and into Amani, an environment to which they quickly adapted....*" I skipped that paragraph and flipped to another page.

"*Rascals are known for their pitiless hunger and amusement in procreating. Real food, although not lethal, does not satiate them...* We already know that." I read diagonally until my eyes fell on the word "procreate." "*They have the ability to procreate in two ways: first, two Rascals can have a Rascul by having sexual intercourses; second, a Rascal's teeth contain venom that is immediately released when teeth pierce flesh. When the alternative happens, a human has twelve hours before the complete transformation turns him into one of them. There is no going back.*"

I was stunned, unable to assemble my thoughts. That's why Xander had left. *There is no going back.* No cure.

Samera just shook her head and insisted that I read more, in case we were missing something. There was a footnote at the bottom of the page that read: "*If you are reading this because you were bitten, the best thing to do—for your loved ones as well as for yourself—is to find an isolated space to hide until your transformation is complete. You might be dangerous to the people around you.*"

As if on cue, Samera and I both started running toward the exit. Maybe Xander hadn't left the HQ yet. Maybe he'd been delayed by a Protector or Michelle herself.

However, my legs didn't grant me to run really far before they started to quiver, forcing me to a slow walk.

"Stay here, I'll find him," Samera told me.

She kept her pace and was out of my sight in a few seconds. Feeling helpless, I grabbed my cell phone and called Xander, but was instantly sent to voicemail. Was he really going to hide? What about his dad? What would we tell him?

I set my foot on the first stair and started to climb, one by one, ignoring my sore feet and dry mouth.

One more step.

Breath.

Another one.

Breath.

After only two floors, I heard several feet running down

in my direction, followed by the voices of Samera and Mrs. Cohen.

"She won't agree with this anymore than I do," my best friend said.

"You girls do not get to decide." Michelle sounded angry. "This is getting out of control—Amya, dear! What are you doing?"

Samera appeared next to Michelle. "Jeez! I told you to stay in the library. You look like you're gonna pass out."

"Mrs. Cohen," said a man with a bruised cheek, "shall I carry her up to your office?"

"In a moment, Ian. Amya, would you sit down with us while you recover your colors? It's time you two explain everything from the hospital to Xander being a Rascal."

I turned to Samera. "You told her?" Panic filled my mind. "But we have to stop him!"

"He's gone," she replied, lowering her head in defeat.

"Girls," Mrs. Cohen said. "I don't know when you started keeping secrets from me, but might I remind you that it is a really bad idea? Now. Are you certain that we are dealing with Rascals here? No one, including me, ever believed such monsters really existed in our Dimension."

More out of duty than choice, we told her everything, from my memory loss to Wyatt's intentions to turn Xander into a Rascal. And finally, to the evidence that nothing could be done to save our friend. Mrs. Cohen remained quiet throughout the entire account, merely nodding or shaking her head a few times. It was only when she was certain that our story was finished that she spoke.

"Well, the matter is set: you are not going to Europe. You are in enough danger as it is. You two will live at the HQ until it is safe to go back to university. Until then, you will make yourself useful to the Protectors…"

"Wait, no!" Samera interrupted. "We have to find Xander."

Michelle shook her head. "From what you told me, Mr. Macfrey doesn't have many hours left before he becomes a danger to us all. He knows his way here. He knows where both of you go to school. Who knows if he won't be working with the other Rascals once he has transformed."

"But—" Samera and I started before Michelle cut us short.

"The discussion is closed. I will do anything in my power to protect my people and that is my final word on the subject. We will talk more *tomorrow*." She turned to her colleague. "Ian, will you show Samera and her friend to a vacant bedroom upstairs, please? There are still a few things I need to take care of. Good night, girls."

She headed downstairs without as much as a glance in our direction. Ian was about to lift me and carry me all the way up, but I protested, asserting that I had enough energy left to walk.

With Samera's help, we climbed two staircases to the bedroom floor and were welcomed by two new Protectors, one of them holding bottles of water.

"Dad!" Samera exclaimed when she saw the second man.

From what I could now recall, Karl Jensen also worked for the Protectors of Amani, although he didn't have the ability to Travel. He was in charge of the safety department, protecting his wife and her family. Xander had certainly trained with him before he became our bodyguard.

"I'm so glad you're fine, Samy," he said when Samera jumped into his arms. "It is nice to see you again, Amya. Glad you're all right." He faced Samera again. "Your mom just called to explain the situation. We'll take care of everything, don't you worry."

"I'm not worried, Dad. I just wish I—we—could help. He's our friend after all."

Karl's face changed when he noticed Samera's bruised eye. "Did he do this to you?"

"No! Xander would never hurt me. It's that guy in the car... I'm okay, really."

He examined his daughter a little more and grunted. "You two, follow me."

"Hm, sir," Ian said. "Mrs. Cohen ordered me to show the girls to their bedroom."

"Well, I'll take it from here, Ian. Thank you."

After my stomach had welcomed the bottled water, Karl

led us to a massive bedroom, again decorated only in white: white sheets; white walls, ceiling, and floor; and white curtains, even though the windows were fake. My eyes fell on the clock in between the two beds. It was close to midnight; no wonder why I was so tired, especially after the wearisome day we'd had.

"There is a phone next to each bed," Karl remarked. "Press one if you need anything."

"What about my parents?" I asked, just remembering that they were still waiting for me.

"I'll take them home and they'll be back first thing tomorrow. They will understand, I'm sure."

He kissed his daughter on the forehead and bid us good night before leaving. There were pajamas on the beds and clean clothes in drawers for the next day. We each took a shower, brushed our teeth, and prepared for a good night of sleep in complete silence. I was so glad to be able to wash my hair at last, and I decided to blow-dry it straight to make sure I'd be presentable the next morning.

We were sitting on our beds in silence when I exploded. "We can't just give up on Xander! I don't care what you parents said. I just can't stand here and wait to see what they'll do. If they ever find him, that is."

"Look, I'm not thrilled by all of this either, believe me, but we have no idea as to his whereabouts and, like Mom said, it's dangerous, especially since Wyatt might still be looking for you." She lay down.

"So you're okay with waiting here and doing nothing?"

"No. Well, yes, sort of. I mean, what else can we do? We can't get out of here without alarming the Protectors and even then, where would we start?"

"I don't know! We could help them find Xander from here."

Samera thought about it. She knew as well as I that the chances of Michelle accepting our help were really slim. "All right," she finally replied. "Let's just take a good night's sleep and see what we come up with tomorrow. You can barely stand on your two feet right now, so we are of no use."

"Fine."

"Night, Amya."

"Good night."

She turned off the light and, ignoring my swirling thoughts and anxiety, I quickly dozed off.

***

A dreamless sleep was exactly what I needed. But I wouldn't have minded if it had lasted a little longer...

"Amya! Jeez, wake up!"

Regardless of how much I love my best friend, for her good qualities as well as for her faults, she can be a little annoying from time to time. As soon as I opened my eyes, she backed away from my face and threw a pillow on me.

"What's wrong with you?" I said, rubbing my eyes.

"Been trying to wake you up for five minutes. Thought you were back in a coma. Something's going on and I want you to come with me. Listen."

I found a sitting position and listened carefully for any noise coming from the HQ. Faint voices and feet running up and down the stairs was all I discerned. Nothing unusual for a business like this one.

"Maybe they're working?" I said. "Ever thought of that?"

"*Or* they found Xander."

"Xander!"

My brain recovered its full awareness, which made me recall the events of the previous night. I got out of bed in two quick motions, put on a dressing gown, and headed for the door. But Samera didn't immediately join me. She looked surprised.

"Are you coming or not?"

She walked in my direction and smiled. "Of course. I just wasn't expecting you to be so energetic. You look great compared to yesterday."

I felt great. Well, better, at least. My legs didn't tremble anymore and my muscles seemed to have recovered their full capacity. "Thanks," I said. "Let's go."

We soon realized that the commotion came from above

our heads, so we headed upstairs, making ourselves as silent as mice. Everyone was gathered in the large room full of computers, but they were too busy looking at their screens to notice our presence.

"Ian, come here, would you?" It was Mrs. Cohen.

We hid behind a wall and listened.

"Yes, that's the exact location they were last night." Ian agreed. "They're still there."

"All right. Karl, prepare your team. You're leaving in fifteen minutes. You shouldn't be more than ten in total."

I turned to Samera. "What do you think they're talking about?"

She shrugged.

There was only one way to find out without alarming Michelle. I closed my eyes and pictured Samera's mother in her usual brown outfit and hairstyle. Surely she was looking at some kind of device... a computer, maybe. There were also a lot of Protectors circulating around her, waiting to receive their order.

It didn't take long before the image I was forming in my head turned into a purple spot, which indicated that I was about to Sojourn into Mrs. Cohen's head.

***

If I send two of my people and Karl brings seven or eight of his, they will be enough to defend themselves, attack, and Travel if necessary.

"*Two and eight, Karl,*" *I tell him, before he walks away.*

Everything is going to be all right, *I try to convince myself. I really hate the idea of sending my people on a mission in Europe right now.* Everything will be fine.

As long as they exterminate them all. We simply cannot afford to let the threat grow.

But what about Sam and Amya? And what about Xander's father? What will I tell them?

I push aside any tension and replace it with a static focus. I'm going to need my two best Protectors for this mission.

"*Ian. You're going. Take anyone else you feel comfortable working with.*"

"*Yes ma'am.*"

He leaves.

I take a last, longing look at my computer screen, before I shut it down, in case the girls wake up and come upstairs. I still wonder how the Rascals managed to find refuge in the Bath Abbey...

***

Shortly after my soul returned to my own body, I grabbed Samera's arm, ignored her protests, and dragged her back to our room. We almost bumped into a Protector heading for the same staircase, but were able to hide behind a vacant desk before he could notice anything.

"For Pete's sake, Amya!" Samera exclaimed once we were in the bedroom. "Mom was about to say something about—"

"Sam."

"We could have waited a little longer. Now, how do you plan on going back there without being seen? We were really lucky."

"Samera Cohen."

"What?"

"They're going to England. The Rascals are there." I knew where the Bath Abbey was because I'd always dreamed of visiting the Roman Baths, which are situated right next to it.

"How do you…? You Sojourned! Magda knew you wouldn't take long before—"

"They are going to kill them."

She looked questioningly at me. "The Rascals? Why should we care? They're not even human."

I ignored the image of Ponytail, which quickly created a heavy rock in my stomach. He had seemed real and human enough for me…

"They will kill them *all*," I repeated.

Samera took a few seconds before she realized how this last bit of information caused a problem.

"But... NO! No, they can't just... How do they know he's with them?"

"Shhhh. Keep it down. Michelle still thinks we're asleep. I don't know all the details, but the screen seemed to show some kind of tracking device. Do they inject you with a tracker when you work for the Protectors?"

"Yes. Yeah, that makes sense." She shook her head in denial. "But why is Xander with the others? He'd never work with the Rascals..."

I shrugged, trying to hide my disappointment and fear. "The old Xander wouldn't... but we don't know how the new one operates."

"But... How?"

"I don't know. Michelle is sending ten Protectors altogether. Two who can Travel and eight with weapons. Your father's part of the team."

Samera paced around the room. "When do they leave?"

"In fifteen minutes."

She came to a sudden halt as the severity of the situation flashed into her features. We had no way to stop her mother from killing our friend. We had no money to get on the next plane to England. Overall, the situation was absolutely hopeless.

Chapter XXIII

Ian Cohen

AFTER THE PREVIOUS NIGHT'S EVENTS, I wasn't too keen on going on a mission with Karl. He had found Jim's body in the bathroom when he'd come back from taking Amya's parents home. Naturally, Karl had alerted the other Protectors, and an investigation was still ongoing. So far, they had found neither fingerprints nor any trace of somebody else's blood on the crime scene, and I'd had time to hide my bloody clothes in another Dimension. But Karl seemed to suspect me above anyone else.

He spent at least two hours asking me questions about Jim, our relationship with each other, and anything I knew about the deceased Protector. Karl told me it was because I'd been Jim's closest friend at the HQ, but I knew better. I could see the way he looked at me. I could hear the silence he forced on me between each question, as if trying to make me feel guilty.

When that was over, Michelle assigned me to keep an

eye on Xander's tracking device. It didn't show his whereabouts like it was supposed to. She told me that it was malfunctioning, as if Xander had removed it or was dead. But she didn't believe both option and she wanted me to alert her if anything came up.

I was trying to keep my eyes open and focused on the screen when the phone in my sock started vibrating.

"I was wondering if you would call me again," I answered.

"Seems like we need your help after all," Meo replied. "We have Xander. He's coming back to life as we speak, which means his transformation is almost completed." As he said that, the tracking device started working again and the red dot indicated that Xander wasn't really far from the HQ. "You're the one assigned to tracking Xander down. We're taking him somewhere far away and your boss can't know about it."

"How do you know that?" I looked around, nervous I was being watched.

"It doesn't matter. All you need to know is that you won't see him again. He is one of us now."

"A Rascal?" I asked.

Getting the question out of my system was a relief. Ever since Michelle had mentioned the name, I'd been wondering if Meo was one too. He had to be. That would explain his superhuman strength and the fact that his body was as hard as a rock and that he didn't bruise easily—or at all for that matter. After the Protectors were briefed on the situation at hand,

Michelle had explained to us what Rascals were and especially what they could do. My conclusion was that Meo was one of them, and his ability was to feed on people's memory. That would explain why Karl and the other Protectors couldn't remember what really happened after the car accident two weeks back.

"Yes," Meo answered, his voice like a robot. "I am a Rascal too."

The sudden realization that I'd been right felt like a slap in the face. I was dealing with people much more dangerous and powerful than I'd ever imagined. I felt simultaneously scared and lucky. Scared that he and his group would one day turn against me. But lucky to have found such mighty allies. For now, that gave me enough hope to keep me going.

"What can I do for you?" I said in a much more respectful tone.

"You can destroy the connection to Xander's tracking device. Make sure they never find him."

"But they'll know. They'll eventually become aware of what I've done. I'm already suspected for the murder of my friend Jim. I can't risk it, I'm sorry."

Meo exhaled loudly and fell silent for a moment. "Okay," he said. "Time is all I need." He paused. "Give me some time and I'll let you know what comes next. Oh, and before you go, tell me what happened to your friend. Who killed him?"

That was a rather odd question coming from him. It almost sounded like he cared.

"I did. I killed him." I was ashamed to spell it out and more so because my voice broke when I did. "But it was an accident. I thought it was somebody else. It was only when the piece of mirror was in his chest that I realized it was him. My only ally among the Protectors."

Meo was silent for a moment. "All right. Now get over it and get back to work," he snapped before he hung up.

***

After only three hours of sleep in front of Xander's tracking device, I woke up and noticed he wasn't in New York anymore. He seemed to be traveling over the Atlantic Ocean. Since Meo needed as much time as I could give him, I decided not to wake up Michelle until I knew for sure where he was going to stop. So I waited some more. Around seven-thirty in the morning, the tracker stopped in the city of Bath, in England.

"How long has it been working?" Michelle asked me as soon as she saw the screen. There was an angry note to her voice.

I looked at my feet. "I'm not sure," I said. "I'm so sorry.

I fell asleep. I was with Mr. Jensen for most of the night, so I didn't get any sleep before you assigned me to keep an eye on the tracker. I'm really sorry."

"Karl? What did he want from you?"

"He keeps asking questions about Jim…" Appearing to be the saddest person on earth wasn't that hard after what I'd done to my friend. I simply had to push my emotions to the next level. "I miss him so much, you know? He was my best friend." I yawned without opening my mouth, in order to bring some tears to my eyes. "And Karl—Mr. Jensen—keeps asking me all these questions… it's just so hard to think about it, you know?"

Mrs. Cohen sighed and put her hand on my shoulder. "I'll talk to him, okay? Get some sleep now. I'll stay here and make sure we don't lose Xander's trace again. If the tracker hasn't moved in a few hours, I'll send a team. Until then, get some rest."

And just like that, Michelle's emotions blinded her from the truth and, I was out of trouble.

Chapter XXIV

"I CAN'T LET HER DO THIS," SAMERA SAID. "I just can't. How is it that you're so calm? I'll go talk to her."

"No!" I grabbed her elbow. "Don't, or she'll know I Sojourned and will probably lock us up in here, until... well, until they've killed everyone."

She dropped onto the nearest bed and sighed heavily. "What do you suggest?"

"Honestly? I have no idea. All I know is that we need to stop this." I looked around, as if I could find a way out of this situation. I'd called Xander already and he hadn't answered. Would he pick up the phone today? I didn't think so. We needed to get to him before the Protectors did. "How can we board a plane without being seen?"

"We can't. They're probably already gone and boarding as we speak..." She mumbled something else to herself and then, as if an idea had just kicked her in the butt, she stood up in one sudden movement and smiled at me. "I got it! Got it, got it, got it!"

"Tell me."

"A convy! We can use a convy!"

"Excuse me?"

She jumped up and down several times and hugged me. "A convy! An underground means of transportation in Red that's, like, twice as fast as a plane. Or more. I don't know. Never seen any, but it was in a book I read as a child."

Her enthusiasm added a load full of hope in my heart. "Where can we find one?"

Samera wrinkled her nose. "I don't know, but we can ask. Somebody in Red ought to know."

Samera drew the curtain to the parallel Dimension and realized that it unveiled the inside of a building, probably its basement floor, since the HQ was underground. She told me that we were lucky, as our room could have been parallel to the Caves, which would have forced us to Travel from another room or even another floor in the Headquarters. At least now we had no chance of running into a Protector before leaving.

Without thinking any further, we changed into warm clothes, stuffed our beds with pillows so that it would appear we were still sleeping, and packed our cell phones, in case Xander decided to call. We even carried a backpack with warmer clothes, given that the temperature wouldn't be in our favor, and plenty of food we'd found in a closet.

"We should get something to eat first thing in Red," Samera said, looking me up and down. "I don't want you to faint today."

She drew the curtain once again, but this time I could see the office we were about to step into. It was vacant, fortunately for us, except for a huge amount of documents piled on one another on the desk and even scattered all around the floor.

"After you," Samera said.

I hadn't made one step before the door in our room opened. "Where do you two think you're going?" a familiar voice uttered.

Gareth's eyes were filled with amazement. Without losing his sight of the open curtain, he walked into the room and closed the door behind him.

"Dammit," Samera muttered before she released her hold on the Dimension. "What are you doing here?"

"I could ask you the same thing. Your mother sent me to see if you were still sleeping."

"Well, get back up there and tell her we still are."

He shifted from one leg to the other, as if trying to look tough. "Why would I do that?"

"Because I told you to."

He put his hands in his pocket and shook his head. "What if I want to come with you?"

"Are you insane?" Samera shouted.

I joined her side and whispered in her ear, "What if he

tells your mom? He's seen the office. He can describe it to her and she'll know where to find us."

Her eyes grew bigger. "But we can't bring this guy with us. I'm not even supposed to Travel in front of a non-field-related Protector. Mom would kill me."

"She'll want to kill you anyway when she realizes we're gone."

Gareth stepped in. "I know how to get to your friend faster than the Protectors."

Samera bounced on the librarian like a tiger, pointing her angry finger at him. "What makes you say that's what we're going to do?"

"I knew you'd want to get him back as soon as I heard what he was. It was just a matter of time. I'm offering you my help."

"How?" I asked, not certain whether we could trust him or not. Michelle might have sent him to learn our intentions.

Samera looked furious. "You're not really thinking of letting him join us, are you?"

She walked to the other side of the room and crossed her arms.

I ignored her reproachful stare. "What do you have?" I asked Gareth.

"I read something—it was in a book I read a couple of days ago—about a way to travel faster than a plane. It was created in the Red Dimension. I don't know much about it except that it works by an underground magnetic field—"

"A convy?" Samera interrupted. "Yeah, we already know about those. Now, if you can't help any more than that, you're absolutely useless."

Gareth was taken aback by her knowledge, but quickly recovered his wits. He frowned. "Do you know where to find one?"

Samera and I looked at each other. I knew her well enough to read her intentions from her eyes without having to Sojourn. She was just about to lie.

"Pff. Of course we—"

"Don't," I finished. "We don't know, but we hope that someone in Red will tell us."

A smile appeared on Gareth's face. He realized we needed as much information we could gather to find our friend, which gave him considerable leverage.

"*I* do," he said, a small smile toying at the corner of his mouth.

"Where?" Samera snapped.

Gareth was surprised by her reaction. "Do you think I'm that stupid? I want to come with you. Once we're there, I'll tell you everything you need to know."

"No," Samera said.

I grabbed my best friend by the elbow, dragged her into our private washroom, and closed the door behind me before Gareth was able to retort.

"We need him."

"No we don't! I'm no travel guide, Amya. This guy doesn't understand how important this is. He just wants to visit the Dimension."

I pondered on her last words and nodded. "Okay. Maybe you're right, but he could be useful. Who knows how long it'll take before we find someone with a convy out there?" I waited for a rebuttal, but when none came, I continued. "All right, think about it. We agree to take him with us, but only for a couple of minutes. In exchange, he'll promise to reveal the location of the convy and he'll immediately go back in Amani, while we carry on to Xander."

She squinted and chewed on her upper lip. I didn't want to bring the librarian into this mess any more than she did, but did we really have a choice? If Samera had never seen a convy while Traveling in Red, it certainly wasn't a common means of transportation.

"Fine. But if he runs away, I'm not going after him and he'll have to stay there for the rest of his life. Now, let's get some food. I'm grumpy when hungry."

Gareth was ecstatic when we told him he was allowed to come. He started asking all sorts of questions like if Traveling hurt, if he needed to prepare in any kind of way, or if staying in another Dimension for too long could damage you.

"Yep," Samera answered the last question, after rolling her eyes to the other two. "If you remain in another Dimension for more than twenty-four hours, you'll die."

Gareth's features betrayed his shock, though he quickly recovered. Later, when he wasn't listening, I asked Samera if what she'd said were true and she merely answered, "Who knows? No one's ever stayed that long in a Dimension that wasn't their own. Anyway, look at him. He'll certainly think twice before doing anything stupid."

***

Shortly after Travelling into the messy office in Red, we found our way to the ground floor and out the street without running into anyone. The building must have been deserted a long time ago.

The street, however, was anything but deserted. It reminded me of the way people described Hong Kong, except that the signs, flyers, and placards were all in English. Lights of every color beamed the street, because even though the sun was up high in the sky, it was blocked by a thousand skyscrapers, every one higher than the ones in New York. The people on the street, wearing the most distinct clothes and hairstyles I'd ever seen, were attending their own business. Ballerinas dressed in white were dancing to a beautiful melody. Two men in suits were heading toward yet another building made entirely of tinted glass, while a sixteen-year-old punk was playing electric guitar and screaming his heart out at every passer-by. There were artists, stylists, nurses, business people, prostitutes, doctors, nudists, athletes, professors, and every imaginable type of people, their styles enhanced by their way of walking and running, by their behavior and expressions, by their fervor and passion for what they did or were about to do. It was truly inspirational and made me want to open a book and read for the rest of the day.

But there was no time for personal enjoyment.

Looking at my surroundings, I wondered why everyone remained in the middle of the street, where a car could hit them at any time, but then I noticed that the oddly shaped cars stood about fifteen feet up above our heads, on a second-floor street.

"It's safer for everyone that way," Gareth told me. "Plus, the cars are magnetic, so accidents are pretty rare. I actually read somewhere that every means of transportation here works magnetically. And you see those buildings around us; they're almost as deep into the ground as they are high out. I read that the Red Dimension…"

Gareth meant to explain a few more interesting facts about this Dimension, but Samera hurried us toward a Chinese restaurant.

"I'll lose my mind if I don't eat," she said.

We ordered some kind of porridge with rice and green peas and Samera paid with what looked like a foreign credit card. Admittedly, I felt pretty foreign myself in that café with the rest of the customers looking like they came directly out of a film noir movie.

"How long have you been working for the Protectors?" I asked Gareth after a few bites, which felt like heaven to my stomach.

He grinned. "A month, but I already love it there."

"I bet!" I'd take his place anytime. "Have you had time to read a few books?"

His smile reached his eyes. "I try and read as much as I can, but there's so much to do that I sometimes spend two days without reading."

Normally, I would have found this inconceivable, but I couldn't remember the last book I'd read. Dismissing the growing nostalgia, I kept asking questions.

"Does your family know you work for the Protectors?"

At that, Samera's head raised from her meal and she looked intently at Gareth, who immediately denied having told anyone about his job. "My parents are dead and my friends aren't really interested in what I do for a living."

"Oh, I'm sorry for your family."

He shook his head. "Don't be. I was born an orphan with no siblings and have taken care of myself all my life. No biggie."

Samera didn't seem very interested in his story and I could discern a note of loneliness in his eyes, which had been triggered by my last question, so I dropped the subject altogether and we were silent for a moment. I couldn't feel bad for him, though, because, from what I'd learned so far, he'd turned out pretty well. Sure, he wasn't all that confident and could be a little tactless sometimes, but he'd found a great job, which would help to build a great future, and he seemed like a nice person.

Several teenagers came in and out of the restaurant and ordered meals I couldn't even pronounce. This one guy, who wore a thick, scary hospital scrub and was followed by an electronic dog, ate a plate full of gray, giggling sausages. He left without paying, but no one seemed to bother.

After taking his last spoonful of porridge, Gareth shifted into his chair. "Hm, so I guess you are waiting for me to tell you where to find a convy, right?" Samera groaned and rolled her eyes. "Right. Well, I saw the information in a book I read a month ago. I was bored and tired with stacking books into the shelves so I just picked the one on top and started reading. It was really interesting and I learned a lot of things. Like, for example, how people in Red vote for a new leader every week, or how their hair and nails grow very quickly. Or that the sun never goes down, and time doesn't exist. I don't know whether I have a Red-self or not, but this Dimension sounds like a lot of fun." He laughed to himself. "It's funny, I read about this guy who had—"

"Enough already!" Samera blurted. "Where's the

convy?"

Embarrassment shone into Gareth's eyes. "I—If I remember correctly, it's on the corner of Cat and Bun."

"Where's that supposed to be?"

The librarian looked down. "I don't know… that's all I can remember."

Furious, Samera stormed out of the restaurant and I was left staring at him, clueless about how to react to his revelation. He'd half-lied to us just to be part of the *voyage*, but his information was still relevant. It would be much easier to find the convy now that we knew its location.

There was one way to gather the last piece of information. I turned to the teenage girl eating at the table next to ours and didn't even have time to pop the question before she shook her head. "I will not buy anything from you kids today," she said. "Just bought the condo at the top of this building," she pointed at the one on the corner of our street, "and it cost me more than I usually invest. So there will be no more expense from me for… at least until I get bored of this one." She stood up, her blond bob remaining firmly around her ears. "Oh, I am playing Violetta at the theater really soon, if you want to come. Not that I care. It was nice meeting you." And she left, murmuring lines to herself.

Gareth opened his mouth to say something, when some guy on a bicycle crashed into the window of the restaurant. I looked outside and noticed that no one paid attention to him, except for Samera, who rushed to his side and started apologizing. Once out of the diner, I realized that the rider had run into the window to avoid my friend.

"Oh my! I'm so sorry!" Samera told the guy. "I was so mad. Didn't see you coming. I'm so—SO—sorry."

"Sam! Are you all right?" I said.

"I am, but he isn't. Oh, for Pete's sake!" she cried when a strong wind followed by heavy drops of rain began to unroll. "Could things get any worse today?"

The man on the concrete stared at her and smiled. He was about twenty-five years old, which was older than most people we'd met so far.

"How many fingers can you see?" Samera asked him.

"Hi," the man said. "I'm Joshua."

"How many fingers?" she repeated, although a ghost of a smile appeared on her face.

Joshua carefully lifted his right hand and reached for Samera's cheek. "None. Am I dead? Are you taking me to Hell?"

My best friend got up and laughed before helping Joshua to his feet. "I think he's fine," she said.

The wind sped up and the rain became a real shower so we went back inside the restaurant with the rider. We were quickly told not to linger inside too much, as only customers were allowed to sit. The fact that we'd been customers only five minutes before didn't count, I guessed.

"Are you certain you're going to be all right?" Samera asked Joshua, who didn't look like he wanted to leave her side anytime soon.

He sat on the nearest chair and brought it closer to hers. "I must admit, my lady, that I hurt my face on the window. Is there a way to reduce the pain?" He pointed to his left cheek with his finger and grinned.

It was hard to tell if Samera was embarrassed or flattered when her own cheeks turned a dark shade of red. She nevertheless complied with his demand and remained close to him afterwards.

"Better now?" she teased.

"It's funny that you ask, because my neck—"

"Oh, enough already," Gareth blurted, and immediately regretted his words. "I'm sorry. Ahem, aren't we supposed to find your friend? I mean… find the streets and all." He cleared his throat a second time.

The injured man seemed to finally acknowledge the fact that Gareth and I existed, but his attention didn't shift from my friend, whose cheek hadn't come back to its normal shade.

"Your boyfriend seems a little jealous," he said. When Samera shook her head and told him Gareth was just a colleague, he added, "May I ask your phone number?"

Clearly, things were getting out of control, so I stepped in. "We're not exactly from here," I said. "However, I'd like to ask you a question. You see, we are looking for the building on

Cat and Bun. Would you be kind enough to indicate the way for us?"

He barely looked in my direction before turning back to Samera, who seemed to have forgotten why we were here. "Is that what you wish, my lady? What exactly are you looking for?"

"That is none of your business," Gareth voiced fiercely.

Joshua smirked. "Is it not, now? Then why are you asking for my help?"

"Because we don't have much time," I said, which sort of caught Samera's attention. "We would *all* very much appreciate if you could tell us where those streets are. Right?" After I realized that my best friend was still too far off the planet Earth to answer, I subtly kicked her ankle from under the table.

"Yes!" she finally replied. "We want to find a convy."

Gareth looked at her in disbelief. He clearly didn't like the guy and especially didn't want him to know what we were here for.

"A convy? You should have said that earlier," Joshua exclaimed. "I know a guy who owns one, and he is indebted to me."

"Really?" I exclaimed. This guy proved to be much more valuable than I'd ever imagined. "Would you ask him if we can borrow it?"

He shrugged. "I could, but only if that's what my lady wants?"

He also proved to be much more annoying than I'd ever imagined as well. He was undoubtedly good looking with his dark eyes, messy hair, and overflowing confidence, but his attitude bothered me greatly.

"Yes," Samera said.

"Excuse me?" Joshua replied, bringing his face closer to hers, until their noses were almost touching. Heat radiated from those two, the same way heat emanates from the oven when my grandmother cooks my favorite biscuits—though it didn't smell as good. "What do you want?" he asked for the second time.

"You," Samera mouthed and then winked. "I want you to ask your friend." She smiled.

Without warning, Joshua stood up, bowed, and cried, "So be it!" He offered his hand to my friend and they headed for the door.

The raging weather had already calmed down to a combination of rays of sunshine peeking through mild drizzle, which in turn favored a double rainbow mirrored on several buildings.

"That's more like it," I said out loud.

Samera turned away from her new friend and smiled at me. "This weather will last as long as the previous one. Consider Mother Nature bipolar here."

Gareth and I walked in silence, following the two lovebirds, whose conversation revolved mainly around Samera's hobbies and life in general. However, I was able to catch a few bits of information on Joshua. He was a professional athlete and liked to paint during his free time. He was also very protective of his cotton plantation, which he grew inside of his apartment, and of his women. Curiously, he didn't specified how many girlfriends he had and it didn't even seem to bother Samera; she, too, wasn't into serious relationships.

As we made our way to another neighborhood, our surroundings transformed; the grass was either yellow or brown, the number of trees diminished, and the buildings lost their utmost heights. Their extremely tall chimneys discharged a dark gray smoke into the atmosphere.

"The industrial sector," Gareth told me. "I've read a lot about the Dimensions. Personally, I'd rather live in Blue, but the Red Dimension is my second favorite. Did you know that it takes these people less than a week to build a building here? Everyone is so enthusiastic about everything they do that once their mind is set on something, nothing will stop them. Every city is as high and alive as this one."

"Every city in America?"

"No. Every city in the entire Dimension, whether you live in Africa, China, Brazil, etc. There are construction lovers everywhere in the world, and architects whose only goal in life is to create new types of superstructures, houses, offices, etc."

"What happens once all the space is occupied in a city?"

"They destroy old buildings and erect new ones." Gareth pointed behind him. "I bet that's what they plan on doing with the building we Traveled into."

It all made sense. Why else would it be deserted?

"What else do you know about Red?"

"Quite a lot, really, but the funniest thing is… well, see for yourself. Look at everyone's nails." The people walking on the street either ran or jogged to their next destination, which prevented me from having a good look at their hands. Luckily, Joshua was patting Samera's back, so I was able to notice that his nails were… red.

"Nail polish?" I asked. "Why would a man paint his nails?"

"It's not painted red; it's natural."

"Natural? How?"

"I don't know. It doesn't make much sense to me either, but people in the Blue Dimension have blue nails and in Yellow… well, you get the pattern. Maybe it has something to do with blood flow or something. I don't know."

We did not speak for the rest of the walk. Samera and Joshua were still deep into conversation and Gareth kept eavesdropping on them and rolling his eyes. As for me, I was lost in my own thoughts. I longed to visit all the Dimensions and remember everything I once knew about them. I wanted to ask their citizens about their culture, their environment, what they ate and read, how they entertained themselves… I craved knowledge so badly.

But saving Xander was much more important. He was a

Rascal because he'd come to help me at the hospital. Since we'd met, he'd always been there for me. And today I swore I would protect him, even if it were from himself.

I also felt responsible for the man I had killed the previous day—Ponytail—but it would be too overwhelming to face this feeling at the moment. I feared I might just burst into tears if I opened that door.

"We're almost there," Joshua said to Gareth and me.

We walked about ten more minutes until we arrived in front of a large, though very short in height, building. It was a sort of hangar, but even larger. One could have stored at least three planes in this thing.

"Here we are," Joshua told Samera. "Give me five minutes. I'll talk to him alone and see if he agrees to meet with you. Where do you want to go again?" Joshua asked Samera, tilting his head to one side.

"England," she answered.

He kissed her hand, bowed and entered the edifice. When he was out of sight, I turned to my best friend and threw my hands in the air.

"Do you even know the guy? What's with the hand-holding and kisses?"

"Of course I know him. His name is Joshua and he smells like Heaven." She wore a dreamy grin.

"You should be careful with him. He admitted having several girlfriends after all. What's his last name?"

She snapped out of her romantic mood and frowned at me. "I don't know, okay? But I don't care. He'll come visit me whenever I'm in his Dimension. Why should it be complicated? We like each other and that's all that matters. Just because you lost your boyfriend I shouldn't stay single, too."

She immediately regretted her last words and clapped her hands to her mouth. But the point was made. I had no right judging her and projecting my own trust issues onto her relationships.

"I didn't mean to say that, Amya. It's just... I'm nervous and tired of this whole thing. Besides, you don't even... just forget what I just said, okay?"

I nodded, though her voice echoed in my head. I had first thought I'd lost Wyatt to my sister, but in fact, he had never been mine. He'd always been a Rascal, feeding on people behind my back and plotting with his family. I'd been simply too naïve to acknowledge the truth until he'd spoken it right to my face. And then I'd left him but it was already too late.

"I don't want you to get hurt," I told her after a moment. "Seems to me like he's got a lot of 'ladies' in his life."

"I'm eighteen, Amya. I'm not looking for a husband right now. I just want to fool around for a while. And maybe, when I'm forty or something, then maybe I'll be ready for something serious."

"Just be careful."

She winked at me and quickly squeezed my hand.

"So," Gareth said, before he cleared his throat, "You guys are really going to England? What if your friend doesn't want to come with you?"

"Then we'll kidnap him," Samera answered. I couldn't be sure if she meant it as a joke or not but it was a great idea, regardless of how improbable it was that we'd ever be able to pull it off without being seen by the other Rascals.

"Have you thought of the Protectors? What if they get hurt because of what you're about to do?" Gareth added.

Samera and I looked at each other. Hearing someone else spit the ugly truth felt like a slap in the face. We both wanted our friend back, but the chance of getting the Protectors in danger was high. What if someone got hurt? Or worst, what if Xander was the one who hurt them?

The image of Ponytail came back in a flash. What if Wyatt killed someone, just to avenge his friend? It would be all my fault...

"Amya!" Samera exclaimed. "Jeez, Gareth, don't talk like that around her. She'll just freak out."

"But he's right! What if everything goes wrong? What if Xander doesn't want to come with us and attacks us or the Protectors? What would we tell your mother?"

"Oh for Pete's sake, Amya. We've already had this conversation. There is no guarantee, but it's worth trying, remember? Life never comes with a guarantee, anyway. We could walk away from all this and go back to the HQ and the

Protectors could get killed anyway. One of them could cross the street in England and get hit by a car. Just like that. Anything can happen, but isn't it what makes life exciting and worth living?" When she saw I couldn't answer, she added, "I'm going with or without you. Are you in or out?"

My brain screamed at me to back away and go home, but my heart and soul were ready to dive in and swim to the other side of the ocean to save Xander. "I'm in," I said.

"Me too," Gareth shouted.

A sharp laugh escaped from Samera's mouth and she was about to dismiss him, but I spoke faster. "Good, because I have a plan and it involves the three of us."

Chapter XXV

"ARE YOU CERTAIN this is going to work?" Gareth asked. "I trust that you know your friend better than I do, and I'm really excited to be part of the plan, but what if Xander is more dangerous than you think? I've read the book, you know."

"Don't chicken out right now," Samera said. "You wanted a little adventure? Well, there it is."

She wasn't keen on letting the librarian join us, but she'd come to understand that the plan, although flawed in many ways, required him as well. We didn't have much time to argue anyway, because Joshua came back promptly and beckoned us inside. "My friend wants to see you."

Inside the hangar, the light was almost nonexistent, aside from a few dimmed bulbs here and there. We had to poke our way around for a while, until our eyes adjusted to darkness. Joshua led us to the third and last floor and asked us to remove our shoes before entering his friend's office. After a few grunts from Gareth and me, we did as he bid and had to stand on cold steel until Joshua finally opened the door to…

Sand.

The room resembled a traditional Japanese restaurant where people eat on low tables and sit on pale cushions, but instead of wood, the floor was completely covered in sand. There was as much as a small wave pool on the other extremity of the office. The ceiling was high and depicted a sunrise, which suited the dim red and orange lighting arrangement. Samera was the first to step onto the heated sand, followed by me and Gareth. My nose soon detected an odor of salted water and fish, like the ocean.

"Whoa! How cool is that?" Gareth whispered to me.

"Very."

"Oy! Look at these!" Samera said, pointing at moving objects in the sand.

There were actual turtles and lizards in the office. They were really small in size, however, and did not seem lethal. I had read somewhere that one could recognize a lethal frog by its effervescent colors. My only hope was that the same applied for lizards and turtles.

"I've never seen animals in Red. They don't belong here," Samera stated.

There was a crack. "That is because I imported them," a man behind us voiced, before he closed the door. "Welcome to my sanctuary."

The person standing in front of us was the opposite of what I had expected. He wore a creamy white suit, his pants were rolled up to his knees, his tie was untied, and he was smoking a cigar. His smile showed his perfect white teeth, but did not reach his eyes, which were circled by deep blue rings and a piercing on the eyebrow. The oddest part was that all of these characteristics did not fit with the fact that he wasn't older than sixteen years old.

"You may take a seat," he said, gesturing toward the cushions.

"Who are you?" I asked. Was this all a joke? This boy couldn't own a convy. I wasn't even sure he owned a driver's license.

He faked being offended and turned to Joshua. "Haven't you told your friends who I am?"

"Right," Joshua said, not in the least bit sorry. "This is Jeffrey. He'll drive you to England. Right, Jeff?"

"Of course, of course. That is what I said. Let us sit down, shall we?"

We all sat on the cushions, making the circumference of the rectangular table, and I saw Gareth hide his shaking hands under his thighs. He hadn't said a word in a while and I feared he was going to back out of our plan at any moment. To my displeasure, the dozen gray lizards gathered around us and seemed to wait for something. What was going on?

Jeffrey crossed his legs and finished his cigar before

stamping it out in the sand. "I assume you don't want to share the reason for your trip to England." His gaze fell on me, which sent shivers down my spine. There was something about him that lifted every single hair on my arms. Something creepy and disturbing. His attitude, maybe. No wonder Gareth was anxious around him. Then Jeffrey looked at each and every one of us, except Joshua, who seemed proud and relaxed, as usual. "Very well," Jeffrey continued. "What do you offer in exchange for my service?"

"I have a little bit of money left on my card," Samera said.

He snorted and cracked his knuckles. "Do I look like I need money?" He gestured around him. "No, I want something more valuable."

Don't flinch, I repeated to myself. I didn't know what about this boy was so scary, but were it not for Xander, I would have never agreed to make a deal with him. *Don't flinch or he'll know you're afraid.*

"Name your price and we'll see what we can do," I told him.

His smile finally reached his eyes as he passed his hand through his hair and then cracked another knuckle. "Powerful people need connections. Loyal connections." At that, the lizards tightened their circle around us. "If I agree to your demand, you will owe me one favor. Each."

"Deal," Samera uttered, before I could even process the

idea.

As for the librarian, he stared at the lizards and seemed frozen by fear. We couldn't make the decision for him. It was unfair; Xander wasn't even his friend.

Disregarding how fast my heart was beating against my ribs and how moist my hands had become, I had to make a choice. "It's a deal for me, too, but I'm not deciding for him," I nodded toward Gareth, whose eyes grew bigger by the second. "Gareth, what do you think?"

He eventually looked at me and signaled his agreement with a slight head movement.

"Wonderful! We shall leave in fifteen minutes," Jeffrey exclaimed before he rose. Samera was about to say something but he didn't let her. "Yes, I imported a watch from your Dimension as well. Very useful in times like this. Now I know what the Amani saying 'Time is money' means." He smiled and left the room.

There was a long moment of silence, in which my entire core relaxed. Regardless of how creeped out I was to owe this guy a favor, we'd finally found a way to Xander.

"Told ya he wouldn't mind!" Joshua said with an inappropriately cheerful attitude. "Jeff is such a nice guy. Everyone loves him, mostly because he has a lot of money and power. He runs a big part of our Dimension."

"Kind of like the President of the United States," Gareth said, seeming more at ease now that Jeffrey was out of sight.

"The who?"

"The President. Jeffrey is like a president… Oh, right! I forgot. You guys don't have presidents—only deputies."

"Who makes the big decisions then?" I asked.

Joshua looked bored by my question. "There is a new deputy every once in a while," he said. "He makes small decisions that are, most often, waived by the next one. Jeff's the only one in charge of the big picture. He has to travel a lot to meet with other powerful rulers on the other shores."

One question was bothering me. "Is he severe? I mean, does he get mad easily when things don't go his way?" *What if one of us refused to give him what he wanted?*

"Definitely. He is very passionate about being right and having the final word. One time, I overheard his conversation with a deputy. The poor guy made an announcement that everyone was allowed to travel to other shores whenever they wanted, which the previous deputy had forbidden, under Jeff's demand. Those who live in Middleshore—your America, if I remember correctly—must stay in Middleshore. We can journey around, as long as we stay within the borders. We've lived like this for a while now, but it gets harder when our twin in Amani travels into another—um—country. It just feels natural to do the same.

"Anyways, I guess the deputy forgot to mention to Jeffrey that he intended to bend the rule. Jeff's the only one who can travel to other shores. He's actually the only person I know who's visited all the shores in Red. He says that it has become dangerous out there; that we are better off in Middleshore. And I believe him." He turned to Samera. "I hope you will be very careful out there. I want you to come back to me in one piece."

I didn't let her answer. "What happened to the deputy? Was he fired?"

"He called Jeff one day, when I was with him, and they were supposed to meet at the corner of Fun and Bat, Jeff's old address. I don't know what happened, but I haven't heard of the guy since. I'm certain he was deported to another shore. It sometimes happens, when someone is too rebellious."

Or maybe he killed him? I was about to ask why people got deported, but my mind caught onto something more important. "Did you just say Fun and Bat?" My gaze fell on Gareth, whose eyes had expanded to their full size. "Cat and Bun? We would have searched for hours for your stupid streets!"

Samera rolled her eyes and snorted. "A nerd dyslexic. Probably the first in history."

Gareth seemed really offended and I immediately regretted my outburst. "I—I might have misread," he said. "I was dyslexic as a child. Reading helped me overcome this condition, but I still confound letters sometimes." He looked apologetic. "We would have never found it anyway, since Jeffrey no longer lives there."

"Jeff moved here two years ago," Joshua said. "I helped

choose his new office."

"More proof that you have good tastes," Samera flirted.

"Indeed, indeed," Joshua whispered as he closed the space between them and cupped his hands around her face. He winked at her and she giggled.

Gareth wrinkled his nose. "Disgusting," he murmured so that only I could hear.

I rolled my eyes. "For once, I agree with you."

We were stuck with these two for the remaining ten minutes and I almost lost my patience when Joshua kissed Samera on the mouth, as if they'd known each other for more than an hour. But I kept my comments to myself. Despite her impulsive personality, Samera knew which lines not to cross, so she clearly felt something for this guy, however superficial. I just hoped she wouldn't get too attached; he didn't seem like the kind of guy you have a meaningful relationship with.

The door of the office finally opened. "Anyone ready for a two-hour trip to Angushore, follow me," Jeffrey uttered, before he cracked another knuckle.

Joshua kissed Samera's hand before letting her go. "I already miss you."

She smiled and blew him a kiss. "You better miss me while I'm gone."

We followed Jeffrey back to the first floor and ended up in a small elevator, made entirely of steel. I'm not usually claustrophobic, but that teeny-tiny space made my heart-beat increase and my hands moisten.

"Where are you taking us?" I asked.

The dimness of our surroundings did not attenuate my anxiety at all. Plus, there were strange noises coming from above our heads, like the elevator would collapse any second.

"Don't you trust me, Amya?" Jeffrey said. My name spoken by him sounded like a threat. Much like anything else coming out of his mouth, really. "Only this elevator can take us to the convy."

He took a set of keys from his pocket and selected a small white piece of plastic. Then, he positioned himself in front of the buttons in order to block our view.

"Don't you trust us?" Samera asked, mimicking his previous tone.

He turned around and smiled. "This is nothing personal. Prudence, my dear fellows, prevents from unfortunate compromises."

He pushed something I couldn't see with his white key and the doors closed, reducing the dim light to absolute darkness. Then we descended to what seemed like a whole other layer under the crust of the Earth. At least, that's how I felt.

Maybe I was claustrophobic after all, because when the thick doors opened again to an intense silver light, I immediately stepped out of the elevator covering my eyes, my heart rate abnormally high. Then I looked away from the blinding bulbs.

With my back turned to what lay in front of my friends, I could only see their reaction: complete amazement. When my eyes had adjusted to the brightness of the room, I didn't waste another breath before I turned around and was face-to-face with a horizontal, egg-shaped piece of...

"Iron metal," Jeffrey said, as he made his way toward the machine. "It is entirely controlled by magnetic fields in the tunnels. We could reach up to five thousand miles-an-hour, which would destroy the exterior material of the convy, and we would possibly catch on fire. The speed needs to be regulated by the pilot. Me. And don't worry, I've done this hundreds of times." He put his hand on the iron egg, which activated a mechanism and opened a door upward. "Let's not waste any time. I've got to be back here in a couple of hours," he said when none of us budged.

"This is genius!" Gareth exclaimed, suddenly at ease with Jeffrey's presence; his fear shadowed by his curiosity. He joined our pilot. "Are there tunnels to every shore?"

"No. Only a few, but I'm working on implanting more every year. At the moment, we could go to Frankshore—your France; Angushore—your England; Slavshore—your Russia; and Cathashore—your Africa."

"Brilliant!"

"It is," Jeffrey agreed. "I owe this technology to the Red-self of my Amani-self's grandfather, Desmund Archer. A brilliant man, I've heard."

I was torn between being impressed by the whole concept and scared of it. Even though we would not travel at five thousand miles an hour, we'd still go much faster than a plane, and underground... the idea wasn't really comforting.

Samera and I were the last ones to enter the convy. "Fancy" was her reaction when she saw the interior design. And I couldn't have agreed more. The seats were made of black and red leather—probably imported from Amani, as there were no animals in Red. There were only four seats in the back, and two in the front for the pilot and occasional co-pilot. It was all confined to a small space; however, we had enough room to lower our seats in case we'd want to sleep or simply relax. TVs were set above our chairs, which made me wonder what kind of films and TV shows they produced in Red.

"Take your seats," Jeffrey told us, once at the front of the machine. "We are to leave in two minutes."

Gareth sat in front of Samera and me. Frankly, he was the only one of us three who looked comfortable and relaxed... even excited. Samera seemed a little restless; she kept looking around as if to find an exit door. I remembered she'd always been scared of taking the subway.

"What if we get stuck in the tunnel and can never find a way out?" she said out loud, so that Jeffrey would hear. "We would just die, wouldn't we? And no one would ever find us."

"That's never happened before," he answered, clearly annoyed by her question. "But there are ladders to the ground level every ten miles—except in the ocean, of course. Just relax and enjoy."

That was some of the worst advice he could have given her—and me, for that matter. Our gazes locked and I could see in her eyes that, just like me, she was hoping our plan to kidnap Xander would work. Otherwise, all this stressful nonsense would be for nothing.

Gareth cleared his throat. "If we get stuck under the ocean, we could always find Atlantis!"

He was clearly trying to cheer us up, but his tactic wasn't working, especially not on Samera. "Only a nerd like you can believe in that stupid myth."

"Did you know that the word *myth* in Greek language means *convey information from mouth to mouth*? Nothing impossible here."

"It doesn't exist, moron." Nervous, she bit her upper lip.

"How would you know? Has every corner on Earth been searched? I've read somewhere that it could be under a big pile of mud flats in southern Spain, or on the Greek island of Crete. Though I don't think that any of those hypotheses are true."

"This is ridiculous. Where do you think it is, then, since you're that clever?"

Gareth smiled. "Well, first of all, Atlantis was known to be larger than Libya and Asia put together, and it was a way to other islands. What if it was directly in the middle of the Atlantic and offered a path to today's America and Africa? It would be huge, right?" When he realized neither Samera nor I was going to speak, he continued. "According to Plato, Atlantis was believed to be the most advanced society of the ancient world. Just think of how incredible it would be to find what remains of them and their culture." He paused. "It's just a shame that all we know about it comes from a few pages from a book written by Plato."

"Exactly," Samera said. "This Plato guy probably created this empire for the sake of his reader's entertainment. I mean, do you believe that Narnia exists? Or Hogwarts? It's all just fiction."

"Plato didn't write fiction, he was a philosopher."

"Still. Maybe he used this imaginary island to convey his philosophical theory or something. With today's technology, someone would have found it by now."

"Not necessarily. It is said that the island disappeared under the ocean in a single day, under violent earthquakes and flooding. The Atlantic Ocean covers approximately twenty-two percent of the planet Earth. With an average depth of eleven thousand feet, how long do you think it'd take to search the entire thing? Forever, if we're optimistic."

Gareth looked at his watch and kept talking, even though Samera looked exasperated. He explained the myth of Atlantis. How its citizens worshiped the god Poseidon, how the island was described by Plato. He went on and on, occasionally looking at the time. When Samera appeared to be bored, he said something that would either challenge her or make her angry. After a while, I started to suspect that Gareth was imposing this conversation on her for a specific reason. She wasn't frightened by the idea of riding under the ocean anymore. On the contrary: her legs were now crossed on her seat and her arms flew freely from one side to another while she expressed her argument. I was certain she hadn't noticed how long it'd been since we left the hangar.

Even I was able to relax, listening to their exchange. The story was interesting and it distracted my thoughts from the real danger we were running into. I became so serene and disconnected from my surroundings that I eventually fell asleep.

Chapter XXVI

Ian Cohen

THERE ARE ONLY TWO TYPES OF LEADERS: the brave and fearless ones, and the cowards whose balls aren't big enough to make the hardest decisions. Karl Jensen is certainly not the first type.

"Any question?" he asked after briefing us on our task as well as on information he'd gathered about Rascals.

Michelle had probably ordered him to get off my case, because his attitude had changed toward me. Unfortunately, it hadn't changed for the better. Every now and then, Karl would look me up and down, as if trying to figure out what was wrong with me. He thought I couldn't see him analyzing my every move, but he was wrong.

"How many are there?" Jonathan asked.

Jonathan was the Protector I'd chosen to bring for the mission. Not because I thought he was good or anything. Quite the contrary, actually. Jonathan was some third cousin of mine.

Twenty-three years old. Not very bright for his age. And much too nervous to have a long career as a Protector. I thought I could get rid of him if things didn't go as planned with the Rascals.

"That is a question I am afraid won't be answered before we arrive at our destination," Karl said. "Some Protectors in England who we believe are still faithful to our cause tried to find out where the Rascals were hidden and how many of them we would face, but since Rascals have a human appearance, they couldn't be certain. The only information they were confident about is that they heard screams from under the Bath Abbey early this morning. Those screams might be coming from humans."

Everyone around me, except for Karl, looked like five-year-old children too afraid to go to bed with the lights off. It was pathetic. They were used to fighting with one another during practice and some of them had experienced real-life combat during a mission, but it had always been against humans. Rascals represented the unknown.

Karl repeated the plan one last time before everyone was released to wander around the private plane we'd borrowed. The bodyguards remained together and Jonathan decided that I was good company. He followed me to the other end of the craft and sat beside my chair.

"I'm a little scared. Aren't you?" he said. "Heck, we don't even know what these creatures are capable of. Do you think Mrs. Cohen sent enough bodyguards? I've never had combat training. Have you?"

He kept looking behind himself, like it was a nervous habit. It reminded me of the way birds peek all around themselves while they eat, their head moving in abrupt motions, like they're always scared something's going to attack them.

"I think it's going to be just fine." *I'll be fine because I'm already working with the Rascals.* That last part I kept to myself and, when Jonathan became aware I wasn't going to elaborate, he leaned back against the headrest of his chair and closed his eyes.

After several minutes of silence, I myself was about to doze off when my ankle started to buzz. My eyes scouted the plane, resting a little longer on Karl to make sure he wouldn't notice me going to the washroom. When I was convinced everyone would mind their business, I headed for the washroom door and closed it behind me as quietly as I could.

"Where are you?" Meo snapped before I had time to answer.

"Hey, I'm on a plane to England," I whispered.

"And you didn't think it was a good idea to call me after you received your orders?" He snorted.

"I didn't know how to reach you. How does this thing work, anyway?" I inquired, looking at the device in my hand.

"It's a smaller version of a coop-hole. Thought you'd figured that out by now. Never mind. What kind of weapons do your people have?"

I was taken aback by his question. Would it make a difference to know what we were attacking them with? They knew we were coming. The Rascals had the advantage.

"Knives and guns, why?"

"Made of what?"

"Excuse me?"

He grunted. "What are your weapons made of? Do you have any idea or should I ask somebody else?"

I doubted anyone else would agree to help him, but I answered nonetheless. "Stainless steel, I guess, and copper. What difference does it make?"

He didn't answer my question. "Good. Do as you're said and we'll take care of ourselves. There might be casualties."

"What about you guys? If you move, don't bring Xander with you or we'll be able to track you down."

"Who said we needed to move? We're good exactly where we are. Besides, I told you. We can take care of ourselves."

I had a question I was dying to ask, but I was afraid to hear the answer. It'd been in my thoughts ever since we'd boarded the plane.

"Will I be part of the casualties?" I finally inquired. I had helped the Rascals, but was I still an asset, or were they waiting for a way to get rid of me?

Meo didn't answer instantly. Apprehension was building

a sharp pain in my stomach, but I didn't have time to hear Meo's answer before the floor outside of the washroom made a crackling sound, indicating that someone was listening. Without a word, I threw the device into the sink, opened the door, grabbed whosever shirt my fingers could find, and pinned the eavesdropper to the now closed door.

I fetched for the knife from my front pocket and placed it under the person's chin. Then, remembering what had happened the last time I'd acted impulsively, I let my adrenaline go down a notch, and I focused on the guy's face.

It was Jonathan. It was *only* Jonathan. I exhaled my anxiety and looked deeply into his fearful eyes.

"I didn't hear anything, I swear. I don't even know who you were talking to," he said, sweat filling his big forehead.

"How do you know I was talking to someone if you didn't hear anything?" His eyes grew bigger and he opened his mouth but nothing came out. All I wanted to do was to beat the memory out of him, but it would be too obvious I was the culprit since we were only ten on the plane and everyone else, except the two of us, was deep in conversation. Instead, I inhaled slowly and wondered how Meo would handle a situation like this without using his memory-draining power. "Don't lie to me, Jonathan," I said. "Let's be honest with each other, now, shall we?" He nodded three times. "Good. Tell me what you heard and I promise I'll tell you what I actually said. Our senses are sometimes affected by our emotions, so I would understand if you heard my words wrong." I lowered my knife, but kept a firm hold on it. That was absolute crap I was talking, but Jonathan bought it.

"I—I," he cleared his throat. "I heard you talk about a device and weapons... and also about Xander and tracking him down."

I fought the urge to silence him completely by cutting his throat, and I laughed. *That's what Meo would do. He always laughs.*

"W—what?" Jonathan blurted. "What did I say?"

"You heard me right, Jonny. Can I call you Jonny?" When he didn't answer, I continued. "Now who do you think I was talking to?"

His eyes shifted from left to right, up and down. He was searching for an explanation.

"Mrs. Cohen?" he finally said.

"Good, good. And why do you think I must speak to her in private?"

This time, he didn't have to think twice before he answered. "Because you are her right arm and she trusts you the most. It was a secret meeting, wasn't it? I'm so sorry," he said, looking genuinely remorseful. "I didn't want to listen, but Mr. Jensen said I needed to keep an eye on you..."

Anger almost made me hurt Jonathan, but I quickly recovered my wits. Killing him right now would only give Karl the satisfaction to be right. And I couldn't let that happen.

"Look," I said between my teeth, "I am willing to forgive you and say nothing to Mich—Mrs. Cohen, but only if you don't tell Karl about my secret meeting with his wife. Do we have a deal?"

Jonathan nodded once. I was about to let him go when he said something else. "I also heard…"

What is it now? "What did you hear, Jonny? Tell me; it's okay."

He did his nervous, bird-like motions, even though we were concealed in a really small space and no one else was around. "Casualties. I heard there would be casualties."

I faked a smile and tried to find an explanation for this. Michelle would never send Protectors to fight if she knew they were going to die. Her plans always excluded the idea of casualties. Always.

"Oh, you must have heard that wrong, Jonny. Mrs. Cohen was afraid for all of you. That is why she called me. I reminded her of the weapons we brought and asked if the tracker had moved from its original place. Xander is still in Bath and I assured Mrs. Cohen that there would be no casualties. No one is going to die today," I told him with a big smile on my face, thinking that if the situation allowed, I would be the one killing him myself.

Chapter XXVII

I WAS LOOKING AT A STILL LAKE encircled by a thousand trees, and inhabited by bufflehead ducks, when an early October chill ran over the peaceful water and up to my neck. I shuddered, two strong arms tightening around my shoulders, before I turned around and saw dark blue eyes looking down at me. Their expression was unreadable and the rest of the man's face was lost in a blur.

"Do you want to go back inside and heat up in front of the fireplace?" Wyatt asked as his features cleared. "It's getting a little chilly out here."

He was merely wearing sweatpants and a T-shirt that said, "Will You Carry Me?" with a man in a bride's arms. I wondered how, on the fifteenth of October and without a proper jacket, he wasn't freezing already.

"The fireplace?" I said. "Don't you think it would be inappropriate to do that at my parents' cottage? They said they'd only be gone for an hour or two. What if they're back early?"

He touched my cheek and smirked. "I wasn't talking about that sort of heating, but now that you mention it… I'm not asking but begging you to come inside. Just think about it as a way to survive the cold. The fire must have blown out completely since your parents left, so we'll have to find another source of warmth. It's only logical, you know, to protect you from hypothermia, or—"

I raised my fingers to his lips. "You know you don't have to convince me, right?"

He leaned in to kiss me. The world started spinning around me, as if we'd been caught in a tornado. Was I in another dream?

It was only when we broke our embrace and my feet were steady again that I heard someone coming in our direction. Wyatt's features abruptly changed from enjoyment to anger.

"What are you doing here?" he asked the newcomer, even before I recognized who it was. "I thought I was clear when I said that no one was to disrupt our weekend."

"I know and I'm sorry," Meo said, as he came to a halt in front of us. "Hi, Amya." He looked apologetic at Wyatt. "It's just that, um…" He seemed to be weighing what he could and couldn't say in my presence.

I recalled that Wyatt was in a special group with a couple of special friends, but the primary goal of this group was out of my memory's reach. And when I persisted in trying to remember, a strong headache formed in my temples.

Meo continued. "There is this thing going on with, um, our red flag." He frowned. "And we need your help for, um, convincing the, um—"

"All right, all right," I finally said. "I'll let you guys alone. I'm freezing out here, anyway."

That is when I noticed that Meo wasn't wearing a coat either. *What is it with guys and always being warm?* "Wyatt, I'll wait for you inside, at the fireplace…"

"I might have to leave with Meo," Wyatt told me, his face wearing the expression of a pleading puppy. "I know he wouldn't have come all the way to Alaska if it wasn't about a serious matter." A curly, golden lock detached from the rest of his hair and landed straight in his right eye. He waited a moment, knowing perfectly well how handsome he was, and then added, "I'm so sorry, princess. I'll make it up to you." He walked toward me with a mild smirk. "I'll make it up to you really soon."

I raised my hands to his neck. "All right. But what should I tell my parents?"

"Tell them that I had a family emergency and that my uncle came to pick me up in his private jet."

Wyatt quickly touched his lips against mine and left with Meo, who nodded goodbye.

When they were completely out of sight, I turned around, took a last look at the lake, and went inside my parents' round, wooden cottage. I was pleasantly surprised when I realized that the fire wasn't completely extinguished; however, there was only one log left, and I instantly regretted not asking for Wyatt's help when he was still here. The stack was about a quarter of a mile from the chalet, toward the parking space. I didn't feel like braving the cold at all, but the temperature would only go down from where it was now, so I put on my big, furry boots and eskimo coat again, and I went back outside.

I had been walking five minutes on the trail to the stack when I heard Wyatt and Meo's voices. Wishing to surprise them, I slowed my pace and tried to be as silent as a cat. It wasn't an easy task, considering I had to step on rocks, tree branches, and a bunch of dead leaves. The voices grew louder as I got nearer... until I could clearly discern what they were saying.

"He'll only help if we agree to make him one of us once everything is under control," Meo told my boyfriend. "What should we do?"

"We agree. And if we aren't allowed to do it, then we'll just have to get rid of him."

As I got closer to the two men, I realized there was a third person standing beside them, his back as straight as a stick. He was much older than the others and did not seem to understand what was going on.

I hid behind a tree and observed the scene.

"Can you still come and talk to him?" Meo asked. "He's

trying to bargain a lot more than we're allowed to give and I'm not sure we should agree with all of it."

Meo looked even shorter than he usually did. It was like he was scared of Wyatt's reaction.

"Fine, but if he doesn't want to listen, we'll manage without his help." Wyatt turned toward the other man. "We need to get to Jeffrey. What's the fastest way?" The man looked abashed, which made Wyatt sigh. "*Comment peut-on se rendre chez* Jeffrey?"

I didn't know my boyfriend could speak French!

"*Suivez-moi,*" the French man answered, as he reached for something in the air next to him and drew open a transparent curtain.

He was about to Travel.

Confused, I stepped back and gasped, watching Wyatt, Meo, and this third man walk to the other side of the curtain and disappear. Samera had told me about her family's ability, but I'd never seen anyone else do it. And more importantly, I wasn't aware Wyatt was familiar with the knowledge of Dimensions.

A chill crept through my veins and I completely forgot to fetch the logs. I needed to go back inside to call Samera and see if she knew anything about what I'd just heard. I needed to find out who my boyfriend wanted to get rid of and why. I started running at full speed, and I was distracted by what I had just witnessed when I lost my balance on a large tree root and fell.

The sensation of falling into a deep and dark abyss engulfed me when I woke up.

"Jeffrey!" I screamed, as my eyes opened to two anxious faces.

"Yes, darling?" Jeff answered from the pilot seat.

For a second, I felt like my heart would pound out of my chest. My hands were drenched, gripping at my seat so intensely that my joints had turned white, my eyes watering on their own.

Samera and Gareth exchanged glances. "Never mind, we found it," Samera told our driver, covering for my previous cry. "She thought she'd lost her ring."

"Mm-hm. We will be on Angushore in approximately ten minutes."

I took calming, deep breaths, reminding me that it had only been another of my vivid dreams. Leaning back on my seat, I tried to relax.

"Are you planning on explaining what just happened?" Samera whispered.

"Nightmare," was the only word that came out of my mouth.

Was it another one of those nightmares in which I recalled something I'd forgotten from my past? Like the one on Princeton campus? If so, I had to inform my best friend. I closed my eyes and tried to recollect every important detail.

"It was about Wyatt…"

I told her and Gareth everything, describing the French man and the way he had behaved around the Rascals. When I was done, Samera was shaking her head, and the librarian's complexion had blanched.

"What do you mean?" Samera asked. "My family took an oath to protect the Dimension of Amani. They wouldn't dare work for the Rascals. That is impossible."

"I'm not sure if we can trust my dream, but we should at least consider it before we try to rescue Xander. You said yourself that your mom thought some Protectors in Europe had gone rogue. That they were starting the Third World War. Sam, this guy spoke French…"

"I don't believe it, Amya. I'm sure there is another explanation."

I thought about my dream and mostly about Samera's statement on why her mother believed the Protectors in Europe to be responsible for the beginning of a war. She'd never mentioned why they were suspected above everyone else.

"Could you explain to me," I told my best friend, "why your mother believes that the European Protectors are somehow responsible for the current conflict?"

She looked down at her feet. "Mom thinks they started making profit on their ability again, just like before the Second World War. Alfonso, her cousin in Italy who is also the head of the Protectors in Tuscany, has always wanted to share his power with the rest of the world. Even as a kid, he begged his parents to let him tell his friends. Mom knows he isn't the only one. It's hard for some people not to be recognized for all they're worth and everything they're doing for their society. Nobody knows about us but we keep doing our job."

"How does that trigger a war?"

"Jealousy? Greed? I don't know. I don't understand why people would go crazy and kill everyone around them and that's why I don't believe in Mom's theory. Some things don't add up."

"Unless the Rascals are involved," Gareth mentioned. Samera and I looked at him. "It's true. Just think about it. The Protectors want to be recognized or whatever and the Rascals offer their help, saying they'll protect them if anything happens, if somebody becomes dangerous to them. In exchange, the Protectors allow the Rascals to feed on their citizens. What happens if a Rascal feeds on too much of your strength?" He stared at me.

"The person could die, I guess," I answered, recalling how long I'd been in a coma. Wyatt hadn't wanted me dead, but what if he had?

"And what if a Rascal fed on your sanity," Gareth continued, "or your memories? On your own beliefs or values? *That* might be enough to make a person go mad."

My gaze fell on Samera, who'd paled immensely. "He's

making a lot of sense. History repeating itself, but this time, Jews aren't the target, everyone enticing to the Rascals is. And that means literally anyone. "In the dream," I continued, "Wyatt said something about…" I pointed to Jeffrey. "He mentioned his name and said he was working for them too. How can he be of any help to them?"

"I don't know…" Samera whispered, shaking her head in denial.

I looked over at Gareth and he shrugged. Then, we fell silent.

"No," Samera finally declared. "Your dream was just a dream. We're all totally creeped out by this guy"—she pointed at Jeffrey—"and anxious about what will happen in England. But that's no reason for accusing my family. There is another explanation and we're going to find out what it is. A Protector would never break his oath."

"Well… That's not entirely true," Gareth said. "I've read about one, in 1975, who decided to bring friends into the Red Dimension for his own birthday party. They all swore they wouldn't tell anyone, but the Protector's father eventually heard about their little escapade from one of his friends' parents. The consequences were severe. His friends and their family mysteriously disappeared. I'm aware that this is a drastic example, but my point it that Protectors are flawed human beings, and they make mistakes like everyone else."

"They are human, but not traitors," Samera snapped, her

eyes like ice stakes.

"Okay," Gareth replied, diverting his gaze from hers. "Let's assume that all Protectors are as holy as Jesus—"

"I'm not in a mood for debate, but Jesus never existed," Samera interrupted.

"—*And* that we don't know the cause of the incoming war," Gareth continued as if she'd never spoken. "Let's just talk about Amya's dream." He paused, thinking about a plausible explanation, like we all were. "Maybe the French Protector had his reasons. Maybe the Rascals are forcing him into sin… or maybe they promised something in exchange for his loyalty."

"Like what?" I asked, intrigued by his new theory.

"I don't know… The book you were looking for at the library said that Rascals live much longer than humans. Therefore, it's possible that someone, including a Protector, would be willing to become a monster in order to live hundreds of years older." Gareth realized that we hadn't come across this information. "You didn't read the entire book, did you? Gosh. If you don't finish a book, you'll miss all the good parts." He sighed. "Due to their slow system, Rascals live close to three hundred years longer than humans."

"Age doesn't matter for Protectors," Samera argued. "Their sole goal is to protect Amani."

Gareth shrugged. "I'm just saying that we should, like Amya said, consider the possibility of running into Protectors who won't be too keen on helping us in England. If I were you,

I'd call Mrs. Cohen immediately and tell her everything. The fact that Protectors might work with the Rascals endangers those she sent to England even more."

"Even if I wanted to call her, cell phones don't work in other Dimensions. Don't you know that, smarty pants?"

"I do, but you must have a coop-hole?"

"A what?" Samera and I inquired.

"A coop-hole. A device created about six months ago that can send and receive waves in and out of every Dimension. It was created by John Atkins, a Protector in Australia." When Gareth realized that neither Samera nor I had ever heard of such a gadget, he added, "Your mother received a box full of those last week. I thought she would have given one to her daughter."

"She hasn't," Samera snapped, not too happy about the news.

"Kids!" cried Jeffrey. "We're almost there. Buckle up."

Chapter XXVIII

THINKING ABOUT CONSPIRACY theories had given me a headache.

"Let's finish this conversation after we find Xander, shall we?" I said. "And most of all, let us all be careful out there."

I looked around for a piece of metal or a ribbon or anything that resembled a seat belt, but nothing revealed itself. *Buckle up.* What did Jeffrey mean by that if there was no seat belt?

In a sudden train of thoughts, a new theory piled on top of the others. What if Jeffrey never intended to drive us all the way to England? What if he really worked for the Rascals and had been ordered to kill us?

I frantically searched under my seat, on its side, and everywhere around it for the buckle, but in vain. My breathing sped up as my gaze found Gareth's. He frowned, as if trying to understand what was going on.

"There's no seat belt," I told him in a low voice.

"I know!" Samera said, mimicking my tone. She too was frantic, hunting around her seat and the wall beside her. "You were right, he works for the Rascals. Holy-moly—crap, what are we going to do?"

"Girls."

"I don't know!" I whispered. "Wait, I'll Sojourn, see if there's an emergency exit or something."

"Good idea!"

"Girls!" Gareth repeated.

"Gareth, not now," Samera uttered. "We gotta find a way out of here."

He sighed. "Girls! The seat belt."

When I looked up, he was holding two metallic fork-shaped objects linked to the ceiling. He slowly pulled on the right one and brought it to small holes on his seat next to his left hip, and did the opposite motion for the other buckle.

Relieved and a little ashamed, I immediately imitated his movements with the belts above my head and saw Samera do the same. I then took deep breaths to calm myself and wondered when I'd become so paranoid.

"I presume you learned that in one of your books?" Samera muttered, as embarrassed as I was.

Gareth laughed and shook his head. "No. I saw the holes in the seat when we entered the convy and assumed their purpose. After that, it was only logical to find the buckles above our heads."

"Clever," I said. "And thanks."

"You are welcome," he replied, looking directly at Samera.

***

The "landing", as Jeffrey called our arrival in London, even though we weren't flying, happened quite smoothly. We did not have two minutes to recover from the ride before he threw us out of the convy and bid us goodbye.

"I assume you know your way from here," he said, beckoning us out of his machine. "We shall meet very soon. Farewell!"

We thanked Jeff and I forced myself to shake hands with him before he left. There was something about his attitude—and my dream—that bothered me.

"All right, we're in England. Where do we go now?" Samera asked me.

Only then did my brain fully comprehend that we really were in England. Sure, we'd been dropped in an underground kind of garage, but one of my wildest dreams had finally come true! Excitement overcame my growing anxiety for Xander and I found myself smiling from ear to ear.

"Let's get out of here," I said, cheerful.

We took the first stairs up and immediately Traveled back to Amani where, for the first time in… maybe twenty-four hours, I fell in love. Books were yet again the cause.

Two years ago, I had decided to make a list of all the places I wanted to visit in England. This place was in my top five. The biggest bookstore in Europe: Waterstones, situated on Piccadilly in London.

Or Paradise, if you'd like.

Six entire floors dedicated to books, including half a mile of shelving, and seats everywhere to enjoy any kind of book one desires.

"Whoa…" Gareth voiced. "This is…"

"Incredible, I know."

"Not trying to be the downer here, but Xander is in danger so there's no time for nerding," Samera said. "It's currently 5:45 in London. We have about two hours before the Protectors' plane lands at the airport. That's if Mom didn't borrow a private jet."

I inhaled the marvelous odor of new books one last time before focusing on our plan. "All right now. We have to find a car."

"That should be easy," Gareth said. "In 2010, more than three million cars were registered to private owners in London."

"Good," I said, before realizing that a detail was missing from my plan. "Please one of you tell me you can drive on the left side of the road."

Samera raised her hand. "I've never done it, but I'd be willing to try."

After experiencing my best friend's driving, I wasn't too keen on letting her take the lead on this. "Gareth?"

Pleased with himself, he answered, "I studied the technique a few months ago, before I was hired by the Protectors."

"Sold." I clapped my hands together, maybe a little too excited by this whole rescue mission.

Samera didn't look too happy, however. As we made our way out of the bookstore, unfortunately leaving thousands of books behind, she kept glancing at Gareth and murmuring things to herself.

Once outside, the sun was set, giving way to street lights illuminating white, ornamented buildings. The pavement was wet, reflecting the purple gleam of the bookstore. And there were so many people and red buses and music coming out of nowhere; I feared we'd never be able to find a quiet place to steal a car. We headed right, following the majority of the crowd on the sidewalk and, only a few minutes later, we were facing a scaled-down and more sophisticated Times Square. But still no parking lot.

"Where do all these people park their cars?" I wondered out loud.

We walked a couple more corners, but luck wasn't on

our side.

"I have an idea," Samera said, after the temptation to take the train crossed my mind. I was convinced, however, that we needed a car to kidnap Xander. Taking a possibly dangerous Rascal onto a train full of people wasn't an option.

***

Samera's idea was actually a good one. Risky, but possible. And that's all we needed. We just had to make sure no one would see us.

Down a couple of streets, we found a more quiet intersection, where only a few cars ventured due to road construction. At the sight of the next car, we all came into position.

As it stopped at the intersection, a group of friends—two men and three women—came out from the opposite street and headed in our direction. It was my job to distract anyone's attention from what my friends were about to do around the car.

"Your turn, Amya," Samera told me, just before she faced the passenger side of the Volkswagen, Gareth facing the driver's door.

I jogged toward the teenagers in a clumsy way and almost ran into the shortest girl. "Watch out!" she warned just before I collapsed on the sidewalk laughing like a drunk cretin, my limbs as limp as possible.

But I was only the diversion. Gareth was to knock on the driver's window, distracting whoever was driving, while Samera Traveled to another Dimension. She would have to jump a few inches off the ground and bend her knees while she Traveled back into the car on the passenger seat, which would scare the poor Londoner out of her vehicle. Once free of the driver, Gareth would take the driver's place and they would go back to Waterstones, waiting for me to join them.

"Bugger! Are you all right?" one of the boys asked me.

"Oh, hi!" I exclaimed, trying to get back on my two feet. "Am I still in London?"

"Oh, you're American," a guy wearing huge, square glasses observed.

They helped me up and gave me a sealed bottle of water they'd just bought at Waitrose. "Thanks," I said, completely bewildered.

"You shouldn't be walking in the city alone at night," a guy wearing black skinny jeans and a stylish brown coat told me. "Are you with somebody else? Did you come with your parents?"

I heard a woman scream from the other side of the street—probably the owner of the car we were steeling—and just before the group around me looked in her direction, I screamed.

"Get off me! No. Please don't touch me!" I shouted at them, pushing them away. "Help! Somebody help me!" I stepped back, gripping hard at my head.

All five of them looked down at me, disgusted by my attitude.

"Calm down. We're not even touching you," one said in a soothing voice. "You certain you're all right?"

"Leave me alone!" I cried, now looking directly into his fearful eyes.

The girl I'd almost knocked over backed away, grabbing her friend's shirt. "It's happening again, Richard," she said, looking pitifully at me. "Those people on the radio were telling the truth. It's a disease. It has to be. I saw another one this morning. The guy got into a fight with someone on the street for no reason. And then he started attacking everyone on the sidewalk." She looked at her friends. "Mom knew a guy who murdered his wife a few days back. Those affected by the disease are dangerous. Let's go."

"But she needs help."

I was speechless. Not only did they believe in my poor acting, but they'd seen someone similar before.

"How? Haven't you heard about Italy? Haven't you seen the footage?" the girl argued. "There's nothing we can do. Let's go."

Richard stared at me, his wary eyes apprehending my movements. "She's already calmed down. Look." He made a careful step in my direction. "Hey. Are you feeling all right?"

I felt bad for them. They all seemed so nice and caring, but that was one more reason why I had to repel them away from the scene. If they noticed my friends stealing the car, they would immediately call the police and our plan to save Xander would go up in flame.

"Leave me alone!" I cried, pushing the guy with the glasses once more. "Leave me alone or…" I got my phone out of my pocket. "Or I'll alert the police."

I dared to stray my eyes away from them and toward the owner of the Volkswagen, and I was pleased to notice that she was gone. She'd most likely ran away from her car and from the crazy girl shouting at a group of teenagers on the opposite sidewalk.

But then a sudden gunshot resonated from only two streets down ours, followed by a hoard of people screaming.

Chapter XXIX

THAT WAS ENOUGH TO SCARE the group of teenagers away.

"Take care, American girl. It's not safe in London anymore," Richard told me before he trailed behind his friends and disappeared around the next corner.

Shocked, my feet refused to obey me. They remained firmly in place, while my ears noticed that the screams were getting closer. I remembered what Dr. Bennett had told me at the hospital about his father. England wasn't as bad as Italy and France and the other countries the reporter on the radio had mentioned, but the danger and fear were still present.

Another gunshot echoed in my ears. *I have to get to my friends, find Xander, and return to America as soon as possible.*

Without thinking any further, my legs finally listened to my brain as they started running to the *rendez-vous* point.

When I finally found my way on Piccadilly, it was easy

to recognize the car Samera and Gareth had stolen because everyone around us shot angry looks at a Volkswagen temporarily parked in a bus parking lane. I got in right before a "Golden Tour" bus honked at us four times.

"C'mon Gareth!" Samera urged.

"Didn't you hear the gunshots?" I asked a little out of breath, as I realized that the pedestrians were paying more attention to our car than to the possible murder scene.

"What gunshot?" Samera inquired.

I shook my head. "I heard two gunshots from a few streets down," I said. "Something's going on and it's coming our way, so we should go. Now."

The librarian looked miserable, trembling all over the place. It was not only his first time driving on the wrong side of the road—and of the car—in London traffic hours. It was also the fear of letting us down in a time that we really needed him. The pressure that if we didn't leave soon, we'd be stuck in the middle of a possible gun fight or crazed citizens.

"Get off!" an angry, middle-aged man shouted at us from the sidewalk. "Get off the bus lane, you idiotic kids," he added.

Gareth started the engine, took a deep breath, and moved the car.

"Come on, come on, come on," Samera insisted.

The traffic around came to a halt and let us, slowly but surely, drive away from our illegal parking space. Gareth followed the Cadillac in front of us, looking frantically around.

"You're doing well," I encouraged. "Do you know the way out of London?"

Without a word, Samera showed me the GPS on her phone. "Okay, now you keep going straight until I say otherwise. Just remember to stay on your left," she said.

I wasn't sure if the streets in England were much narrower than in the United States, or if it was just an effect of driving on the wrong side of the road, but it made the ride even weirder and more stressful. I wouldn't have changed places with Gareth anytime and I was convinced Samera was glad to be sitting on the passenger seat after all. At least, the farther we got from Piccadilly, the safer.

"Try and pass that big old red bus, would you?" Samera asked. "It's blocking my view of street names. What's with the idea to put the names on the buildings, anyway?"

Gareth looked over his right shoulder and attempted a slight right between two cars. The one behind us had to break suddenly, but succeeded in avoiding any accident.

"Okay, stay on that lane, it's the fastest. Just follow the guy in front of you," Samera told him.

After a few minutes of driving, the tension in the car finally dropped. Even Gareth's hands had ceased trembling. The danger was behind us, and when I was certain that we were going in the right direction, I leaned back against my seat and enjoyed the view.

The architecture of London was just incredible. Every

building more detailed than the previous one. Some old fashioned sat next to constructions from the twentieth century, much like a family photo including many generations. The result was nonetheless harmonious and beautiful.

"To our left, we can see Green Park," Samera said, looking at the GPS on her phone.

"Green Park? We're so close to Buckingham Palace!" I exclaimed.

Of course, Buckingham Palace was also on my to-see list. I'd been obsessed with the Royal Family ever since I was ten.

We passed by the Victoria and Albert Museum, the Natural History Museum, and a rich neighborhood with expensive cars, such as Lamborghinis and Ferraris. I even saw a velvet car, which made me wonder how the owner ever washed its exterior.

After an hour, we were finally able to leave London and carry on to our next destination. We didn't stop for dinner; we ate the snacks we'd stuffed in the backpack this morning. There wasn't enough food for the three of us, however, as Gareth hadn't initially been part of the plan, but I gave the librarian half of my share. A cramp of anxiety was slowly building in my stomach, anyway, taking most of the empty space.

"Hey, I meant to ask you," Gareth said, looking at me through the front mirror after he'd finished his granola bar. "Did you mention earlier in the convy that you could Sojourn?"

Had I? I was normally careful with that word around strangers, but the stress of the last few days might have made me slip. Was it a bad thing? After all, Gareth wasn't a stranger anymore. Besides, he couldn't know what that meant, unless Michelle had already told him about my family.

"Maybe. Why do you ask?"

He frowned. "You're a Seraph? No way! I thought they didn't exist, but you really are one!"

"A what?" I asked.

"Gareth, what are you talking about?" Samera added.

"A Seraph… Wait. You don't know what it is? A Seraph?" When neither Samera nor I answered, he continued. "Okay, maybe you're not one. It was in the book on Rascals. Oh, never mind then."

Samera sighed. "What's a Seraph, Gareth?"

Although the librarian seemed disappointed in the fact that I wasn't a Seraph, he was still pleased to be able to teach us something new. "When Rascals were admitted into our Dimension, they unbalanced the tension between good and bad in the world. It is believed that God, or whoever is up there, gave special powers to a few people on Earth. Powers for good, against the Rascals' bad nature."

"What kind of power?" Had that power been given to my family? Was I a Seraph?

"I guess the author of the book never met one. He wrote that people with good intentions rarely manifest themselves, as opposed to those with evil ones, like Rascals. But he was able to get his hands on one piece of information. He mentioned in the book that a friend of his had overheard a conversation with someone whom they suspected was a Seraph. This person used the word Sojourn… That's why I thought that maybe you were one."

I was shocked. A Seraph? Why had I never been informed of that? Why hadn't my family told me? Or maybe they didn't know either. After my sixteenth birthday, I remembered asking my grandmother about our special ability, and why we were so different from everyone else. She'd said something about being blessed and lucky, but she'd never seemed to understand the reason more than I did. This ability had been transmitted to every generation in my family for centuries and no one had ever known why—why we were in possession of such a great power.

"Wait," I said, latching onto something Gareth had mentioned. "Are you telling me there are others with that ability? Other families like mine?"

"So you really are one!" he exclaimed, almost letting go of the wheel. "Whoa! I feel like I should bow or something. I'm in a car with a Seraph." He laughed. "This is incredible!"

"Calm down, nerdy," Samera said with a smirk on her face.

"Right." He cleared his throat. "Hm, yeah, I think there are others, but I'm not sure, really. The book was more about

Rascals than you guys. But can I ask what *Sojourn* means? I swear I won't tell anyone."

Uncertain whether I was allowed to tell him or not—I mean, no one had ever come up to me knowing more than I did about my power—I stared at Samera, eyes wide open. To my disappointment, she only shrugged her shoulders and shook her head.

"I don't know, girl." She turned to Gareth. "Why do you want to know?"

"I'm curious, that's all. It's not every day I meet someone who holds a heavenly gift."

Heavenly gift? It sounded way cooler than it really was. And way more important. I'd never really done anything with my gift. Nothing meaningful, that is. Was I supposed to? Were Seraphs predestined to become heroes or help human kind in some way?

"I can only send my soul into people's bodies," I blurted out. "That way, I sort of become them; I see what they see, hear what they hear, and see their thoughts."

"That's awesome!" the librarian proclaimed. "Like reading someone's mind, but in a cooler way."

"Sort of."

"Can you do it now? I want to see what it's like."

"On you?"

"Yeah!"

I considered his request for a moment. I had never

Sojourned to impress anyone. Not that I could remember, anyway. It wasn't a game or a tool to make friends. Especially after what Gareth had just told me. This gift was a means to do some good on Earth. But at the same time, it was not like showing Gareth would hurt anyone. Plus, I was still a little out of practice since I had come out of the hospital.

"Fine," I said, as I focused on what the librarian was looking at. The road, his hands, Samera.

The purple spot came so fast that I almost didn't realize what was going on before my soul was out of my body and in Gareth's.

***

I wonder if it's going to hurt. The theory of putting two souls in one body has never been scientifically tested on anyone. Would she allow me to do some tests on her? Probably not. Yeah, she probably won't want to...

I focus on the road, but I am way too excited to drift away from my speculations. Will she alert me before she Sojourns, or will I feel it? I wonder if she'll be able to speak to me in my head.

I peek in the front mirror and all I can see is her

forehead. Maybe she's still debating. An emotion—alarm—
distracts me. As long as she doesn't see...

***

The shock of the image I saw in Gareth's mind sent me right back into my own body, like an elastic band snap back effect.

A boy. It was a boy who looked exactly like the librarian, but whose eyes were troubled and scared. Was that a memory of Gareth when he was younger? Of the way he used to be? What could have made such a young boy look so horrified, imploring for help?

"I'm ready, Amya. Anytime you want," he told me, ignorant of my discovery.

All this time I'd known about my ability, I had dreaded being confronted with a situation like this. Invading someone's privacy. I couldn't tell him. Or could I? After all, he'd been the one begging for me to Sojourn. No, I had to make him believe I hadn't seen anything important.

"It's already done," I said, forcing a laugh. "I got out when you started thinking about science. I mean, how boring can someone's thoughts be?"

It worked. Aside from being a little embarrassed, he looked just fine. No sign of undesirable confusion or misconception. Samera made fun of him, but she stayed nice about it and they even exchanged warm glances. The subject of Seraphs was dropped when they began a conversation on Star Wars, which I couldn't have followed even if I'd wanted to. In any case, my mind was too preoccupied by Gareth's past and our mission to kidnap Xander, so I kept to myself for the rest of the trip.

***

We finally arrived in Bath and chose to park the car at The Circus.

"The Royal Crescent is just around the corner, guys," I said, excited to walk on the streets where Jane Austen had set two of her published novels, *Northanger Abbey* and *Persuasion*.

From there, I knew where the Bath Abbey was located. I'd studied the streets to the Roman Baths a thousand times on Google Map for when Wyatt and I were to visit England together. I knew my way to the Jane Austen museum, to the Victoria Park, and to the Holburne Museum of Art. But none of that mattered. Only Xander did.

"Gareth, I hope you didn't forget your phone in the car," Samera told the librarian, as we jaunted down New Bond Street. They seemed to get along pretty well since their cooperation in the car.

"No, I haven't," he said. "Don't worry."

We remained silent throughout almost the entire walk, too amazed by the yellow-beige buildings that went on and on, looking all the same. Only the color of the doors changed. It was when we turned the corner of Northgate Street that we caught a glimpse of the colossal Bath Abbey. And that was our cue to start walking faster.

Because we weren't certain where the Rascals and Xander were hiding, and mostly because we didn't want to run into Wyatt, our plan was to draw our friend out on the street and immediately push him into another Dimension, where we'd be able to resonate with or simply kidnap him.

First, we needed to find a spot to hide Samera. Only I could be visible, as my intention was to call Xander and let him find me. Gareth put on a scarf to cover his head and he mingled in the crowd.

I used his cell phone to call Xander. This way, he wouldn't recognize the number, which enhanced our chances of him actually picking up. On the left side of the Abbey was a shopping building—gift shops, a music store, etc.—and I decided that its left extremity was a good enough spot to wait for him as well as to hide from the hordes of tourists surrounding us.

"Xander speaking," my friend answered on the second ring.

His cold voice froze me in place. "We're here," I

muttered.

"Who's—Amya?"

"Come out on the street. I want to make sure you're okay," I said, my voice trembling.

I'd been thinking about this moment for hours now, but I never would have imagined Xander to sound so different... so harsh. I feared he would inform the other Rascals instead of coming on his own. Samera had said that he'd be more likely to listen to me than anyone else. Hearing his voice right now didn't boost my confidence on the subject.

"Where are you? Please don't tell me you've come all the way here—"

"Follow the gift shops," I said just before I hung up.

"How was he?" Samera asked from behind me. "Do you think he'll come?"

I pondered on the question for a few seconds—my heart pumping hard—and decided to tell the truth. "I don't know."

***

A mild rain had started to fall on the beautiful city and it was so cold that even after putting our warmer clothes on, I could hear Samera's teeth chattering and see our breath in the hue of the street lights.

It was ten-thirty and I was starting to lose faith. Xander wasn't coming and the Protectors would soon be here to kill the Rascals. To kill him. Gareth was still waiting, walking around a tree or in front of the Starbucks, where I was convinced he would have gladly entered for a nice, warm coffee. Samera and I occasionally exchanged a few desperate words, looking at everyone twice to make sure it wasn't our friend.

"I'm tired of waiting. Let's take a look inside the Abbey," she said.

"He could be anywhere... but maybe it's our best shot."

I was about to wave my hand at Gareth to come closer so we could discuss our options, when I perceived black sneakers with a yellow stripe on the sides. And my heart skipped a beat.

Xander.

"He's here," I told Samera through my teeth. "Stay put."

He walked slowly in my direction, as if assessing the danger. And all I wanted to do was run into his arms and never let go. I hadn't realized how worried I'd been until now. He was here and he was safe. That's all that mattered.

My legs made a couple of steps to join him, but Samera's faint grunt reminded me that he needed to come to me for our plan to work.

And he did, looking sexier than ever.

"What are you doing here, Amya?" he said, gazing at our surroundings with his watchful eyes.

This was when Gareth was supposed to push him, and

Samera was supposed to open the curtain to another Dimension, but the former was out of sight. Not knowing how to respond, I stared at him and blinked repeatedly. He frowned and got closer.

"What is it? Are you all right?"

Where was Gareth? "Yes. You?" I replied.

He seemed confused, his bright blue eyes looking me up and down. "Gosh, Amya. You're freezing." He took off his brown leather jacket and handed it to me. "Come on. Take it."

I wasn't uncomfortably cold, but I nonetheless accepted his offer and put the jacket over my already warm sweater. What else could I do? I wasn't prepared to have a conversation with him all alone. Besides, I never thought he would behave like the Xander I knew, as opposed to like a monster... like Wyatt.

In one swift movement, Samera stepped from behind the corner of the building. "Don't get any closer," she warned him.

"Hello to you, too," Xander said, not in the least bit surprised. "I was just wondering where you were hiding." He scanned the perimeter around us. "You two have to leave or they'll see you."

"Come with us," I finally murmured. My voice sounded like it'd been customized on a computer.

"I can't."

"Why?" Samera inquired. "Because you're one of them now? You're besties with Amya's ex, is that it?"

Xander took a step back, his eyes darkening. "You don't understand. You must leave. Now."

"Not without you, we won't," I said firmly and took a step forward.

"Then I'll have to call Wyatt and the others. They want you back anyway." His gaze was fierce and sharp, but I knew in my heart that he was bluffing.

"You wouldn't," Samera started to say but was interrupted by a third party.

"Why, welcome to England, princess." It was Wyatt… and five other Rascals, who were gathering around us. I'd been too busy looking at Xander to notice their arrival.

Chills ran down my neck when I saw something else in the corner of my eye. Gareth was by their side.

"I'm so sorry," he mouthed.

Sorry? Why? What was happening? I didn't have time to panic before I heard a noise like someone getting hit behind me, and then everything went black.

Chapter XXX

AN EXCRUCIATING PAIN behind my head…

Silence all around…

What happened?

My limbs move on their own, trying to reach for something…

"Amya, princess. I'm here. Don't you worry," a voice said.

The voice is smooth and familiar.

Someone else grunted next to me before I opened my eyes. It was dark, darker than it had been outside. And that's when it all came back to me. Xander, the Rascals, Gareth.

"Sam?" I said when my eyes fell on the flamboyant red hair next to me. "Sam. Wake up."

I tried to make sense of my surroundings. My hands were tied up in front of me and I was sitting on a cold gray floor, my back against an equally cold cement wall. Samera was in the same position, but she hadn't woken up yet. On a chair in front of us was Wyatt, looking intently at me and smiling at his victory.

"Welcome back, my love," he said.

"Where's Xander? What have you done to him?"

Wyatt's eyes became black like liquid coal on a sunny day. "Who needs him? I'm right here," he said, his jaw tightening.

"Where?"

Reluctantly, Wyatt pressed a button on his phone and two Rascals momentarily arrived with Xander in between, supporting himself on their shoulders, like he'd drunk too much.

"Do not worry, love. I merely drugged him," Wyatt explained before the two guards pushed Xander on the floor next to me. "That's what happens when someone betrays my trust."

I crawled closer to my friend and took his pulse. His heart was barely beating and he was sweating all over, blood spilling down his nose. "Xander, are you all right?" I murmured in his ear.

His head tilted until his eyes locked with mine. "I'm sorry," he whispered. "Thought I could protect you better from here."

These simple words removed a heavy weight I'd been carrying ever since he had left the library at the HQ. Xander wasn't becoming a crazy monster. He hadn't left to work for the Rascals, against everything he'd always believed in and cared for. He'd left to protect us. And I felt stupid for considering any other explanation. But was he a Rascal? Had he found a cure?

"I have to admit that I almost believed him," Wyatt said. "Little bastard is a good actor. When I decided to bite his arm, all I wanted was for you to stop idealizing him. Then, Gareth texted me after Xander left the library and that's when we got hold of him. But he convinced me he was an asset to my group. Even after all the torture, he never seemed to change his mind, so—"

"You what?" I said, gripping at Xander's arm.

"Torture, my love. I had to make sure he wasn't a coward or a traitor. I had to make sure his transformation had changed him. Anyway, all that work for nothing." He sighed. "Kill him," he told his guards.

"No!"

One of them took a step forward but I positioned my body in front of Xander's, even though I knew the Rascal would have the upper hand if it came down to fists. But he didn't have time to make another move before Gareth came rushing into the room.

"Where is he? You said you'd release him if I brought her to you!" he shouted at Wyatt, who looked uninterested in the librarian's pleas.

The realization of Gareth's betrayal finally hit me. I recalled his invitation to join him and his friends at a party the previous evening. It'd been a ruse. He'd been texting Wyatt all along. Plus, he knew so much about Rascals, I should have known something was off. And his claim that he wanted to come with us merely for an adventure…

"How can you live with yourself?" I spat.

He flinched but his attention was quickly brought back to Wyatt. "Where is he? We have the right to leave now. You said—"

"Yes, yes. I said some things and—oh, whatever. Julian!" Wyatt shouted behind him. "Bring the boy."

The boy? What boy were they talking about? Was it the one I'd seen when I Sojourned into Gareth's head earlier? Who was he?

This boy Gareth kept referring to arrived seconds later. He must have been no older than eight and had bruises all around his eyes and chin. Behind him was the man who'd tried to capture me in Samera's car. Ponytail.

His dark, emotionless eyes fell on me, like a bucket of ice-cold water running down my spine. I hadn't killed him. And just then, I wasn't certain if I was relieved that he wasn't dead or frightened that he'd survive to such a hard hit.

"See," Wyatt told the librarian. "Little boy here's just fine."

On the contrary, the boy looked so scared, every one of his limbs trembled like a leaf during autumn, and unshed tears threatened to leak out of his eyes any moment. Gareth looked at Wyatt like he wanted to murder him in the worst possible manner and then, with much tenderness and caring features, his eyes fell on the boy. It had to be his brother; the resemblance was uncanny.

"It's going to be all right, Billy," he told him.

The boy nodded once and locked eyes with Gareth.

"Touching," Wyatt said in the most sarcastic tone. "Now, I asked you another favor in exchange for little Billy here. Did you do it?"

"Yes. She has your phone." Gareth pointed at me, without making eye contact.

"I know she has my phone, idiot. That's how I learned you were in Bath, remember?"

After raising from his chair and making a few steps in my direction, much like walking toward a defenseless prey, Wyatt slowly slid his hand in the front pocket of my jeans and reached for the cell phone Gareth had lent me to call Xander. He remained close to me for an instant, his nose touching mine, but I didn't dare to avert my eyes; it would have given him too much pleasure to see me flinch under his stare. I looked firmly into his dark pearls and waited for him to back away.

I was relieved when I heard Samera whisper, "You sick bastard." She'd woken up and she was all right.

Wyatt didn't even look at her. He went back to his chair and verified that Gareth was telling the truth. I wondered what he'd done to his phone.

"I swear, it's all there," Gareth said. "Please let us go

now."

My crazy ex-boyfriend closed the phone and smiled. "It really is all there. Fine. You may leave."

Ponytail—Julian—opened the door behind him and signaled Gareth out. He let go of the boy and stepped aside.

Before leaving, Gareth's eyes met with Samera's, imploring her for forgiveness. No doubt she had already picked up on who the little boy was, why he was here, and mostly why Gareth had been forced to betray us.

She kindly smiled at him. "You save that brother of yours. At least it won't have been for nothing." She paused. "But if I die here tonight, I'll sure as hell haunt you for the rest of your life."

"I'm so sorry." He locked eye contact with her for a little longer.

A little too long.

Wyatt sighed. "I'm bored," he said as his gaze fell on me. "Julian, give Mr. Williams a reason to be sorry."

I didn't have time to blink that Ponytail pulled a knife from behind his back, gave it to Billy, and grabbed his arm.

"What are you doing?" Gareth shouted as he moved toward his brother. He was immediately stopped by Wyatt, his determination and struggle a mere annoyance against the Rascal's strength.

In the meantime, Billy's face turned to gray, his expression blank. He was now holding the knife tightly into his trembling left hand.

"Billy, come here," Gareth pleaded. "Come, Billy. Give me the knife."

But Billy wasn't listening. He looked at Ponytail and then gazed at the floor, a tear escaping from his haunted gray eyes. I didn't understand what was going on. Ponytail was no doubt feeding on him, but what did he feed on?

I recalled the way I'd felt in the car, as if Julian had been draining away my faith and hope. But I knew from the look on Billy's face that it wasn't the same.

"Ha!" Wyatt exclaimed. "We never cherish our emotions enough, do we?"

"What is he doing, Wyatt?" I asked. "Stop. Let them go! Please."

"Julian is having his dinner, the same way he did on *Nevada Macfrey* three years ago." He said the name with mischievous eyes and a wide smile.

What did that mean? I heard Xander grunt. He tried to get up, but the drug was still restraining him from any movement.

Emotions. Feeding. Nevada…

Feeding on Nevada's emotions.

Oh no.

It all made sense. Nevada must have met Julian in Florida. Xander told me about a mysterious boy she'd been dating during the holidays. It had to be him. He had fed on her emotions… her joy and hope! He had fed on her joy and must have left just enough for her to make the trip back to New York. And then, she couldn't live unhappy and she couldn't hope to get better. She had seemed so depressed in the school hall. That is why she decided to kill herself.

As if to prove my theory, little Billy pointed the blade of the knife toward his wrist.

"No!" I cried, echoed by Gareth's scream.

"Gimme the knife, Billy-Bee. Come on," the librarian repeated over and over again.

Samera and I tried to help, but the two guards kept us down. Gareth fought against Wyatt's grip. He tried to kick him in the shin, to punch him in the face, but there was nothing he could do. Wyatt was apparently feeding on him too, because Gareth's movements slowed and he was soon unable to stand on his own.

"Wyatt, stop!" I pleaded. "Let them go!"

"What fun would that be?" he said, clearly enjoying the situation.

He only released Gareth when the latter fell to his knees, barely strong enough to support his weight on his hands. Billy's eyes were full of sadness and pain. There was nothing else left; no joy, no fear, no hope. He carefully brought the blade to his wrist and began to cut deep into his flesh, blood streaming down his forearm.

Gareth cried, his rage and despair expanding throughout

his trembling body. "Please stop. Billy Bee. Please. I need you to stop…"

But Billy only cut deeper. It wasn't long before his face turned white and he collapsed on the floor next to Wyatt's chair.

"Billy!" Gareth whispered, crawling his way to his brother. "Please don't be dead… Billy Bee, please… I need you." The rest of his sentence was incomprehensible through his sobs.

I couldn't stop myself from weeping for the boy. He was so young and looked so fragile, especially now, lying on the floor, his lifeless corpse like a doll. Gareth shielded his brother's body with his own, spilling his rage and grief through his eyes the same way Xander had with his sister.

"What a nice family reunion," Wyatt said.

Against Gareth's protests, Wyatt urged the two guards to get rid of Billy's body, like someone gets rid of a used carpet. One of them took the upper body while the other carried the legs. They had to push the desperate librarian away before they could leave through the dark staircase.

With the remainder of his strength, Gareth joined Samera's side on his hands and knees and buried his head on her shoulder for comfort. The expression on his face made me wonder if he would ever recover.

"Now, where were we?" Wyatt exclaimed. His nonchalant attitude froze the blood in my veins. How could he be so cruel? "Oh! Right. Julian, would you bring Xander closer to me? I'd like to show something to Amya."

Still too weak to fight against the Rascal, Xander lay mostly still, only his head and hands struggling to get away.

"Leave him alone!" I cried as Samera and I stood up to defend our friend. "Wyatt, why are you doing this?"

He laughed. "Oh, Amya. You don't remember, do you? That's at least one thing Meo took care of properly." He paused and halted Ponytail. Taking a sharp object from his pocket, he said, "If you can't be mine, you won't be anybody's."

In one sudden motion, he threw the knife at my drugged friend. There was no time to realize what was happening, before the blade struck Xander in the chest, forcing him to curve into a fetal position and scream out his pain.

I dropped to my knees. "Xander. Xander!" I cried, tears already down my chin. "Oh my God. Xander, open your eyes!"

His eyelids still shut, he took my hand between his and brought it to his jacket, the one I was wearing. I felt a small glass container in its right pocket. Then, he pulled me to him, his mouth almost touching my ear.

"Drug," he whispered, patting the jacket. "Throw it on Wyatt and escape by another Dimension."

The container probably held the same drug Wyatt had used on Xander.

"You're coming with us," I told him. No way had we done all this to leave him behind. No way was he going to die tonight.

My attention returned to Xander's wound. *Should I remove the knife or not?* I pondered hastily. I'd read in a fiction novel that sometimes the wound needed to remain concealed or the person would die from losing too much blood. How would I know if it were the case? How was I supposed to make that decision?

"Look at him!" Wyatt shouted, startling my inner hysteria. "Look down his eyes, Amya. He is just like me. He's a monster too!"

I looked down, but Xander still refused to open his eyes. Was he really a Rascal? I gently touched his cheek, my cold fingers moving down to his chin. "Open your eyes," I said. "I need to know."

He shook his head and swiftly removed the knife from his chest, letting out a sharp cry.

"For Pete's sake, Xander, what are you doing?" Samera asked, furious, pressing her tied hands over Xander's wound.

"Open your eyes!" Wyatt screamed, still seated. "Show her what you've become."

There was blood on Xander's black t-shirt, and everywhere around my hands, which meant that I wasn't doing a really good job at helping him. The odd part was that the pain seemed to have gone away. He was breathing slowly and his thumb moved on my palm, the same way he'd caressed it at the hospital.

When he finally opened his eyes, they were dark blue

and so intense, they could have sent lightning bolts to anyone who dared cross their gaze. Samera removed her hands from his chest and his wound seemed to have stopped bleeding. For a moment, I could have sworn it had started healing already.

"See! I told you," Wyatt continued. "He isn't your little lover anymore? He is a Rascal."

Another Rascal entered the room, which distracted Wyatt from us. With the guards around us gone, it seemed to me like the ideal moment to escape.

"Okay, let's get out of here," I told my friends. "Sam, can you open two Dimensions at once? One with each hand." She nodded. I looked behind me to make sure Wyatt couldn't hear, but he was too busy yelling at the Rascal. "Blue toward Wyatt and whichever else for us. Gareth and I will carry Xander."

The librarian's features lit up when he realized he was part of the escape plan. He didn't say anything but it was obvious he was relieved. I just hoped he'd recovered enough of his strength to help.

"Xander." My gaze fell on his now-clear, beautiful blue eyes. "Are you ready?"

He squeezed my hand and the ghost of a smile crossed his face.

All at once, Samera got up and opened the curtain to the Blue Dimension with her tied hands and I, with Gareth's help, pulled Xander onto his feet. If my deductions were exact, we were under the Bath Abbey, which meant that we were parallel to a load of water in Blue.

And I was right. As soon as the curtain was slightly opened, a thick wall of water was projected onto Wyatt, Julian, and the third Rascal who'd just come in. They were surprised at first, but promptly recovered their wits. Julian was submerged by the flow while Wyatt shouted at the other to let me leave under no condition. The third Rascal hadn't made two steps in our direction before I took the flask from Xander's jacket and threw it on him. It immediately exploded, letting a greenish liquid out, covering the guy's face. After merely two seconds, he dropped into the growing lake.

The water was now equal to our knees and I was starting to weaken under Xander's weight. "Sam, open the other Dimension," I shouted over the sound of the flooding and Wyatt's anger.

"You can't leave me, Amya," he cried. "I won't let you!" He hit the wall next to him. "I'm doing all of this for you... for us. Please don't..."

Ignoring Wyatt's plead, Samera tried several times, but her hands were tied too tightly together to open a second Dimension without closing the first. And Wyatt was too close to us to stop the flow of water. He would easily be able to follow us into the curtain. I had to think of something.

"The knife," Xander murmured in my ear. "I left it on the floor."

Without thinking any further, I pulled Samera under Xander's arm, which made her lose her grip on the curtain to the Blue Dimension. Wyatt immediately started to make his way toward us, so I bent down and looked for the knife as fast as I could. It was even darker underwater than above, but I tried to focus on any glint of light that would reflect the bulbs of the ceiling.

Samera must have been able to open the curtain once more because the current increased, making my search even more difficult. However, it slowed Wyatt and Ponytail down as they were pushed by the stream toward the staircase.

"Hurry!" Samera shouted.

"I'm trying, but..."

I hadn't noticed before but there were fish swimming at our feet. Actual red and silver fish.

Or was it...? *Could it be?* The silver fish wasn't a fish, it was the knife!

In one quick motion, I half-swam, half-walked to the wall behind us and grabbed the knife. When Samera realized I'd finally found it, she let go of the curtain to the Blue Dimension.

But what was I supposed to do with the knife? I couldn't just throw it at Wyatt. And Xander was too weak to help. But we had to use it in order to slow the Rascals down. In order to leave this place.

"Give it to me," Gareth ordered. He didn't let me think twice before he stole the knife from my hand and instantly threw it at Wyatt, who looked as surprised as I was.

The knife only caught his thigh, but that gave us enough window to Travel to another Dimension. And the last thing I saw of my ex-boyfriend was his eyes as black as the night, looking directly into mine with a promise of revenge.

Chapter XXX

Ian Cohen

ONCE IN THE CITY OF BATH, I calculated the distance we would have to walk in order to arrive at the Bath Abbey from the post office. We were less than half a mile away from our destination, and Karl decided that we would Travel in the Yellow Dimension to make sure no one would see us coming.

"Who knows how many of them there are?" he said to the rest of the Protectors. "Maybe some have been assigned to guard the outside area of the Abbey. There's no such thing as being too careful."

I obediently opened the curtain and everyone stepped into Yellow, making sure no pedestrian would see us. We were about to start walking southeast to the Abbey when Karl's coop-hole rang. *Subtlety reigns*, I thought.

"I must have forgotten to turn it off," he apologized before picking up. "Karl." His eyes grew wary, a crease formed in between his two brows, and before he hung up he said, "I'll take care of it, Michelle. Don't you worry, I'll find her."

There is only one person capable of making Karl worry to a point where he needs to be quiet for a moment before he is able to gather his thoughts together. That person is his daughter, Samera.

"Mr. Jensen," one of the bodyguards said. "Mr. Jensen, is everything okay? Has something happened to your wife?"

He turned to us to make an announcement. "My daughter is in England as we speak. She is most likely here to find her friend Xander, who has recently been turned into a Rascal. Mrs. Cohen tracked her down as soon as she realized she was not at the Headquarters anymore. She is in Bath. Therefore, I want all of you to forget everything I said on the plane. We are to attack the Rascals, kill them, and burn the remains. All of them, no exception. Then we are not leaving England without my daughter and her friend Amya. They are our priority. Did I make myself clear?"

The Protectors shouted "YES" in unison and I was left wondering if Meo knew the girls were here. We started running in the direction of the Abbey, across a tent full of babies in their cribs, some screaming *gabee* or *bada* as we passed, meaning they'd just pooped their pants or were hungry. Critters, two Banimos and an Ocelito, flew by us, crying out their freedom. It was dark in Yellow, but the Dimension never ceased to amaze me with all its wonderful colors and gaiety, such a contrast to the way I felt inside.

When we finally reached the space I thought was parallel to the Bath Abbey, Jonathan opened the curtain to the Dimension of Amani and we all hurried in. Although the Abbey was empty of people, we could hear screams from below our feet. Cries of anger transformed into shouted orders, and soon enough, steps were heard coming in our direction.

"Find your position," Karl ordered. "They are coming."

Our bodyguards scattered around, hiding behind the furniture. Some crouched under a pew while others leaned on the humongous white pillars, facing whichever direction the voice was coming from. Everyone had their guns ready. I did too, even though I was supposed to remain withdrawn from the action.

"Meo!" an angry guy cried from downstairs. "Meo! Where the hell are you?"

I thought I'd heard a laugh from above my head, but since no one else seemed to have noticed, I figured it was the product of my imagination. I could clearly hear, though, four pairs of legs making their way out of the basement.

"Meo! Meo, for Satan's sake," a young man with curly blond hair said before he came face-to-face with Karl.

I had just enough time to hear a laugh from behind my back before the gunfire began; Karl fired at the blond Rascal, and four other bodyguards attacked the rest of them. The shots echoed in the Abbey, making my skin shiver with anticipation. I began walking toward the Protectors and realized that the

Rascals were fighting our guards even though their bodies were filled with bullet holes. Some had only been shot in the shoulders or legs, but two of them—including the blond one— were hit in the stomach and they still looked stronger and more alive than the rest of us.

I saw a Rascal with three bullets in his shoulder beating the life out of a Protector. When he realized how weak the Protector, Danny, was, the Rascal pushed Danny on the floor and kicked him away. I wondered if he was dead. Danny's face was covered in blood and his right leg was bent into an unnatural position. The red-haired Rascal leaned on a brown wooden pew, brought his left hand to his right shoulder, inserted his index finger in the wound, and started extracting bullets. It didn't even seem to hurt.

Witnessing this made me comprehend how inhuman Rascals were. Out of sudden fear, I aimed my own gun at the blond Rascal's head, but did not shoot. I was certain he was high in the Rascals' hierarchy. They had all looked at him before they'd launched at the Protectors moments earlier.

My hands were sweating and I wasn't certain if Meo would want me to hurt his boss—or whoever he was—so I remained in place, looking at the Protectors fighting against immortal beings. None of them seemed to have noticed me anyway. The gun shots multiplied and soon enough, the Protectors had their knives out and were fighting two or three against each Rascal. Karl was deep into hand-to-hand combat with the blond one. Jonathan was hiding behind a pew, looking like he would faint any moment. Three Protectors were up against a Rascal with a ponytail and the rest of the bodyguards were cuffing the two remaining Rascals after they had shot them in the head. Although they seemed dead, my gut told me they wouldn't stay dead for long. Their limbs had already started twitching on their own.

My eyes darted back to Karl, who seemed to be avoiding any contact with his opponent. He looked exhausted and just about to give up when his eyes found mine with a pitiful expression of gratitude. At first I wondered why he was grinning at me. The blond Rascal was just about to inflict a fatal blow to his head, but Karl's gaze didn't inch away from mine.

No matter how much I disliked Michelle's husband, I wanted him to turn around and block the blow. I felt the urge to shout "Watch out!" but my throat felt dry and it was like the world stopped for an instant.

Just for a split second.

Such a small amount of time to make such a big decision.

I knew why Karl was looking at me like that. I was the one holding a gun pointed directly at the blond Rascal's head. For all I knew, I was probably the only one with a gun still full of bullets. I was also the one standing there with no one else around to distract me from my aim. And most importantly, Karl believed I had killed Jim, so he was convinced I wouldn't be afraid to take the shot. To kill somebody again.

What Karl didn't know, however, was that I needed this blond Rascal's support in order to become the leader of the Protectors. Were I to kill him, his people—or monsters if you will—would never help me. That included Meo.

At the same time, I could not let Karl die. The Protectors must have seen what was happening, all waiting for me to save our commander. If I didn't fire, I'd lose all credibility to my co-workers.

During that split moment, that half-second, I saw Jemina, my twin sister, in Karl's eyes. She was pleading for my help, all arrogance vanished, while she struggled to swim out of the lake. While I let her drown to her own death and to my liberation.

"Shoot," a voice whispered in my left ear, startling my inner demons. "Shoot. He'll survive anyway."

That was encouragement enough for me to pull the trigger. The bullet flew directly into the blond Rascal's cheek and he was projected backward onto the fence surrounding a dead man's statue. Then I turned to my left and saw Meo's white, crooked grin and dark brown eyes.

"Why hello, Ian," he whispered.

"Why did you want me to do that?" I asked, dumbstruck and still a little out of breath.

He didn't answer. "I didn't tell the blond one, Wyatt," he pointed to the Rascal I'd just hit, "that you were coming. I lied to you. He doesn't know we've been in touch." His laugh was just loud enough to echo through my core, but it didn't reach the Protectors who had started gathering the wounded Rascals together. Karl squinted his eyes in order to find me in the semi-darkness, but before he could, Meo grabbed my combat gear and shoved me onto the white pillar behind which he'd been hiding. He came close to me, still holding the brown material of my shirt, and added, "Wyatt won't agree to work with you until you prove yourself. I've seen him do it to others. He uses them and then kills them without mercy. Besides, Protectors don't usually help us willingly. He will never believe you're truly on our side."

My heart rate was losing it and I was short of breath, but I still managed to say, "Why do you care whether he kills me or not?"

Meo's smirk reached his eyes. "I believe you are a valuable asset. I also believe you will be much more valuable once you're the head of the Protectors in New York."

His answer created a mixed feeling inside of me. I was relieved to know he was truly going to help me with my personal quest, but at the same time, it also meant that he was working with me merely for the sake of our mutual goal. It was all about business. I wondered why that affected me so much.

"What should I do then? How can I win Wyatt's trust?"

Meo laughed louder this time, and I heard footsteps coming our way. "Wyatt trusts no one. Except me, perhaps, but he still keeps that to a certain level. No, you need to prove your reliability. And most of all, you need to gain some credits with the Protectors. Without them, you'll never be elected as their leader."

I let out a nervous laugh. I had never thought of that. I'd always believed I would become the head of the Protectors by playing on Michelle's weaknesses. Was it possible to make my family like me so much that they would want me as their leader instead of Michelle? Play on my strengths instead of her weaknesses? "How am I supposed to do that? I've killed one of them, Meo. I'm still wondering why no one has publicly accused me yet."

"Believe me. They'll come around. Until then, I won't be able to convince Wyatt of your worth until you're powerful enough on your own. Get people to like you, and most of all, know your true allies."

"Ian?"

I heard Karl's voice from only a few feet away and feared he would hear us. Meo, however, didn't mind anything. As usual. He peeked behind the pillar just enough not to be seen and then brought his face directly next to my left ear, which gave me shivers up and down my spine. It wasn't the kind of shiver you have when you're cold, though. Nor did it feel like a shudder you experience when you're scared. The feeling was somehow sweeter and expanded to my fingertips and toe nails. It almost felt like the tip of my hair curled in reaction to my inner state.

"I've seen you on the bridge," Meo whispered, covering my ear with warm steam. I closed my eyes, trying to contend the strange feeling growing within me. "You're stubborn and you're strong for a human. Use that to your advantage."

His words gave me hope. I already had a plan. I would convert myself to Judaism and thus become one of them in a way I'd never been before. I would become part of their community, their well-protected inner circle. Little by little, I would gain their trust. Little by little, I would be there for them in a way that Michelle couldn't be.

"Ian?"

"Yes?" I said, the warmth still contouring my left cheek.

"Ian? Oh, there you are." It was Karl. I immediately opened my eyes and saw his concerned features in the shadows. "Are you all right?" He walked across a pew and halted in front of me. Had he seen me with Meo? Did he think I'd been attacked? "You did well, Ian. You did the right thing."

What was he talking about? Was he approving my alliance with a Rascal? I didn't understand. My head was throbbing as I was trying to find an excuse for being seen with a Rascal. *He attacked me, but it happened too fast for me to react and shoot him?* No. That sounded lame even in my head.

I blinked a few times, the same way you try to blink away a bad dream. "I don't understand, Mr. Jensen," I said.

"What you did back there. You saved my life, Ian." He put a hand on my left shoulder and I shrank back with an involuntary gasp. My mind couldn't get around Meo's words and comprehend Karl's at the same time. "Ian, it's okay. You did well. It was either me or him. You made the right decision."

And then it struck me. Karl wasn't angry. He hadn't seen Meo at all. He thought I was in shock after sending a bullet into somebody else's head. He thought I felt bad about it.

I muffled an upcoming laugh into a cough because it was the only thing I could do to repress my true feelings. I was happy. No. I was more than happy. I was elated—overjoyed, even. I had a plan and powerful people to back me up once the plan was in motion. Plus, after seeing me like this, Karl would assume it was the first time I'd "killed" someone. His suspicions about Jim might even diminish or vanish completely. He thought I was in shock, for God's sake! Ha!

Karl brought me to the others. As we walked, I was in a sort of daze where everything was more colorful and more luminous. For the first time since we'd Traveled into the Abbey, I could appreciate the flower-like patterns carved into the ceiling, much slike fashionable tornados engulfing the pillars in their beauty. Several of those pillars had lost some of that beauty because of the holes created by lost bullets, but Michelle would send a team promptly. Every detail would be back in order before the sun rose tomorrow. That was how powerful Michelle was. That was how powerful I'd soon become.

"Xander wasn't with them. We need to find my daughter," Karl said once we had gathered with the other

Protectors, looking down at four unconscious Rascals. He spilled his portable gas tank onto the monsters and set fire to it.

But nothing happened. The match was doused once in contact with the Rascal's skin.

"Try with my lighter," John told our commander, while supporting his brother Danny on his shoulder. Danny was half unconscious, half dragging himself on one leg because the other one was undoubtedly broken.

Karl brought the flame produced by the lighter to the pile of monsters again, but was left with the same result. Frustrated, he kicked the closest Rascal limb and grunted.

"How are we supposed to get rid of them now?" he muttered. "We can't just leave them here."

Our commander was losing it. I had to step up. "What's our priority, Mr. Jensen?" I asked. The answer was obvious to me. He had mentioned it earlier.

Karl stopped pacing around and faced me. "We need to kill those *things* once and for all," he replied.

I shook my head. "I understand. But what's our priority? Kill them or save your daughter?"

I had no idea what could kill a Rascal, but I didn't want Karl to find out. Not today anyway. I had to convince him to leave them alone.

"We've checked their pulse," he continued. "They're not dead, Ian, which means that they'll come back—"

"And when they do, we'll be ready. For now, I believe

your daughter's life matters more than theirs. We should find her now, before it's too late."

He stared at me for what seemed like a full minute, breathing rapidly by his nose, much like a bull does before it charges on a red flag. "Fine," he said at last. "Let's find Samera and Amya. Then we're going home."

Chapter XXXI

WE STEPPED INTO WHAT LOOKED LIKE A CAVE crowded with stalactites and a few stalagmites. When Samera released the curtain, the snippet of light coming from the basement in Amani died out, leaving us in complete darkness.

"Why did you lead us to the Red Dimension?" Xander grunted, his words echoed by the walls. "You know we shouldn't venture into the Caves. It could be dangerous."

"There was too much water coming from Blue and we would've hit a wall in Yellow: only rocks and mud," Samera replied. "Did you want to drown or be buried alive?" She waited for an answer to her rhetorical question. "I didn't think so, either."

"How are we supposed to get out of here, now? Who knows what we'll run into..."

Gareth untied our hands with difficulty, as the ropes were interlaced in such intricate and tight knots, it was hard for him to loosen them. Then Xander, Samera and I opened the flashlight mode on our cell phones. The Cave walls were only wide enough for two people to walk side by side and we had to hunch over to avoid most of the stalactites.

We hadn't made ten feet forward when an acute, piercing sound echoed from the path in front of us.

"What the hell?" Samera said. She was the one supporting Xander on her shoulder, and even though—feeling much better—he was able to walk slowly, she had to stop and take a few steadying breaths. "We can't go in that direction. I have no intention of meeting with whatever just made that noise."

The noise echoed again like a wincing door. I remembered Xander telling me that people in Red walked into the Caves before they died and never came back. Whatever was hiding here was expecting somebody ready to die.

We all agreed to retrace our steps and decided to attempt the other direction, the one we hoped led to the exit. Everyone remained silent, too focused on finding a way out and listening for any noise. In the meantime, I thought back on what had happened in the basement and felt such pity for Gareth that I couldn't help but ask him how he was holding up.

He shrugged and looked up as if to stop himself from crying again but rebel tears escaped from his blinking eyelids.

"You did everything you could," I told him.

"But it wasn't enough." He looked away and started

walking a little faster than me, doubtlessly to hide his emotions.

"Guys," Samera said before she stopped again and leaned against the wall. "Listen to this. Xander, repeat what you just told me."

He took a deep breath and said in a low voice, "We have to find a way out quickly. There are Protectors in Europe who work for the Rascals. They will be able to follow us as soon as they get hold on one of them."

This realization hit me hard, but it must have been even more difficult for Samera, who trusted her family more than anyone else in the world. It meant that the dream I had had in the convy wasn't just a dream. And Michelle was right about Protectors going rogue. My next question was out before I had the time to think about it.

"Does someone named Jeffrey Archer work for the Rascals?"

Xander looked surprised. "How do you know? Did you recover your memory?" A glint of hope sparkled in his eyes.

"No, but I keep having these dreams and flashes of things I forgot." I thought about the images I'd seen at the hospital. The window with the red eyes was about Nevada and my first day as a Seraph—the name still sounded so unfamiliar. The second, Wyatt in front of a lake, was about the Protectors working with Rascals. "Has any of you ever dressed like a ninja turtle for Halloween?" I asked my two best friends, thinking about the third image.

Instead of answering me, Samera and Xander stared at the floor and remained as silent as the rocks surrounding us. Upset by their secrecy, I was going to repeat the question, but the acute cry we'd heard earlier echoed from the dark passage we were heading toward, followed by another behind us; however, this time, it sounded much closer to our immediate location. As the noise was repeated over and over again in both directions, panic rose in each one of us and we stood frozen in place for what seemed like forever.

I started to look around for an opening or crack in the wall that would allow us to either exit or hide, when I thought of something else that could actually work.

"Sam, can you open the curtains horizontally instead of vertically?" I inquired.

She shrugged and said, "Never tried. Why?" She looked composed, but I could see from the patterns her fingers made on her thighs, and because her teeth kept biting her upper lip that she was fighting to keep calm like everyone else.

"If we're lucky, the basement of the Abbey wasn't too deep into the ground. We could try to Travel upward, see if we end up on solid ground."

We quickly walked to an area where the ceiling was the highest. Gareth and I were able to raise Samera on our shoulders, allowing her to touch the rocks above our heads. She then opened the curtain to the Yellow Dimension, exposing a beautiful night sky.

"It worked!" Samera exclaimed. "Push me up, I'll keep the curtain open for you guys from there."

I used all my strength to keep myself from falling, as Gareth and I—with a little help from Xander, who, thanks to a Rascal's fast metabolism, was feeling much better already—worked against gravity to lift Samera as high as it was humanly possible. She succeeded in getting her hands onto solid ground and pulled herself up, letting go of the curtain.

Samera disappeared, leaving us in absolute darkness once again. The cries of whatever creature was coming toward us were getting so close, I could hear their feet running in our direction, like a dog chasing after a bone.

Hurry up, Sam, I mentally requested.

When the curtain opened anew, not only was Samera in the hole above us, but she was also surrounded by five more heads.

"Thought we'd need some help," she said with a big smile on her face, echoing the children's around her.

Several hands reached out for us and, against his protests, Xander was the first to go.

"Your turn," I told Gareth when Xander was safe above ground.

"No, you go first. If someone has to stay behind, it's me. I am the only one who's got nothing to lose anymore. Billy was my only family and he's gone."

"No one's staying here. Now, get up there and—"

"He's the tallest," Xander interrupted. "You won't be able to jump high enough if you're last." He hung his hand in the air. "Grab it, Amya."

I didn't want to leave Gareth on his own. He was depressed and I was afraid he would stay in the Cave on purpose as a way to punish himself for what had happened to his brother. Nonetheless, Gareth agreed to use his thigh and hands as stairs for me to climb on. When I reached Xander's and a red-haired boy's warm fingers, I realized that the librarian would never be able to jump high enough. He would have needed to be more than seven feet tall to make it. I told him to hold on to my feet while the others hauled me up on the grass.

"No, they won't be able to lift us both. I'll find a way. Just go," he said.

I didn't have a choice. Xander and the boy didn't let go of me until I was kneeling next to them, looking down the hole.

"Jump!" Samera told the librarian. "Come on! Just jump and we'll catch you."

He tried. He jumped three times, getting so close to our fingers that I thought he would eventually succeed. But he lost hope too fast. Discouraged, he sat down and crossed his arms.

"I give up," he said, before his head rapidly shifted from one side to the other. "Wait. Something's coming." He turn the flashlight on his phone back on, got up, and started to look around. "They're so close now. I can almost hear them breathing."

The wincing noise must have come from less than a mile away from him. It now sounded like pigs crying their lost hope at the slaughterhouse.

"Xander, Sam, grab my feet," I ordered. No way was I going to let Gareth down there all by himself. "Slowly push me down the hole and as soon as I say so, pull as hard as you can. I'm going back in."

Once my friends had a firm grip on my ankles, I crawled to the opening of the Dimension and started my way down, head first.

"Jump again, Gareth. I'll catch you."

He didn't even look up. His head moved from left to right but the rest of his body seemed frozen in place.

"Gareth!" I repeated louder, even though I knew he could hear me.

"Don't, Amya," he finally answered.

"What's going on? Come on, jump!"

Without saying a word, he took a cautious step back and lifted his hands in the air, as to reach mine. And that is when I noticed what was in front of him. The creature that'd been running in the Cave. It wasn't like anything I'd seen before. Its size resembled a rat's and it was standing on four feet that looked almost like claws. Its nose was long and humpy, but the thing had no ears, only small crevices like lacerations.

"What's taking so—?" Samera started to say, before she caught sight of the horrible creature. "Holy moly—crap…"

Ignoring her, I focused on a way to get Gareth out of this. "Back away slowly. I'll come to you," I told him.

But Xander didn't let me. "You don't know what this ugly thing can do. You stay right here."

"But—"

"I'll go," he said.

Although Xander hadn't recovered completely from the drug, he was taller and much stronger than me. The only problem was that I doubted Samera, the children around us, and I would be able to support his weight. And what if the creature jumped on Gareth before Xander was able to pull him up?

We still had to take our chances.

Xander wasn't two feet into the hole before the creature cried out and charged at Gareth, its nose peeling off into several rows of teeth, like a shark's. It took a bite at our friend's shin and immediately attacked the entire feet, moving fast and meticulously around the bones. Frightened, the kids released their hold on Xander's feet causing him to fall head-first on the vile creature.

"Xander!" I shouted over Gareth's screams.

Xander was up on his two feet in a split second, before the rat-like monsters cried once more. The one who'd been crushed by my friend shook its head violently before its body divided into two creatures of the same size. The other one soon imitated it. Then, the four beasts thrust themselves on the helpless guys' legs, crying their victory and taking away more flesh than they could actually digest. That, I realized, was how they got rid of the bodies once our Red-selves died.

Gareth kicked them and Xander tried to crush them with his feet, but they moved too quickly.

"We have to do something!" I cried.

Samera was dumbstruck, looking at the scene like a spectator at a Shakespeare's *King Lear* representation, and the children seemed too scared to do anything. The younger were sent to a nearby tent while the older kept screaming at every bite the creatures took on my friends.

I was thinking of breaking a branch from a nearby tree and jumping back into the Red Dimension to help Xander and Gareth against the beasts, when I heard birds flying above our heads. Looking up, I discerned Ocelitos and Banimos, at least five of each. Without being asked, they flew into the hole and, the latter species attacking the awful creatures with their strong gorilla arms, the former critters were able to carry the two men out of the Cave and onto the ground with the help of their strong eagle wings and cheetah claws.

Everyone but Samera gathered around the librarian and Xander, and several more children arrived with towels and some sort of brown ointment to cover the wounds. Gareth kept screaming and pushing everyone away. As for Xander, his flesh grew back in a few seconds, though his skin tone paled, making the black of his pupils even darker.

"Calm down," Samera told Gareth once she'd made sure

all critters had flown back into the Yellow Dimension. "Hush, now… Hush, keep your strength."

Gareth's body was shaking like he was in hypothermia. The spasms were so strong, I thought he might break his bones on the ground. We kept him from peeking at his lacerated legs. Surely, the sight of your own bones deprived of any flesh wasn't the most soothing sight when in shock.

"It's okay," Samera told him. "You're going to be fine." She caressed his damp forehead and squeezed his hand. "When you're better, we're going on a hunt for Atlantis, okay? Do you hear me? We'll find it, I promise." She kept talking about the mythical island until Gareth's agony was so insufferable that he lost consciousness.

Chapter XXXII

"WE NEED TO TAKE HIM to a hospital," Samera urged. "Like, now. He's losing too much blood."

"I know, I know, but we can't go back to Amani or the Rascals might find us," I told her.

Gareth was shivering, his teeth chattering desperately. Xander carried him to the nearest tent, followed by a dozen kids and the critters. Samera and I remained outside while she looked into the Blue and the Red Dimensions to see if it was possible to Travel from our location. We decided that we were more likely to find a doctor nearby in Red, and then we ran to the tent to notify our friends.

Xander was sitting on a chair a few feet away from Gareth. Both wore a ghostly complexion, and I feared the former would pass out as well. I walked across the room to Xander and touched his forehead. It was glacial, like the inside of a freezer. He removed my hand and muttered that he was fine. That he only needed to gain back his strength.

"How? Do you need food? Water?" I asked, but he didn't answer. He merely looked away. "Tell me. I can't be of any help if you don't."

"I don't want your help," he snapped.

I was about to tell Samera to shake some sense into him when I understood what was going on. He was a Rascal now. His body responded differently from ours, so his cravings were undoubtedly particular. *Real food, although not lethal, does not satiate them,* the book had said.

There was no certainty that Xander was still himself. Maybe the Rascal in him was just waiting to destroy his humanity. Or maybe becoming a Rascal didn't really change who you were, but simply enhanced your personality: your fears, your hopes, and the way you behaved. But I didn't have time to wait for an answer. Trusting Xander completely, I set a chair in front of him and took his hand.

"Feed on me."

Shock and outrage replaced his exhausted expression. "Are you insane?" he said, getting up, although he was forced to sit down again or he might have fainted. "No."

I squeezed his fingers. "We need you awake and sane." I turned to Samera, who was keeping an eye on Gareth. "Tell him, would you?"

Her brows met above her nose and she tilted her head. "I don't know, Amya. I don't know if it's safe…"

"See!" Xander exclaimed.

I grunted. "Don't listen to her. Look at me," I said. Somehow, I felt the urge to get even closer to him. "Look at me," I repeated. "I trust you, okay? You wouldn't do anything to hurt me."

"No, you know I'd never hurt you..."

"So, please... *please* believe me. You need this."

"You don't even know what I feed on," he said.

I looked intently into his eyes. "Tell me."

He avoided my gaze and stared at his hands instead. "Emotions," he said in a cold voice.

The news was a jolt to me and it must have been even worse for Xander, particularly since that was exactly what Ponytail fed on. The power that had killed Nevada and Billy.

I tried not to react impulsively, which would have scared Xander even more. "Does it have to be joy or hope, or can you choose another emotion?"

"I can choose, but—"

"Then do it."

Xander brought his free hand to his hair and scratched his head. I could feel that he was going to concede. He didn't really have a choice. He needed it.

Finally, after he was confident about his decision, he asked, "What emotion do you wish to lose for a short period of time? The effect won't last forever. New events will trigger new emotions and you'll be back to normal in no time."

"Is that what happened to her memory?" Samera inquired. "She was able to recover some information from her past because it was triggered by something?"

"I don't know. I think memory is a much more complex element. Wyatt seemed to be saying that she shouldn't be able to remember anything that Meo drained from her. But he must have unintentionally left traces of it, which can now be triggered by words, smells, or even dreams."

"Like the fact that Jeffrey works for the Rascals," I said. "We should have never made a deal with him."

"Wait, you two have met Jeffrey?" Xander voiced. "Why in the world would you make a deal with him?"

"We didn't have a choice," Samera exclaimed, insulted. "He was the only one in Red who owned a convy."

"What are you talking about?" Xander looked confused. "Jeff doesn't own a convy. Jeffrey Archer. Are you sure we're talking about the same guy? Jeff is a CIA agent who lives in Amani."

Silence befell all of us. Only the kids taking care of Gareth and murmuring songs to themselves continued their activity.

A CIA agent.

"A CIA agent?" I said out loud. "What is a CIA agent doing with Rascals?"

Xander sighed, he looked exhausted. "Remember what we heard on the radio yesterday? With all that's happening in

Europe? Well, that's all part of a plan. Some kind of diversion while the Rascals do the real damage. The thing is… I didn't stay with them long enough to know what they were really up to."

"What do you mean by a distraction?" I asked.

"With the help of Protectors in Europe—" He turned to Samera. "Most of those Protectors' families are being threatened; they're not willingly helping the bad guys—Rascals Travel in the other Dimensions and kill people's Blue and Yellow-selves."

"That is awful! No wonder why people in Amani go crazy and murder everyone," Samera uttered. "They're not used to being influenced only by their Red-self and they go insane under the pressure. That's not good. That's really not good…"

"Exactly," Xander continued. "But it's even worse than you think. That's where Jeffrey comes in. Being a CIA spy, he writes all sorts of reports to his superior about Europe going through hell, so that the United States government will panic and maybe even start a Third World War with European countries. Humans are too easy to manipulate." He paused. "Anyway, I wish I knew what the Rascals are doing in the meantime, but I don't."

"How old is Jeffrey?" I asked. "The one from Amani."

"Hmm… I haven't met him personally, but Wyatt was talking about him like he was in his sixties. And that's exactly why he was willing to help. He thinks Wyatt will turn him into a

Rascal so he can live longer. But I seriously doubt that's going to happen."

Sixties… Our Jeffrey isn't older than seventeen, eighteen top, I reflected.

Gareth moaned from the other side of the room and I heard a branch creak outside the tent. Expecting the Rascals to have followed us to the Yellow Dimension, I put my finger in front of my lips and whispered for everyone to be quiet. Maybe they'd turn around if they couldn't hear us. My heart was beating so fast that I could feel it up to my ears.

Another bunch of branches broke closer to the entrance.

"Feed on me *now*," I ordered Xander. "We'll need your martial arts ability against them this time. We won't be able to just Travel."

Reluctantly, he covered my hand with his and closed his eyes.

"EVERYONE ON THE GROUND!" I heard a man shout, followed by a clickety-clack sound, like a gun being cocked.

But the feeding process had already begun and I realized that I wasn't really afraid of whoever had just broke into our tent. However, Xander carefully moved aside from his chair and sat on the floor, which was covered in dead leaves, forcing me to do the same.

"Dad!" Samera cried.

I should have felt relieved that we were surrounded by

Protectors, and good ones at that, but all I wanted to do was to laugh.

So I burst out laughing and Xander instantly released my hand. I stood up and saw that all the guns were pointed directly at me.

"Hey!" I exclaimed, amused by the look on everyone's faces.

"Samera, what is she doing?" Karl asked his daughter, before he noticed Xander next to me. "You..."

Karl pointed his gun at my friend and sent three of his men to cuff him up.

What are they doing? I thought. *They're ruining all the fun!*

I put myself in front of Xander and shook my head. "No no no no no. Don't hurt him. He is my friend. You know, he could be your friend, too, if you were a little nicer."

Maybe they don't have any friends and they're sad about it.

I put my hand on one of the men's arms and he looked up at me, confused. "Mr. Jensen," he said. "What should I do?"

"Don't mind her," Karl replied. "Samera Cohen, what happened to Amya? Is she drunk?"

"Drunk drunk drunk drunk drunk?" I repeated. "I'm not drunk. I simply want everyone to be happy. Happy happy happy!" I made my way to Karl and gently patted his cheeks. "You're not happy. Loosen your face a little. It'll help."

Why does everyone seem angry?

I leaped to the Protector next to me and patted his cheeks too, as if to soften his expression. "Here," I said. "Teeth were created to be shown. Show them to me." I smiled to show mine.

But he didn't want to show me his teeth. I heard the kids around me laugh and Samera said something to her father, something secret that I couldn't hear. Then the Protectors ignored my protests and grabbed Xander's arm in a really rude manner before they cuffed him and pushed him out of the tent. Two others carried Gareth out as well, soon followed by Samera and me.

Before I left with the angry men, I thanked the children who'd helped Gareth and I received a load of hugs. They were so nice and friendly that I had no desire to leave their side.

"Amya. C'mon. We gotta go," Samera told me. "Dad says they were able to slow the Rascals down in Amani, but they're still alive. Bullets don't seem to kill them…"

Nevertheless, I felt happy and lightheaded, as if thousands of little puppies were gathered around me, licking my face and biting my ears.

Right then, the image of the ninja turtle next to a giraffe flashed in front of my eyes, only it lingered on the features under the red mask. At first, they were blurry, but the picture soon cleared, exhibiting pale blue eyes and a full lower lip. Xander's. It wasn't like the other flashes I'd had, as I didn't quite recall seeing him in that costume in front of a giraffe. What I could remember, however, was how happy I'd been at that exact moment. That image represented one of the best times I'd had in my life and I had no recollection of it.

I unwillingly trailed behind my best friend and Traveled in the Red Dimension like she asked me to. The sun still illuminated the city, as if it were closer to midday instead of midnight. We walked to a building and climbed many stairs until we reached the street full of cars. I wondered how the Protectors had found us, though I guessed it had something to do with their tracking device. If they had created cell phones that could send waves in any Dimension, they'd probably found a way to do the same with tracking systems.

There was an oddly shaped ambulance waiting for us outside the entrance. It resembled two cupcakes glued together. Two men took over the librarian, and another Protector who was full of bruises, and the rest of us were split into three cars. Against my protests, Xander was forced to sit in a car surrounded by Protectors, including Ian, while Samera and I embarked in the one driven by her father. She sat on the passenger seat, and I at the back between two armed Protectors.

"You two are in big trouble, young lady," Karl said before he started the engine. And those were his last words until we arrived, two hours later, at a building made entirely of glass.

During the ride, I had time to think about the crazy day we'd just had. Gareth was on the verge of dying from blood loss and Xander was believed to be a monster. But he wasn't. I was a hundred percent certain he was still himself. Samera and I had broken about a dozen rules to escape the HQ and rescue our friend and we… well, Gareth's brother died because of us tonight.

All of this transformed my peppy mood into a more neutral, pensive one, and I ceased smiling like an idiot and singing weird songs in my head. At the end of the ride, I was back to normal.

From inside the building, we took an elevator to the basement floor and I had just enough time to realize where we were heading before the doors opened to a sound of knuckles cracking; Jeffrey was waiting for us.

Samera didn't lose a second before she turned to her father and uttered, "He's working for the Rascals! Don't trust him."

"What are you talking about?" Karl said, frowning. "Jeffrey is the one who saved your lives today. Were it not for him calling your mother, we wouldn't have known that you three had left the HQ and you might still be in Yellow, waiting for the Rascals to find you. He came back to Angushore and waited here for you all day, in case we needed him."

"No, Dad! He is passing for a CIA agent in Amani. I don't know how he does that, but he's found a way to Travel…"

Jeffrey looked scandalized by her accusation.

"Unless…" I wondered out loud. "Unless his Amani-self works for the Rascals. Not him."

After I explained everything Xander had told us about Jeffrey, the one living in Amani, we decided to give the Jeffrey standing in front of us the benefit of the doubt. After all, he was, once again, helping us, and his age didn't match Xander's description. Jeff and Karl exchanged greetings and Gareth was carried by Ian and three other Protectors into the convy. Thanks to the doctors in the ambulance, the librarian wasn't losing any more blood, but he still needed medical attention, and rapidly. The bruised Protector was also allowed in the convy. After looking more closely at the deep lesion on his cheek and because his face was more purple than it was beige, I was surprised he could still stand on his own.

"Michelle will be waiting for them at your office," Karl told Jeffrey, once the latter was ready to depart. He turned to Ian and the Protectors next to Gareth. "Stay with him and make sure he doesn't wake up. The doctors told me they had to remove a damaged muscle in his leg. Please, just keep the morphine high in his blood."

Once the convy gone, the rest of us went back upstairs and Traveled to Amani. According to Karl, we were only a few minutes from the airport, where we would board the first plane to New York. Xander, Samera, and I didn't have our passports, but none of that mattered. Michelle knew really powerful people all around the world. We were in the air, on a private jet, in less than an hour.

The adrenaline down, my mind and body felt like

sleeping would be the best option, but I still needed to know one more thing. My gut told me that Xander wouldn't be free to walk away when we landed in New York. They were probably going to put him in jail or interrogate him for hours, at least until they were certain he was harmless. I needed to get my answers now.

There were five armed Protectors gathered around him, and Karl was sitting right in front of me, so I couldn't just walk to Xander and have a little chat with him. I tried to remember the theme song of the ninja turtle TV series and the name of the turtle who wore a red mask. Raphael. Yes, that was it.

Raphael is cool but crude, the song said. And I remembered Xander telling me Raphael was his favorite.

"I need to go to the washroom," I told Sam's dad.

Karl's eyes lifted from his book and he nodded his authorization. I got up and headed toward the middle of the plane. Xander appeared to be sleeping, but I still hummed the ninja turtle theme song in case he was listening. Just like I'd expected, he slowly lifted his head and gazed at me, but I ignored him. I went straight to the washroom and it is only when I walked back that I halted in front of his seat.

"Raphael and Benny will be thrilled to see you again," I said, hoping he would get the allusion to Benny the giraffe in Yellow. "They told me they couldn't remember," I touched my temple with my fingers, "the last time you were together. At Halloween, was it?" Surely, if Xander had dressed as a ninja turtle, it'd been for Halloween.

Xander peeked at the Protectors around him and, seeing as they were busy looking at some small computer device, he looked directly at me and nodded once.

It had worked! I was finally going to know the meaning of the third flash I kept having. Pleased with myself, I walked down the aisle and sat next to Samera, facing Xander. When I had made sure no one would notice what I was about to do, I stared at my friend and Sojourned into his head, the purple spot building a nice feeling in my mind.

***

You asked to see this, Amya. Just remember that…

Amya, Samera, and I were invited to a party hosted by an old classmate of mine. After two hours of waiting for the girls to get ready, we are finally on the balcony, about to knock on my friend's door. Naturally, Sam is the most excited of the three, jumping up and down in her fairy costume.

"This is gonna be so much fun!" she says.

"Mm-hm," Amya mutters. She is already looking at the clock on her cellphone.

I don't feel like going in either. Tonight was Sam's idea.

"I might not be sticking around for more than a couple

of minutes if Eveline is here tonight," I say.

Eveline is my friend's little sister. She had a crush on me two years ago, when we were still in high school. On Valentine's Day, she'd told everyone we were a couple, and when I had denied it, her brother made sure I'd regret breaking her heart. It was ridiculous, obviously, as he knew perfectly well I'd never liked her. Anyway, she has made it her purpose ever since that day to make me feel guilty every time we see each other, even though she has a serious boyfriend now.

"Please don't leave without me," Amya pleads.

She recently broke up with her boyfriend and it's like she's always on the edge and nervous about everything. She's assured me all is fine, but I can feel she's not telling me the whole story.

Samera snorts. "Jeez! You guys don't have to come if you don't want to." Without a second glance at us and without knocking on the door, she turns around and goes straight into the big blue house.

Amya looks at me and shrugs. "No one's forcing us to go," she says.

"But you're all dressed up for the night," I reply, admiring her Ilsa Lund costume, from the Casablanca *movie.*

"Why don't we go to my parents' and watch Friday the 13th*? They're out of town for the weekend."*

I have a much better idea.

We drive to the Protectors' Headquarters and wait for

someone to open the tree to the stairs leading inside. Michelle is in her office when we arrive.

"Mrs. Cohen," I say. "Will you allow us to spend the night in Yellow? I'd like to show Amya something."

"That's your big plan?" Amya says before Michelle can reply. "Xander, you know I don't like that Dimension. Everyone is too… cheerful."

Without a word, Michelle leads us back outside and opens the curtain to the Yellow Dimension. "Have fun." She winks before I drag Amya in with me.

We step into a tent where Banimos and Ocelitos are sleeping in a pile of fur and feather. I grab Amya's hand and silently take her outside, where we can admire the three moons. They are so thin, looking like they'll disappear any minute.

"Whoa, that's beautiful," Amya whispers.

There are kids playing Celtic music in a tent nearby, but Amya doesn't want to join them, so we sit on the grass, under a tree with orange leaves, and gaze at the moons. After several minutes, Amya feels like dancing, but I know it is close to twelve o'clock, so I stand up and ask her to wait for me.

My feet quickly make their way to the tent where the music comes from and I convince the children to move the party outside.

Amya's eyes are radiant when she understands what is going on. There are close to ten musicians and twenty dancers, from the age of five to fourteen. For once, Amya doesn't care if she isn't a good dancer; she grabs my hand and pulls me into the middle of the crowd.

"Thank you for that," she tells me, a big smile on her graceful face. "I needed this."

I say nothing. It feels like a reply would somehow weaken her words. Instead, I circle her waist with my hands and lift her up in the air, while spinning her around like a child. She laughs and looks at the sky, her arms like wings, ready to fly off.

When I put her down, our gazes lock for a moment and I feel an urge to kiss her, but I know it would be too soon. She admitted that one of the reasons why she broke up with Wyatt was because she still had feelings for me, and she knows I've never loved anyone but her. Still, I simply bring my hand to her chin and brush my thumb against her lips while she closes her eyes. I know that when she's ready, we can be together.

The music stops at 11:58, and the children let every Benny out of its assigned enclosure. Just about a dozen giraffes join our gathering and look up at the moons. At 11:59 and thirty seconds, everyone is quiet except for Amya.

"What is it?" she asks. "What's going on?"

I smile but keep gazing at the moons. And then, at precisely midnight, blazing golden fireworks set off, one after the other, transforming the dark night sky into a mine of gold. My eyes immediately shift to Amya's amazed expression. She looks like she's at peace with the world, her smile finally reaching her bright eyes.

Without averting her gaze from the fireworks, she slips her arm under mine and leans against my shoulder. Together, we contemplate the sky, until the twelfth explosion has completely dissolved into the dark smoke.

***

"Amya! Jeez, you're sleeping with your eyes open now? Or are you're Sojourning?" Samera asked me, which brought my soul back to my own body.

I gasped, my mind still in Yellow with Xander. "We were together, weren't we?" I said out loud.

"Hm?"

I turned to my best friend. "Xander and I were a couple before the incident? Wyatt called him my lover in the basement and... and at the hospital, when Xander visited me the first day I was conscious; I Sojourned and I remember him thinking how he loved the girl behind the tree. That girl was me! We were together!"

My heartbeat increased and I started to breathe fast... too fast. How had I not realized that earlier?

"Calm down, Amya. What's the problem?"

"You knew? You knew and you didn't tell me!"

"He didn't want anyone to tell you..."

"Why?" I snapped. I'd been in a relationship with my friend and they thought it wasn't important enough for me to know?

When I first met Xander in high school, I'd felt such a connection with him, but he'd quickly made himself clear that we would never be more than friends. He'd said he didn't want to lose what we had. I'd given up and gotten used to our friendship. We'd grown like two peas in a pod. And it was all totally fine.

The knowledge that he'd changed his mind made me so angry because I couldn't remember anything. Not a single day spent with him as his girlfriend. Not a single kiss... *Nada*.

"He was waiting for you to remember on your own. I think he doesn't want to force things... to force you to love him again."

To love him again... Did I still love him? Did I feel anything other than friendship for Xander? I shook my head. "I don't know if..." I paused. "Too much has happened and I can't remember, you know?" What would I tell him?

Samera's dark brown eyes looked intently into mine. "It's okay. Like I said, he doesn't want to rush. Don't worry."

I couldn't make myself glance back at Xander. Too many emotions were swirling and intermixing in my mind. I needed to clear things out before anything happened. And yet something still didn't add up.

"Wait," I said. "When did you say I broke up with

Wyatt?"

Samera thought about it. "I didn't. But if my memory is correct, you ended things with crazy ex-boyfriend in mid-October last year. Why?"

"Nothing. Well, it's just that I remember studying Jane Eyre with Wyatt in his bedroom." I paused, recalling the first time we had sex. "We started analyzing the Brönte Sisters' works only in November. It doesn't make any sense. What happened to me from the time I broke up with Wyatt in October and the day of the incident in April? The only few memories I have are with Wyatt."

"Can't be. Wyatt disappeared for months after you broke up with him... until April 20th. And you started officially going out with Xander in November. Even then, you'd never told us why you were afraid of Wyatt so we couldn't have figured out he would eventually reappear to feed on your energy and leave you in a coma. I guess this Meo guy had already drained your memory."

"The fact that I don't remember is understandable. What I don't understand is why I remember things that never happened. Am I still a virgin?"

Going to the movie theater; that night in Wyatt's bedroom—and all the other nights; the surprise party for Xander's twenty-first birthday; Christmas at Magda's; and everything that happened after I broke up with Wyatt... were all these memories fake?

Samera laughed and looked at her father who was deep into conversation on his phone. "I don't know, Amya. You should ask Xander, not me. This whole thing is weird, though. I think we should mention it to Mom." She smiled. "Not that you don't remember if you're a virgin or not, but that your memories were somehow faked or implanted."

I agreed with her idea, though I didn't say so. "But shouldn't I have told you if Xander and I had... you know? You're my best friend."

"I guess you should have but you didn't. Anyway," she added, looking rather uncomfortable with the subject. "I came to tell you that my father just called Mom and told her about Jeffrey—the one from Amani. Other CIA agents are hunting him down as we speak and since we know what is going on in Europe, Mom will pull the right strings with the right people to keep the Protectors' families safe. Wyatt won't be able to manipulate us anymore. He won't be able to Travel either, so the insanity will ultimately stop. She also promised Xander will not be executed. Her decision did not please everyone at the HQ, but it'll do for now. They will throw him in jail until they know what to do with him. Don't worry, they'll soon realize he's still the same guy. It's all going to be fine. I'm probably going to be grounded for the rest of my life because I lied to Mom for, like, the first time ever..."

She kept talking, though my mind hung onto a statement she'd just made. *It's all going to be fine.* Somehow, after all that had happened since we left the hospital, I believed her. Even though I still had many inquiries unanswered and even if I knew for sure we would be punished for everything we'd done today, Xander was alive and the world would go back to normal.

Epilogue

Ian Cohen

GARETH AND THE INJURED PROTECTOR named Dany were taken to Dr. Goldbridge as soon as the convy arrived in New York. Michelle had been waiting in Jeffrey's beach-like office with four bodyguards. Once at the Headquarters, I was assigned to prepare a prison cell for Xander. Everything was to be cleaned up and made comfortable. I didn't understand why we were keeping him alive. Her instructions had been clear: every Rascal was to be killed. But again, every single one of them was still alive. I made a mental note to ask Meo if Rascals were immortal and, if not, what could kill them.

I reluctantly—with the help of John, Danny's brother—carried a mattress from the rooms on the second floor to Xander's new home: an eight-by-eight cage-like space, toilet included. But hey, at least he had a comfortable mattress and warm sheets. Because no one ever used that prison cell, there was dust everywhere, and I didn't feel like cleaning, so I told

John that Michelle needed me upstairs.

"I don't mind," he replied. "As long as I can keep myself busy. Danny's still in with Goldbridge. He got himself a pretty severe concussion and…"

He kept talking, but I didn't listen. I didn't care, really. I nodded when he was done and told him how sorry I was and immediately headed upstairs to the second floor. I needed to call Meo and ask him what our next step was. Then I planned on going to sleep. It was close to four in the morning, after all.

I climbed the stairs two by two and when I'd made sure I was alone in the washroom, I tried to figure out how the device worked. There was a small screen and only three buttons: a green one for picking up and a red one to end a conversation. The third button had the number ONE printed on it. I decided it was my best guess, pressed it, and was rewarded with the sound of a ringing tone.

"Ian?"

That didn't sound like Meo at all. Actually, it couldn't have been more opposite to his sarcastic way of speaking, which was perfectly normal since the voice didn't come from the device. It came from the door. My heart stopped beating for at least two complete seconds.

"Ian. Are you in here?" Michelle repeated.

Without a word, I quickly hid the device back in my sock and washed my hands to make her believe I'd been too busy to answer her. What did she want with me?

"Mrs. Cohen," I said, stepping outside the men's washroom and closing the door behind me.

She wasn't alone. Two bodyguards were at her side and had their arms crossed in front of them. What was going on? Sweat started to form around my temples. What if somebody had seen me with Meo in the Abbey?

"It's about Jim," Michelle said, her voice like a robot, as if she was assessing my reaction. As if she thought I was going to run away.

For an instant, I actually thought about it. Somebody had finally accused me of murdering my friend. I was in trouble. But then I knew that I'd never make it out of the Headquarters without being apprehended. Not with those two bulky giants, that was certain. I swear I heard one of them groan like an animal.

I was going to end up in the jail, next to Xander Macfrey.

"Follow me, Ian," Michelle ordered.

I reluctantly trailed behind her, closely followed by Tweedle Dee and Tweedle Dum, but my mind contemplated every possible option. Were I to escape by the main entrance— that's if I was able to outrun Michelle's new bodyguards—she would have me found by the police or the Secret Service if she had to. I could always Travel to Red—I knew the Headquarters gave in a deserted building—however, Michelle would simply have to follow me and send her bodyguards onto my trace. The problem, I realized, was them. I had to get rid of them.

We walked down two floors, to the training equipment and crossed a pile of gym mats, several boxing dummies, and a banner with the Protectors' mantra written on it: Protecting Amani For A Better Future. I thought of using an ancient sword on the weapon armoire against the guards, but instantly concluded that I didn't stand a chance. I wasn't a hundred percent sure whether it was a real sword or just a decoration, and besides, I wouldn't have known how to use it.

We were only a few feet away from the last corner, the one that led to the cell I'd prepared for Xander Macfrey. The one that led to my fate. I wasn't going to be able to help Meo anymore. I was never going to become the head of the Protectors. Every dream I'd had ended in this room.

Michelle unlocked the door to the prison with her key card and she stepped in, her body stiffening at every step, as if she didn't want to do this. Maybe I would be able to convince her I was innocent. *Get people to like you*, Meo had told me. *And most of all, know your true allies*. Michelle wasn't one. She was too weak, because of her daughter. She would do anything to protect her.

"This way," she said, leading me directly to a vacant prison cell.

I was on the verge of asking why she was taking me to jail when the device in my sock buzzed against my tibia and I had to cough to cover the droning sound. Luckily, it only buzzed once, possibly indicating that I had received a text message, not a phone call.

We passed in front of Xander's future cell and were just about to face mine when I saw what was inside. Or, more precisely, who. At first, he looked like a scared child crying for mercy, but then I noticed his clean combat gear and his right arm wrapped in a bandage. I hadn't noticed that Jonathan had been hurt in the Bath Abbey. I didn't even remember seeing him fight anyone at all.

"I am sorry for the secrecy, Ian," Michelle said as she faced me. "No one must know about this. I am only telling you because Jim was your best friend." I frowned and shook my head as a way to convey my confusion. "Jonathan came up to me an hour ago and confessed his act." She stared at me with such pity that I had to stop myself from looking behind my back to make sure she wasn't talking to somebody else. I also wondered for a second if it wasn't just a joke, until Michelle added, "You are looking at Jim's killer, Ian. I am so sorry."

I was speechless. Bewildered. Astonished. I couldn't believe my ears.

Michelle put a hand on my shoulder. "I will hire more bodyguards for all of us, especially for you and me, and everyone at the Headquarters will be interrogated about Jim's death even more thoroughly. We will find out if Jonathan had a partner. Until then, you will be escorted everywhere by Dick and Max, your two personal wardens." She nodded to the two bulky mountains behind me. "Jonathan admitted that he meant to kill you, not Jim." She paused and examined my reaction, which was blank. Utterly impassive.

"Why?" I managed to ask.

"He didn't say, but I have my theory. You are my second, Ian. You, of all my family members are the one I trust the most. Therefore, if someone wanted to weaken the Protectors of Amani, they would have to get rid of you first."

It didn't make sense. None of it did. Why would Jonathan confess a crime *I* had committed? I needed answers.

"May I please have a word with him in private?" I asked Michelle, forcing my voice to quiver.

I think she'd have agreed to anything right that moment.

"Of course," she said. "Just be careful."

She nodded at my two new bodyguards and followed them outside the prison, leaving me alone, facing a disturbed bird in a cage. I knew there were cameras around, but I wondered if they recorded sounds as well as images. Without taking any chances, I moved closer to the bars and whispered Jonathan's name. When he didn't move, I cleared my throat and said his name louder. I hadn't expected what I witnessed when he turned around. His face was covered in tears, his hair flat on his head and his skin—his skin was bloated, with red scratches surrounding his stiff features.

As soon as his eyes found mine, he jolted up and bounced on the cage bars, which, I was afraid to admit, scared the hell out of me. Tears ran down his cheeks like a waterfall, covering his gashes with salty water.

"Ian," he murmured, tilting his head on the left, his face distorted by pain.

He invited me to get closer to the cage with a movement of his hand, which made me realize I had stepped away from it. The person in front of me couldn't be Jonathan. Only his eyes were recognizable, although their dark green color was now filled with uncontrollable madness.

I took a deep breath and tried to ignore my fears. "What happened?" I asked. "Why did you kill Jim?"

A loud moan came out of his mouth as he bent his head backward. "I didn't mean to," he cried. "I—I didn't want to."

I walked a little closer to the animal facing me, still wondering what had happened to him. He had been such a fragile person, timid and weak. Killing somebody by accident could have done that to him. It could have easily broken him, shattered his nature into pieces. But the fact was, he hadn't killed anyone. I had.

"How did it happen?" I inquired.

His head moved in quick motions all around himself and when he finally looked at me, his eyes were sad—so sad, I was afraid he would simply drop dead in front of me. I believed that, considering how much he had changed in less than twenty-four hours, nothing he was about to say would surprise me.

He stretched his arm out of the prison cell in one abrupt motion, trying to reach me. "Come closer," he whispered. "And

I will tell you."

I immediately shook my head. My heartbeat was pumping fast enough already, there was no need to get more excited. "Just tell me what you did to my friend," I ordered.

"I—I..." He dropped to the floor. "I don't know!" he cried in a high pitched voice. "I remember holding this piece of mirror in my hand and then, just a few seconds later, it was in Jim's chest, piercing his heart."

Jonathan moaned once more, covering his crimson face with his trembling hands. How did he know about the mirror? How could he remember that scene when he hadn't been there? I needed more information.

I made a few steps in his direction and slid to my knees. "Jonny," I said, trying to gain his trust. "Jonny—"

But he didn't let me finish. His moist hand gripped at my shirt and he pulled hard, slamming my face into the metal bars.

"It was you!" he cried. For a moment I thought he was talking about Jim's murderer. "You were supposed to be there, not Jim! I remember needing to kill *you*! YOU!"

I heard steps coming our way. Michelle must have been monitoring our little encounter. She was sending guards to my rescue.

Jonathan's mouth opened to say something, but then his eyes cleared, as if he recognized me for the first time. "Ian," he whispered. "I remember something else…"

During that exact moment, he almost seemed sane again.

"What?" I asked. "What can you remember?"

He rose himself up and brought his mouth in between the bars. I stood as well, but this time, I remained firmly in place, in case it was a ruse to lure me into his grip again. Tears flooded his chin and shoulders, but he didn't care. He stared at me for a moment before his mouth opened anew.

"Implant."

"Excuse me?"

"Implant," he repeated. "I don't know why but I remember you must be the only one to hear these words. 'Memory implant.'"

Memory implant? What was that supposed to m—? *Oh.*

Then it all made sense: why Meo had told me not to worry about the incident with Jim. Why Jonathan's arm was injured. And mostly why he had gone insane with a memory that wasn't his own.

Jonathan hadn't killed Jim. I had. And I had told Meo, who'd then implanted my memory into Jonathan's mind. He had probably done it in the Abbey, twisting his arm while he transferred the images. Meo had asked me how I'd killed Jim. It wasn't because he cared. He only needed information to make someone else's confession believable. The arrow had stopped on Jonathan, probably because he'd been the only Protector in the Abbey who wasn't already busy with another Rascal. He'd been vulnerable to Meo's motive.

And that information he'd received—those images—they

were eating Jonathan alive.

Meo had also told me I needed to gain the Protectors' trust. If somebody within our organization wanted to kill me, it would trigger pity from the others. Meo knew that by implanting that desire into Jonathan, I would become more likable to my peers.

And his plan had worked. Moments later, two guards were at my side, pulling me away from the madman and ordering me to wait outside. *I don't know what happened to Jonathan after that. Was he beaten for attacking me? Did they inject some kind of calming serum into his blood? I don't know.*

All I knew was that I was given a second chance. And I sure as hell was going to take advantage of it.

About the author

Lydhia Marie was born in a small town in Quebec, Canada. She discovered her passion for writing later in life during her last summer as an English student at Bishop's University. To be honest, she wasn't much of a reader before she started her degree, but this hate for words transformed into a passion for reading, and then morphed into a need for writing. Strange but nonetheless true.

After finishing her first draft, she attended a three-week creative writing course at the University of Oxford, where she realized that her first manuscript was very badly written. Fortunately, the idea behind the writing was "so unique and different," according to an early critique of the novel, that she decided to write the entire manuscript anew, from a blank page to the epilogue.

She enjoys books that transports her into a new world and characters that are both original and relatable. But most of all, she loves spending time writing or reading with her dog, Bookie, on her lap, looking adorable with his legs in the air and his belly ready to be rubbed.

For more information, you can find her on
Facebook: Lydhia Marie – Author
www.lydhiam.webs.com
Twitter: @LydhiaMarie

Made in the USA
Middletown, DE
02 July 2015